# TAKE TO
# THE LIMIT

# TAKE TO
# THE LIMIT

DAWN RYDER

St. Martin's Paperbacks

This is a work of fiction. All of the characters, organizations, and events portrayed in this novel are either products of the author's imagination or are used fictitiously.

TAKE TO THE LIMIT

For information address St. Martin's Press, 175 Fifth Avenue, New York, NY 10010.

ISBN: 978-1-250-13270-3

Our books may be purchased in bulk for promotional, educational, or business use. Please contact your local bookseller or the Macmillan Corporate and Premium Sales Department at 1-800-221-7945, ext. 5442, or by e-mail at MacmillanSpecialMarkets@macmillan.com.

Printed in the United States of America

St. Martin's Paperbacks edition / September 2017
St. Martin's Paperbacks are published by St. Martin's Press, 175 Fifth Avenue, New York, NY 10010.

10 9 8 7 6 5 4 3 2 1

*For Alexandra. . . .*
*Thanks for all the hard*
*work, I can't shine*
*without you!*

# CHAPTER ONE

Rick Sullivan liked the scent of blood.

And the taste, too.

His mouth was full of it and he only spit it out to intimidate his opponent.

*Let him see how much he liked bleeding . . .*

Around them, the guards were shouting. They had their hands hooked into the battered fencing that served as a cage for matches. There was money on the table, lots of it, folded around the rungs of the wire while he and the prisoner across from him fought.

One of the guards fired off a shot from his gun at the ground to get them fighting again. Sullivan waited for his opponent to lunge at him before he twisted and brought his fist up into the underside of the man's jaw. There was a crunch and a gurgle as the bone broke and the man went down.

The guards roared. Some with victory and others spouted profanity. Sullivan absorbed it all, taking note of who had won money on him. Information was the real thing he was after, not the scraps the guards would give him for providing them with entertainment.

Still, later that night, he sipped at the tequila he'd won and smiled at the woman between his knees. Mexican jails were shit holes, but that just meant there were loopholes for him to slip through.

Carl Davis and Tyler Martin could bet that Sullivan would be slipping out of the jail they'd left him to rot in. No one double-crossed him. Martin was going to learn that even all of his Secret Service agents wouldn't make a difference. Because when a Sullivan came for you, there were only two choices: make your peace with God or placate the devil.

He enjoyed the idea of seeing Carl Davis beg for his life.

But he fucking loved the thought of killing him.


America . . .

The party was winding down. At least the first phase was.

Somewhere around ten, the toddlers were sleeping and mothers were gathering up the last of the swim towels. You could feel the vibe changing. The carefree demeanor that had presided during the day was being overshadowed by the darkness and the cravings it somehow granted permission to. The summer weather was perfect for it, negating the need for layers of clothing. As soon as darkness was added, people shifted closer to each other and ventured deeper into the shadows.

Bram Magnus leaned against the house, the stucco still warm from the heat of the day.

Or maybe it was from his temper.

A couple moved further off into the darkness, unaware

that he was watching. The way the female looked around before taking a few more steps into the night, it didn't take a genius to deduce what sort of party they were in the mood for. There was a flash of trim thigh as her short dress flipped up with her hurried steps, a sultry sway to her hips that was unmistakable. She leaned in closer to her companion, his fingers tightening around the curve of her hip before he slid his hand further down until he was gripping her thigh beneath that short skirt.

LeAnn let out a husky laugh. Bram recognized it, which pissed him off.

The problem was, he realized he was mad over the fact that he'd always known LeAnn's feelings for him didn't run deeper than lust.

"Jesus . . ." A bag of trash hit the concrete but Jaelyn surprised him by controlling the rest of her emotions. Her eyes flashed wide but returned to normal faster than he'd have given her credit for. He'd never pegged her as having much nerve. But she stared back at him, steady as could be.

Impressive . . .

"I'm sorry, Bram, I didn't see you."

Jaelyn's voice trailed off as she heard a soft laugh and recognized it as her sister's. Bram watched her face, wanting to know if she knew what her sister was about. Jaelyn turned toward the sound and frowned.

"Your sister is busy," he informed her dryly.

"But you're her boyfriend . . . oh, never mind." She bent to pick up the trash bag but only made it halfway there before straightening. "Look . . . I'm really—"

"Sorry? Don't be," he said with a shrug. "Better this way."

"I can't see how."

His temper was sizzling, and another soft laugh drifting on the night breeze turned up the heat. "It's simple enough. I'm shipping out at daybreak, and it looks like I'm doing it as a single man. No strings attached."

She started to bite her lip. There was something on the tip of her tongue; he watched her contemplate whether or not to voice it.

"Yeah, that's your MO, isn't it? Always playing it safe."

He knew he was being a dick by saying that. Pushing her away with a cutting remark because . . . well, the flat truth was, there was something about her that made him feel less than worthy.

Her eyes narrowed as she sent a harsh look straight at him.

"If you're trying to show a contrast between the way I live my life and the way you show up here whenever you want to feel like you have a relationship . . . you're damned right I'm the opposite of what you and LeAnn have been doing," Jaelyn informed him. "For the record, I don't call it playing it safe. I call it having integrity and not using my grandfather's home as a place to get your fix of family love while you invest nothing of yourself."

Direct hit.

Bram felt his lips curving slightly in response. She was kicking his ass and doing a good job of it.

Her eyes narrowed as she took in his grin. She let out a snort and reached for the bag of trash again. "Fine. Hope you and LeAnn are deliriously happy with your . . . relationship."

LeAnn and her lover had moved off into the night. Bram found it suited him because Jaelyn was far more interesting.

He wanted a fight and was being an ass. But a flare of

hunger entered her eyes, deflating his initial surge of temper. It left him poised on the edge of something volatile, something he felt like he'd known had been simmering inside him but had been ignoring. For all the right reasons, of course, but tonight, there was a boundary missing between them. That knowledge set something loose inside him.

"Your sister seems to have vacated the post of being my girlfriend, so you won't have to worry about seeing me again."

The trash bag dropped once more. Jaelyn faced off with him like she didn't notice that her head barely reached his chin.

"Are you really torn up about . . ." She gestured toward where LeAnn had gone. "It's not like you put a ring on her finger."

"Your sister doesn't want a ring weighing her down."

"No shit," Jaelyn retorted.

Bram chuckled.

Jaelyn rolled her eyes. "Right, you think I don't cuss. Know something? I don't give a fig for your opinion. You were using LeAnn as much as she was you. At least I won't have to worry about you showing up and messing with my grandfather. He thinks the world of you, and you're just here to get your fix. Judge me as you will, but I see through you."

He'd been cussed out by the best—seasoned brass and underworld thugs—but there was something about her Lucy Ricardo insults that shamed him.

"You're not a prude after all."

"You've got nerve." She made a scoffing sound and sent him a glare. "Know something? Just because I think sex should be more than physical doesn't make me a prude. My grandparents loved each other. Maybe you've just never seen how amazing that looks, but I have and I'm not settling for"—she was gesturing at him—"for what you're clearly willing to settle for. I am going to find a man who curls my toes and—"

He pushed away from the wall and wrapped his arms around her. He was being presumptuous at the least, a huge prick at the worst, but the flicker of heat in her eyes drew him to her. Maybe it was plain old desperation to cling to the living before he shipped out to a place where life was cheap and easily smashed.

*Like hell it was that simple . . .*

Whatever had broken free inside him was growing, stretching, as it gained freedom. It was hungry and needy, as well as uncontrollable.

Bram trapped her arms at her sides, sliding one hand up her spine to capture her nape before claiming his kiss. He needed to hold her, needed her to feel his strength. A soft gasp got muffled between their lips as he pressed a deep kiss against her mouth. He forgot what his intentions were when the taste of her swept through his brain, knocking his better judgment out cold.

The only thing left was the feel of the woman in his arms. The way her lips moved beneath his, the way her body curved to fit against his, was mind-numbing and exhilarating at the same time. She was warm and soft, and he teased her lips with a sweep of his tongue because he needed to know what she tasted like. The thin, summer dress she wore was nothing but a frail barrier between her hard nipples and himself. He slid his hand around and cupped one breast, feeling its weight, and brushing his thumb over the puckered tip. The soft sound she made snapped him back into focus.

What the fuck was he doing?

He opened his arms, fighting that thing inside him with every ounce of self-discipline he had. All he wanted was to press her against the side of the house and keep pressing until he was deep inside her.

God . . . he craved her . . .

Jaelyn staggered back a pace, her respiration agitated, her eyes wide.

That was why she tasted so good. She was everything pure, everything his hands were too dirty to touch.

She was waiting . . . and he was a damned bastard for touching her when she was pure and he was a hell of a long way from it himself.

"I had no right to do that." But he wanted to do a whole hell of a lot more.

His jeans felt too tight, his cock swollen and demanding. Her taste clung to his lips as he forced himself to walk away before he lost his grip on his discipline.

Before he took what he wanted . . .

"Hold it right there, Bram Magnus."

Surprise made him stop. The husky sound of her voice was something he'd never heard before. Or expected to.

But he liked it. Liked it a hell of a lot.

He turned to face her and felt his arousal spike when he found her standing only a pace from him. There wasn't a hint of outrage on her face, only a glimmer of something in her eyes which promised him hell.

He liked the look of that, too.

"Kisses . . ." She closed the gap between them, captivating him with the way her hips swayed. She stepped up to him and settled her hands on his chest. ". . . aren't meant to be one-sided."

She stroked him, moving her hands up and over his

collarbones to his neck. It was slow, so damn slow he
wasn't sure he could remain still but it was worth the effort. Her touch sent shivers down his spine, the kind he
hadn't felt since he'd been a raw youth in the troughs of
his first love.

Back when he'd believed in love, that was.

She believed in love, though. He saw it glittering in her
eyes, and it threatened to buckle his knees.

"Always shared, Bram . . . it's called . . . making love."

When her hand reached his head she rose onto her toes
to complete the kiss but he was still too tall. She gently
pulled on his neck and he had no problem complying with
her demand.

Shit, he could take orders from her all night so long as
she was touching him.

This time their kiss was sweeter but not because it was
slower. It was in the way she explored his mouth, teasing
him with soft pressure while tracing his lower lip with the
tip of her tongue before thrusting shyly inside. That was
his undoing. He wrapped his arms around her and captured her neck so he could turn her head to suit his
desire. The kiss became hard and blistering hot. Control vanished as he fit her against him, pushing her back
into the shadows and against the warm stucco of the
house. He ravished her mouth with his lips and tongue.
She moaned, the little sound pushing him further over
the edge as she arched up against him, pressing against
his cock and trembling when she felt the hard proof of
his desire.

He pulled his head back, stroking her back as he detected the ripple of reaction. Her eyes were wide, her lips
open as she panted.

"I shouldn't have started this," he said.

"Well, I've decided to finish it." She surprised him with how determined her tone was. Her fingers fisted into his shirt, pulling a handful of his chest hairs in the process. The little tingle of pain intensified the moment, feeding the savage side of his nature that was all too close to the surface.

"Jaelyn—"

"Shut up." She surprised him again—actually, stunned was a better way to put it. She was the sweet sister. The family-supporting, apron-wearing sibling who always embodied the model of a good girl.

But there was one hell of a woman hiding inside her.

He cupped her jaw, holding her head in place as he studied her gaze. It was hot enough to blister him, giving him a peek at the woman he'd never taken the time to notice she was.

Hell, maybe he'd ignored it because he'd been stupid enough to chase her sister. A hundred missed opportunities flooded his brain as he watched the way her face turned sultry with the help of her lips still wet from his kiss.

"Jaelyn—"

She kissed him again. There was nothing shy about it. Their mouths met with a hunger that curled his damned toes as she pressed up against him from knees to chest without a hint of hesitation.

And then, she was gone, slipping along the side of the house while he was lost in the moment. He blinked and pushed off the stucco in a flash only to find her watching him with her hands propped on her hips and a very confident little smile on her lips, while her hard little nipples pushed out the soft jersey of her dress, proving she was every bit as turned on as he was.

She was stunning in that moment.

"Good-bye, Bram Magnus."

She reached for the bag of trash again but he nabbed it before she got a grip.

"You'll see me again, Jaelyn. Count on it."

*"Count on it . . ."*

Jaelyn heard Bram's words ringing in her ears as she made it back into the laundry room.

*Ha! You mean after you ran for your burrow . . .*

God, why couldn't she feel as confident as she wanted to be? It was such a stupid twist of reality that a person could be so sure of how they wanted to be and yet when faced with an epic uprising moment of hard, blunt reality like the one she'd just encountered, her damned emotions would liquefy.

He wouldn't be coming back.

She needed to get real about that fact and fast, before the feelings he'd unleashed inside her settled into her bones.

Fuck.

Yeah, she cussed.

And it felt like Bram Magnus was a really good reason to lay out some mental profanity as she found herself having to force her fingers to release the doorknob.

It was over . . .

And it was better that way . . .

Okay, logically it was way wiser to be in the house, even if it branded her a frightened little rabbit, than . . . well . . . she shuddered as her mind was all too happy to offer up what she might be doing with Bram.

Hell, he'd curl her toes alright.

*Yeah, and leave you at the crack of dawn . . .*

Jaelyn ended up laughing at herself as she made it back into the kitchen.

He was a true man-animal.

Seriously cut and hardened and untamed.

And she was jealous. It was true.

But no one had it all.

Getting a taste of him would be epic but it would haunt her, too.

Life was just a bitch that way. Bram wanted to play midnight games, sure enough, but he wouldn't be sticking around. Man-animals like him prowled.

*Untamed.*

The word suited Bram so very well. There was a way about him that just drove her insane with curiosity. Both for the feeling of him against her and the need to know him. She'd been itching to tell him off for a while because of the way he seemed so detached.

*Ha! You think you can save him . . .*

He wasn't a baby bird.

She snorted and realized she was looking out the kitchen window.

Bram didn't need to be brought in for protection from the night.

But she did.

Oh, it wasn't that she thought she would go to hell if she indulged in sex. If that was the case, she was damned already for how often she masturbated. She had a healthy sex drive, that was a fact.

But there was something more in life.

She'd seen it in her grandparents and in a few of her friends who had met their soul mates.

Bram would laugh at that idea.

Maybe.

And then again, maybe that made her just a little sick to her heart to think he wouldn't understand something like soul mates.

*You're back to wanting to save him . . .*

Yeah, but she was in the house, so, safe for the moment.

*Safe from yourself . . .*

It was the logical thing to do.

So why did it suck so bad?


"Need a hand?"

Bram jerked around, earning a smug little grin from Dare Servant. The Shadow Ops agent was halfway concealed in the dark, positioned so he could see anyone coming toward them.

"Your knees look a little unsteady, Magnus."

Bram lifted one foot off the ground and sent a kick toward Dare. It was crotch level, perfectly executed, and controlled so that he stopped just a couple of inches shy of the target.

Dare snickered at him and shrugged.

"I don't need a wingman." Bram joined Dare in the shadows.

"Saxon Hale didn't ask for your opinion," Dare replied as they walked across the lawn toward a car. "You might have noticed he's the team leader."

Bram opened the passenger side door and got into the car as Dare slid behind the wheel and turned the key.

Dare looked over at him. "The Raven is dead but Tyler Martin and Carl Davis are very much alive and looking for retribution."

Dare looked at the traffic as he pulled the car away from the curb.

"One could hope Tyler and Carl have learned their lesson to leave the Hale brothers alone."

"Don't count on it," Dare replied. "Tyler Martin sold us out for his position with Carl Davis. Tyler isn't going to leave a loose end like us dangling."

"Saxon Hale's Shadow Ops team is more than a loose end," Bram remarked. "We've kicked Martin's ass three times now."

"All the more reason for Saxon to send me along to sidekick around with you." Dare made a turn and headed for the interstate on ramp. "Real shame about your cheerleader girlfriend there."

Bram only shrugged and looked out the window.

"The sister though . . ."

Bram snapped his head around and held a finger up in warning.

Dare Servant ignored it.

"A little bit of a dick move there on the side of the house . . ."

"I know that," Bram said with a grunt.

"Still, it looked like it worked out in the end. She knows how to make a move." Dare let out a low whistle. "Wouldn't have guessed that by the way she takes care of that old man."

"You sound like more of a dick than me," Bram said. "There's nothing wrong with being devoted to family."

"You're doing your best to run away from yours."

Bram glared at his fellow agent. Even with his attention on the traffic, Dare noticed.

"Just calling what I see," Dare said. "You're playing with our teams because it gets you out from under Daddy's shadow."

"There's more than one way to do that," Bram said to defend himself.

"Right," Dare responded back. "Like taking another tour in Afghanistan?"

"Kagan hasn't offered me a badge," Bram said. "I was there in New Orleans with you and the Hale brothers going against the Raven. Don't expect me to sit around waiting for a formal position to be offered. I've given Kagan a nice long sample of what worth I bring to his Shadow Ops teams."

"No argument," Dare replied seriously. "Which is why you have a wingman." He cut Bram a look. "Don't want you to get waxed because Tyler knows your habits and decides to lay you out in the city morgue to make sure the rest of the team knows he's still coming for us. Or even just to let us know he's watching. He's that sort of a prick."

Bram took the reprimand. He'd stepped right back out into the light and he knew better. Dare was politely reminding him that he couldn't sit on the fence. Shadow Ops teams weren't for weekend warriors. He'd played the game. He'd been dabbling his fingers in the murky underworld of classified missions since he'd come face-to-face with Saxon Hale when the man was assigned to investigate Bram's family.

It was an odd arrangement, to be sure, and maybe part of Kagan's hesitation in offering him a badge was due to the fact that Bram hadn't made it clear what side he wanted to be on.

Army or Shadow Ops.

He wanted the badge. But it meant choosing a life that was separated from the one he'd known. It didn't mean he couldn't have happiness. Saxon Hale had a wife, as did Vitus Hale. Both married women they'd met through missions. Hell, his own sister was married to a Shadow Ops agent.

But they'd followed their men into the world of changed names and no contact with their previous life. For the Hale brothers, their wives had already been victims of fate. Their choices stolen by circumstance and underworld thugs like the Raven.

Bram should never have gone back to the Sondors house. Dare was right but it was Jaelyn's words that stung. She'd called it right on the money. He'd gone there looking for a taste of home.

That fabled thing deployed soldiers dreamed about when they'd been scared so long it felt normal.

He'd wanted to see Jaelyn making her grandfather's coffee and wearing an apron that made her look like a prude when she was anything but. And maybe, just maybe he'd been daring her to tell him off for the way he was playing games with her sister, LeAnn.

He grinned. She'd done that. sure enough.

Dare let out a grunt. "Don't look like that, Bram." The Shadow Ops agent sent him a long look. "I like having you on the team. Don't go getting attached to a woman."

"She left me in the yard."

"I noticed." Dare pulled into the parking lot of a house. It was quiet and normal looking. Just the kind of place Shadow teams liked to use as operation centers. "Let her go. Kagan will offer a badge soon enough."

Inside the house two junior agents were working at computers. They looked up and nodded as Dare entered. He was their team leader at the moment. Kagan was giving Dare a little room to stretch his wings. It was touching in a way, because five paces into the living room Bram realized Dare had set them to tracking him—

To watch his back when he'd been too stupid to realize he was crossing back into the open. His relationship with LeAnn was something that could be traced.

Stupid.

Sure was.

And yet, as he finished showering and lay down on a bed in one of the rooms, he just couldn't quite swallow the idea of never going back.

He needed to.

He pulled a picture from his wallet and looked at it for a long time.

He was a dumb ass. Shit for brains.

The picture was of LeAnn and Jaelyn. He'd never taken the time to contemplate why he was carrying around both of them.

He should have.

LeAnn might be fine with an open relationship but Jaelyn had been right about her grandfather and the way Bram had been showing up to get a taste of normalcy. Milton Sondors was crusty and happy-go-lucky all the time. It was kind of nauseating in that way a sweet old man could be. Damn if it didn't tickle Bram to be around him.

Yeah, well, that was an excuse to be around Jaelyn, too.

He realized the truth as he forced himself to put the picture on the side table.

He'd been drawn to her.

He was taken in by her dedication to her family, which might be confused with being subservient by someone dim enough not to see that she was the backbone of the family.

He needed to leave her behind. Let some guy who hadn't gone off and played dangerous games find her. He needed to leave the picture behind when he left in the morning.

Mexico . . .

"I want out of here."

The guard only gave him a bored look. Rick Sullivan smiled at him. "Fine. Just thought you were the type of man who would like to profit from an opportunity. One I can make for the right man. A friend."

"What opportunity do you speak of?"

Ricky moved closer to the man. "You could make a lot of money betting against me in the next fight."

The guard's eyes narrowed as he caught on. "With your record, the odds are very much in your favor."

"Every man loses once in a while," Ricky said. "Law of mathematics. At least, that would be how you explain the fact that you bet against me, when everyone knows my record."

The guard was considering it. Rick enjoyed watching the way the guy rolled it around his brain. Hell, Ricky just loved knowing he was dicking around with the man's principles. Some people were so damned much fun to mess with.

"It would be very hard to get you out of prison. Yours is a sentence of life."

"So, I'll make sure I don't lose until I'm bloody enough to be taken down to the doctor. Share a little of your winnings with him and slip me out with the dead. I won't stick around for anyone to know I'm still alive."

The guard was weighing his options. He just might toss Ricky in the hot oven in the middle of the yard during the afternoon heat, but it was a risk worth taking. But messing with him, when there were plenty of other prisoners who would provide entertainment. The guy knew Ricky could earn him money but only if Ricky was in condition to fight.

That was really all it took to get what Ricky wanted from a man like the guard. He had to weigh the options and make sure the one Ricky wanted was the better deal. Tyler Martin might have paid someone to toss his ass in jail for life but that someone wasn't this guard. This guy hadn't gotten a slice of the pie Martin paid with. Rich men like Martin never learned that if you left your dogs too hungry, they'd turn on you if someone offered them more meat.

"You have a deal. Next fight." The guard shot him a sneer. "Double-cross me and I will make you wish you were dead."

Sullivan contained his glee. The guard wandered on, leaving him hugging the victory close. Tyler Martin thought he was safe in Washington, DC. Along with that prick Carl Davis, who was about to be elected president. They'd sold Ricky out, used him to do their dirty work, and left him to rot.

Big mistake.

Because he was alive and that meant he could do more than survive, he could thrive.

Step one was to get out of prison. Ricky popped his knuckles and made a fist. He punched the concrete wall, smiling at the pain and chuckling when his flesh began to harden against it.

Absolutely perfect.

His watch started chirping.

Magnus rubbed a hand over his eyes. The room was lightening with the approach of daybreak. His watch started its second cycle, and he turned his wrist so he could silence it. He sat up, rejecting the urge to close his eyes for a few more minutes.

But his discipline faltered when he found the picture facing him. Jaelyn was smiling, and even the sight of LeAnn didn't bother him as much as the idea of leaving the picture behind.

He knew he should.

He went toward the bathroom, hoping a shower would sober him up enough to cowboy up and get on with what needed doing.

### Six months later . . .

Jaelyn sat up, the bed squeaking. Her forehead was dotted with perspiration and her nipples were hard beneath the old T-shirt she'd worn to bed.

She was a rotten sister.

A horrible excuse for a human being.

But that didn't erase the memory of Bram Magnus's kiss from her mind or the feel of his hands from her body. She lay back down, frustrated with the way her dreams tormented her. It was a torment because the man hadn't contacted her even once since that night. After six months, even the excuse that he was in a war zone wasn't holding water anymore. She just wasn't his type. Which made her madder, because he was the type of man she'd never forget the feel of. He'd known exactly how to touch her, kissing her with a skill that still had her dreams full of him.

She snorted and punched the pillow but it didn't improve her mood any. She wanted Bram to come home to her, she wanted to know how much hotter the passion could get between them. She wanted . . .

Yeah, right.

It wasn't going to happen.

It was exactly what she deserved for jumping her sister's boyfriend the second she could. Karma was a bitch. Just because her sister had it coming didn't make her crime any less awful. Considering the circumstances, he didn't owe her squat. He was likely relieved he didn't have to deal with her.

Bram had never noticed that she watched him. There had been plenty of times she'd considered that a blessing. But there was still part of her that wanted him to notice the way she watched him.

Hell, what girl wouldn't?

He was hard-bodied and focused in a way that curled her toes when he looked her way. She would swear she could feel a buzz in the air when he walked into a room. He was a man-animal with solid principles who made a woman feel like there was nothing on his mind except her.

So she'd jumped on her opportunity to taste him. It hadn't been the brightest thing she'd ever done.

*Yeah, but she'd loved every second of it . . .*

For a moment she grinned, like a kid with a handful of cookies.

"Intimacy" was no longer a word with a definition floating around in her brain. It was a hard, pleasure-packed action. One she was hungry for more of.

Shit . . . they'd only kissed . . .

Yeah, well, it seemed to be enough to keep him firmly in mind half a year later.

And there was no way she was ever getting more.

Still, she found herself unable to truly regret it.

Sometimes, it was best to live in the moment before it got away.

## Cobra Fire Base, Afghanistan

"You got a girlfriend?"

Communications Specialist Gideon had a hopeful gleam in his eyes. He waited for Magnus to answer with an intensity that was slightly edgy. His eyes brightened but otherwise he held perfectly still, like he was setting a trap and waiting for the right moment to pounce.

"I got a girl."

"Yeah?" Gideon hit his knee and leaned closer. "Can I see her picture? Blonde or brunette?"

Magnus slid the firing pin back into his rifle, keeping his mouth shut while he ensured his weapon was in prime condition. Inattention could translate into a flag-draped coffin being sent home to his father, or wherever his father was at the moment, anyway. He could sure as hell bet it wasn't home.

Gideon was a civilian, one making big bucks to put his neck on the line in a hot zone. The guy was a typical sub-contractor. One who marketed his degree to the military and was getting his student loans forgiven in the process. Sure, he was making the dough but he could care less about any duty, which left him going stir-crazy while Bram and his men were on a mission.

"You like them curvy or thin? Your girl got tits or melons?" Gideon pressed him.

Bram shot him a warning glare. "She's a lady. Mind your mouth."

Gideon offered him a sheepish grin. "I get it. Nothing

better than a good girl to keep your dreams peaceful, so long as she knows when to be naughty." He waved an open hand between them. "Where's her picture? Come on, buddy, share the wealth. The chicks only wait for you uniform jockeys. I'm shit out of luck until I get back stateside."

Gideon sat down on the bunk next to him, his face too bright with excitement for Bram's comfort. Hell, the guy's lips were wet from being licked. There was lonely and then there was too lonely. Bram lifted one hand and pointed to his temple. "I keep it right here. Private."

Gideon's face darkened. His lower lip actually began to protrude just a fraction of an inch before he curled it back toward his teeth.

"How come you don't have a picture?" Suspicion coated his voice along with disappointment. "If she's waiting for you, why don't you have a picture?"

The cot shook when he stood. Bram finished reloading his weapon before lying back and taking up the spot Gideon had sat on. He placed the rifle across his chest with a hand resting gently over the trigger guard.

Gideon sniffed before shaking his head. "You don't have a girl waiting on you." His voice turned grumpy, and he shuffled his feet against the floor. "You're not alone, buddy. No need to lie about it. Lots of us don't got a girl. Why did you think I wanted to look at yours? You didn't need to jerk me on like that. It's just not right to mess with a fellow comrade. Maybe I ain't a soldier but my ass is still on the line . . ."

Gideon moved off, still grumbling. Bram crossed his booted feet at his ankles and ignored his frustrated comrade.

Gideon was right, Jaelyn wasn't his girl. But that didn't keep him from dreaming about her.

Right or wrong didn't really matter at the moment. Jaelyn kept him alive. She was the water for the dried-out parts of his soul. Without her, he'd watch that last part of his civilized personality evaporate and drift off into the sand surrounding him.

His lips pressed into a firm line as he swept the area once more before closing his eyes. He didn't sleep much. It was a good habit to adopt in Afghanistan. But there was more than fear of impending attack that kept his eyes wide open for eighteen hours in a row. Every time he closed them, Jaelyn was waiting for him. Her dark eyes, framed by inky long lashes. The memory of the way her body moved beneath a summer dress, her hips swaying under a thin layer of cotton. Sultry and seductive with its feminine sway. She didn't employ any practiced method of seduction; she just flowed like a woman. Just the memory enchanted him.

And turned him on.

His cock twitched as her laughter floated through his brain, its silver tinkle sending blood toward his rising erection. Reaching into his shirt pocket, he pulled out a folded photo. Cupping his hand around it, he kept it cocooned away from the eyes of the rest of his comrades. It was like looking through a window into life. He was stuck in the desolate desert and right there, sitting on his palm, was a frozen moment of springtime. Just looking at it was like feeling the spring breeze hit his face, carrying away the harsh desert heat. He could smell the fresh grass, practically feel its satiny smooth blades gliding between the toes of his bare feet.

Jaelyn wasn't waiting for him. The girl in the photo looking at his camera only had a smile of friendship on her face for him. He kept the picture of her and her sister as a reminder of just how big of a fool he'd been.

He hadn't lied to Gideon. It was more a matter of declining to admit what an idiot he was. Jaelyn wasn't waiting for him because he'd been too stupid to notice what a treasure she was when he had been close enough to touch her. Afghanistan changed that. It was the kick in the ass he needed to recognize what really mattered in a girl.

Woman, actually. Right there was the difference. Jaelyn was a woman, one who didn't waste time on games. She'd been right there and he'd been too much of an idiot to recognize her for what she was.

He saw it now. The memory was eating him alive but he preferred that to being alone.

His cock was hard now. Stiff with longing as his lips rose into a hint of a grin while he continued to let his memories of Jaelyn parade through his mind. He rationed the time he let his guard down, only allowing himself a few moments before he slept to indulge in his mental obsession.

In those few, private moments he allowed his mind to enjoy the sweet anticipation of the day he'd be able to show her how much he'd learned since leaving her.

He wrote her letters she hadn't answered but he was still going to pen another one tomorrow. He had no way of knowing if the mail got to her. A low grunt escaped his lips. He was reaching. His buddy Mercer got his letters just fine. Still, he wasn't going to let the lack of response bug him. Quitting wasn't in his vocabulary.

He would write another letter tomorrow.

Tucking the picture back into his shirt pocket, he made

sure to button it to keep the photo secure. He patted it, and heat spread through his chest as he fantasized about her dark hair being spread out over him.

His cock throbbed behind his fly and his lips curved up higher. Anticipation might be good, but the moment he touched American soil, he was going to search out Jaelyn and live his dream. Reach out and touch it . . . touch her. Dig in his heels and court her like she deserved for not running around with every guy the way her sister did. He'd been the stupid one who was too immature to notice the gem sitting in front of his nose. He knew better now, felt the newfound knowledge rippling through him like a river.

Court her . . . That was what he was going to do. With flowers and carefully planned dinners and every sappy thing he could think of or find in a book to help him plan. Until then, he'd write to her and he'd picture her reading his letters and smiling because he took the time to reach out to her.

Yeah, he had a girl and he was going to show her just exactly how much she meant to him very soon.

It wasn't right.

Some guys just didn't understand the bond necessary to survive in a war zone. If a guy wouldn't share the picture of his girl with another guy who didn't have one, he couldn't be trusted.

Gideon watched Bram strip off his vest. A ripple of relief crossed his face but it vanished a second later when the stench of his shirt hit his nose. Gideon grinned. Damn officers liked to think they were so much better than a normal guy like him but they stank just as bad after a few days without a shower. Gideon waited. He was good at waiting. Better than most guys. His mamma had always had some mean-assed boyfriend sleeping with her while he was growing up, and they were always quick to take a swing at him if he woke them up before they were ready to get out of the sack. So he'd learned to be quiet. Real quiet, like a ghost. He knew how to watch and wait for the perfect time to get what he wanted.

He stared at the vest lying over the half wall that served as a shower stall. There was a neat row of them on the east side of the base. Large hoses were secured to four-by-four rough wooden beams. They curled around to spray down into the stall. A hastily laid concrete slab with a drain set in its lowest point completed the bathing faculties. Bram's boots appeared, along with the rest of his clothing. He stripped down quickly, ignoring the fact that his bare ass was on display. There were no female personnel at Cobra Fire Base. If you wanted to wash off the stink of the desert heat, you did it right out in the open.

Bram reached up to pull on the chain to release the water. It cascaded over his face in a white, frothy spray. He stared up into it and shook his head when the water hit his face.

It was time.

Moving across the sand, Gideon approached the showers. Water splashed down onto the concrete but he ignored it. Bram wiped the water from his eyes and looked at him out of reflex. Gideon began mimicking the motions of stripping down to bathe. Bram dismissed him, reaching for a bar of soap that he started to work over every inch of his skin from the top of his head down.

Gideon ignored the itch from his own skin. He stood close enough to the vest to finger one pocket. The snap opened with a tiny pop. Bram tugged on the chain, raising his face upward once more.

In a swift motion, Gideon pulled the small picture out of the pocket. He tucked it inside his own vest before the water stopped flowing. He had to wait to look at it. But it would be better that way. He licked his lower lip as excitement began to twist through him.

"You showering or what, Gideon?"

Bram eyed him with water still streaming down his face.

"Yeah, just thought I saw a bogey."

Bram jerked his head around, scanning the horizon. Gideon began stripping. He draped his own vest over a stall and couldn't resist giving it a little pat. Sweet anticipation spread its warm glow through him. She was his girl now. Because he'd been slick enough to steal her picture, that made her his. A man got to keep what he stole, that was one of the oldest laws on earth. Gideon reached up for another chain and yanked it hard. Cool, life-giving water covered him. He kept the pressure on that chain for a good minute, enjoying the fact that he could take a shower when there were people just over the rise who were worried about getting enough to drink.

He didn't feel sorry for them. Didn't waste his time on anything that didn't have to do with him and what he wanted. Nothing else mattered.

Life wasn't fair, so there was no reason for him to be.

Mexico . . .

They'd buried him in a shallow grave. Sullivan woke up gasping. When he sucked in a breath, he got a face full of burlap from his shroud. He could smell the dirt he was lying under and strained to move it. He fought for his life, struggling against the hold the earth had on him. He broke free with a snarl, clawing at the burlap and ripping it as two of his fingernails went with it.

He fucking loved the pain because he was alive to feel it. His entire face hurt like Satan himself had kissed it and that made Sullivan laugh. Yeah, the devil didn't want him in hell, at least not just yet. He crawled out of the hole and happily kicked the dislodged soil back into place. A rough cross was hammered in at the top of it.

Ricky turned his back on it and walked away from the lights of the prison. His lip was split but he started to whistle as he went because he was on his way to happiness.

Vengeance was going to make him very, very happy. Tyler Martin was going to regret leaving him for dead. And while he was extracting what was due him, Saxon Hale, Vitus Hale, and Captain Bram Magnus owed him plenty for getting Carl Davis pissed off at him.

Yup, it was payback time.

Time for the devil's due.

## America

"Hurry up, Jaelyn!"

LeAnn stomped into the kitchen with the grace of a truck driver. Her candy-pink miniskirt swishing over her thighs didn't look sweet or innocent. Neither did the scowl on her sister's face. LeAnn always knew how to make the male population squirm and she enjoyed doing it, too. But it was an act, one that wasn't employed behind the closed doors of the house.

"Can't you iron faster? It's preliminary tryouts today,

and there is going to be a line a mile long. I could lose my spot if I'm not there to defend it."

Jaelyn held up the iron and a puff of steam rose between her sister and her. "By all means, show me how it's done."

LeAnn instantly changed her demeanor. Her face brightened with a soft smile designed to coax. "Oh, Jaelyn, you know I'm a complete flop when it comes to making things nice. I've got to shine . . ."

"I know it's important. Two minutes, if you want it done right."

"Great!"

Jaelyn pressed the iron back down onto the little white top spread out on the ironing board. There was a hiss and another puff of steam. Her sister smiled and turned around to look at her face in a wall mirror. LeAnn lifted one perfectly manicured finger, expertly smoothing out her eyeliner on her bottom lid.

Her makeup was perfect. The sort of thing you saw staring out of a magazine. Of course, that made sense. There were dozens of the things stacked up in the house, and she invested serious time in makeup classes. Jaelyn could admire the dedication, even if she didn't see the personal value in doing it herself.

But they were alike when it came to their taste in men.

Jaelyn felt the sting of guilt as she lifted the little top off the ironing board. LeAnn grabbed the top and inspected it with a critical eye, then a rare, genuine smile crossed her lips. "You're the best, Jaelyn."

For a moment, time shifted, returning them to when they'd been kids and best friends. Just a blink, though, and there was a scamper of high heels on the entryway tiles. Her sister stopped long enough to shrug into the top before she opened the door to vanish down the walkway in a cloud of perfect hair.

"She's an alien."

"Morning, Grandpa."

Her grandfather lifted a gray eyebrow at her. His lips were pressed into a hard line of disapproval but he shook his head, dismissing the matter. He made his way to the coffeepot and poured himself a mugful. He looked at her over the rim through the rising steam.

"I refuse to accept that any kin of mine can run out my front door without even saying good morning to me," he drew a long sip from the coffee and shook his head. "Nicest thing I can say is, that girl must be alien spawn. I've got to be succumbing to old age for letting her live under my roof while she treats me like I'm already dead."

Rolling her eyes, Jaelyn reached for a skillet. "She's just impulsive. LeAnn loves you."

It was a weak excuse but Jaelyn didn't want to admit to her grandfather just why she let LeAnn walk all over her.

Guilt. It was chewing a hole in her.

Cracking an egg, she dropped it into the heating pan. It sizzled while her grandfather glared over the rim of his coffee mug at her. His face might be wrinkled by time but his gaze was still keen and cutting into her.

"Don't ask," Jaelyn advised him.

Adding two more eggs to the pan, she tried to let the promise of breakfast distract her grandfather.

"Does that mean the date didn't go well?"

No such luck.

"It didn't go . . . bad . . . ," she muttered. Unless she

wanted to admit that Richard Sherlot's kiss didn't even curl one of her toes.

Not even a tingle, actually.

"That young man was put together rather nice."

Jaelyn pointed the spatula at him. "The deal was, I'd go on the date. I did. A postmortem discussion was not included in the agreement."

Jaelyn fluttered her eyelashes and held on tightly to her poker face. Her grandfather's eyes twinkled, the finger aimed at her beginning to wave back and forth. Jaelyn shrugged.

Slipping the eggs onto a plate, she delivered it to the table in front of her grandfather with a flourish.

"You should be out where the boys can chase you instead of cooking for me."

"I need to check the rolls."

Jaelyn grabbed a dish towel and wrapped it around her hand. Her grandfather grunted and she opened the oven door to avoid the conversation, ducking out of the way as heat escaped. She gave her full attention to the cinnamon rolls bubbling on the center rack of the oven. She didn't need to see the look on her grandpa's face, didn't need to hear him tell her to find a boy.

She didn't want a boy. Disgust blossomed inside her, disgust for her own fascination with someone who wasn't going to be thinking anywhere near as much about her. It had just been a kiss . . . God, she was pathetic.

She should have slept with Richard just to get her fascination with Bram out of her system.

Except that the entire idea made her feel like a quitter.

She wanted to fall in love and have amazing sex, not just sex. Was it too much to ask?

Jaelyn shook her head to clear it, earning a grunt from her grandfather.

"Kenny Gardener has a couple of boys. I'll give him a call and—"

"One more word about setting me up and I won't make the icing," Jaelyn warned, looking over her shoulder at her grandfather. He narrowed his eyes at her. "One blind date a month is my max."

"You play rough."

She allowed her hand to hover over the power switch on the mixer. The icing ingredients were already carefully measured and waiting for the whipping blade to cream them together. Her grandpa only got home-baked rolls on the weekend because during the week she kept him on a strict low-fat diet. His eyes were bright as a boy's on Christmas morning as the scent of hot sugar and cinnamon filled the air.

Fine, she was being rotten again but every girl had her limits. She flipped the switch and the mixer started up.

The phone rang, too. Her grandfather nabbed it.

"Why yes, Richard, Jaelyn's here . . . she was just telling me about your date . . . Nope, it's not too early at all."

Milton smirked at her as the icing came together and he held the phone out to her.

She knew the look. Her grandfather looked sweet and innocent, but she'd learned to play hard from him. Seriously, Milton could sweet-talk a gang of old ladies into shining his shoes. She took the phone because she knew when she'd been one-upped.

Milton beamed and used the opportunity to cut himself a huge slice of cinnamon roll twist that he happily slathered with icing. Coffee mug in hand, he carried his prize toward the living room table as he winked at her and Richard started talking.

She really needed more coffee.


"Mail call."

Bram kept his gaze on his tablet but his attention wasn't on the information being displayed. Men were pouring out of their tents and work areas, high-tailing it on the double to where letters and packages were being handed out.

He was waiting, too, eager, poised, needy.

Shit.

He was practically drooling like a dog waiting for a bone. Just one damned meatless bone to prove he wasn't invisible.

The private finished off his bag of mail without calling Bram's name.

What did he expect? He'd jumped on her the second her sister tossed him aside. A girl like Jaelyn wouldn't settle for a guy who thought of her as a consolation prize.

He forced himself to focus.

He would still write her another letter.


LeAnn climbed into her car Monday afternoon and frowned. The mailman was blocking the driveway. Clicking her fingernails against the steering wheel, she watched him stuff a folded bundle of sale circulars into the mailbox. With a rattle, the mail truck moved on to their neighbor's box.

Backing up, she stopped at the curb. Getting out of the car she pulled the mailbox open. The letters were all sitting inside the circulars. Flicking through them, she pulled out the ones addressed to her. A little huff passed her lips as she found one with an overseas stamp on it.

Magnus. Captain Bram Magnus who had been overseas so long the man seemed to have forgotten whose
boyfriend he was. LeAnn scowled at the letter. It was
addressed to Jaelyn again.

She took it anyway and closed the mailbox. Climbing
back into her car, she tossed the letter onto the passenger
seat. Punching on her music, she merged into the traffic.

Boyfriends did not dump her.

Oh, she'd read every one of his letters to little Jaelyn.
Each one made her madder than the last. He was hers. No
boyfriend of hers was going to do one thing for any girl
except her, and that included her sister.

Especially since little Jaelyn wasn't as innocent as she
put on. Magnus had penned such a nice apology for kissing her. LeAnn was the one owed an apology and she was
going to get what she wanted.

Actually, what she really wanted was to . . . well . . .
she couldn't grasp the right word for it. In some part of
her brain, she realized Jaelyn deserved a guy like Bram.
But that made her realize maybe she didn't.

She clicked her fingernails and pressed the accelerator
down.

She wasn't going there. Nope. Life was hard and sharp
edged. It wasn't her fault and she wasn't going to spend
her time apologizing for playing hard in order to get what
she wanted. Men did it all the time. Even Bram. He'd show
up anytime he wanted attention, expecting her to be there,
and she had been. But she wasn't going to miss out on life
while he was away.

He certainly wasn't. Nope. Bram was earning his position and so was she. There was no way she was going to
be shamed into becoming a groundhog that waited for
spring to show up.

## Cobra Fire Base

Gideon licked his lower lip. Sneaking a final look around, he unsnapped his vest pocket. Shoving two fingers into it, he felt the worn edge of the picture. Excitement sent adrenaline pumping through his veins. His hand actually shook when he pulled the picture free.

"Hot damn."

His voice was raw and his mouth went dry. Behind his fly, his cock filled until it was hard.

"Sweet little pair of pussycats."

The captain was a bastard for not sharing.

Bastard.

Gideon stroked the picture with the tip of his index finger. But which one belonged to the captain?

Gideon peered at the photo until he noticed the way the pretty girl had her skirt raised up to show off some thigh.

Got you.

He pushed the picture deep into his pants pocket.

Yeah, he knew which one. Because he was smart. Smarter than the idiots wearing uniforms. Maybe they got the glory but he was getting the paycheck. A man with money could get any girl he wanted, no matter who took her picture to war with him.

# CHAPTER TWO

LeAnn captivated the opposite sex. Jaelyn watched her over the table of food laid out in honor of her grandfather's Memorial Day picnic. It was the only holiday he took so seriously. He claimed it was his way of remembering how lucky he was to come home from Vietnam.

LeAnn was in top form, too. Her cut-off jeans showed off her legs and the waistband dipped in the front to show off her tight tummy. She looked like a queen and she was being attended to like one as well. Every unattached guy was near her. But there were no other young women near LeAnn. They stood in groups a fair distance from her sister. There was one thing you could count on and that was that LeAnn didn't share. Not when it came to members of the opposite sex.

The entire extended family was running around the park, kids chasing each other with squirt guns and babies being adored. The younger teens stood around in awkward groups trying to figure out who they were, their hands shoved deep into their pockets.

There were times Jaelyn felt like she was still at that age. All nerves and doubts. Confidence only a thing much talked about, yet still out of reach. She sighed and looked over the food. LeAnn wouldn't be lending a hand to make sure no one came down with food poisoning. That left the sorting of potato salad and sour cream–based dips to her. She scooped up a few that looked past their prime and dumped them into the trash.

"Bram!" LeAnn suddenly let out a squeal loud enough to get Jaelyn to look back at her. In spite of the numerous guys sitting with her, LeAnn jumped to her feet and ran across the grass toward an approaching man.

He was a man, too.

Jaelyn couldn't help but stare at his wide shoulders that were packed with muscle and truly were worthy of being called brawn. There was something about the way he moved that was downright sexy. His body didn't move in the same way as the others surrounding LeAnn. He had more purpose and a lot more discipline. His gaze was keen. So sharp, Jaelyn felt it slice clean through the distance separating them. She'd never noticed what a brilliant blue his eyes were. Pristine, like a mountain lake. And you could feel the power of the water, like some sort of magical spirit cleanser.

Which was ridiculous, but that didn't change the way Jaelyn felt her stomach tighten.

Bram Magnus stared straight at her, his long legs cutting a path across the grass toward her. For a moment, she felt locked into that gaze, transfixed like time had frozen and her entire world tilted off center. But LeAnn's head interrupted when she flung herself into his arms.

Jaelyn looked down at the bowl of potato salad in her

hands. Disappointment slammed into her. It was so strong she blinked back tears. It felt like he was being ripped off her.

Stupid . . .

Watching him like a thirsty hiker looking at a waterfall was idiotic to say the least.

Still . . . She looked up and had to fight the urge to cringe. LeAnn had her hands wound around his neck while her body wiggled against his, slowly and with a sensual motion that left no one guessing just how intimate their relationship was.

"Well, well, well," her grandfather said as he abandoned his selected chair in the shade. "Welcome back, captain."

Bram set LeAnn aside like a child. Jaelyn stared at the ease with which he moved her sister. It confirmed just how much strength he really had hidden beneath the fatigues he wore. Her sister looked unsure for a moment, her eyes slightly wide, but Bram didn't spare her any attention. He focused on her grandfather and shook the hand offered to him with firm confidence and none of the awkwardness that many of the guys surrounding her sister so often displayed. He was sure and sound in his motions, confidence radiating from him.

And she was about to start drooling.

Jaelyn turned around and walked toward a large trash can. She dropped the overwarm salad in her hands into it without really remembering what she'd decided was wrong with it. She needed something to do, needed to keep moving before she turned around and stared back at Bram again.

Clearly fate had decided to give her a taste of what she

wanted. She was tingling alright but the guy had gone straight to her sister.

So Bram was a dead end.

Picking up her pace, she headed for her car, intent on rummaging through the odds and ends that were still locked inside it. She'd refill the napkins or pull out a bag of chips or anything else, just so long as it kept her from acting like a fool and throwing herself at him.

Maybe she should try another blind date.

It beat drooling over a man who only wanted a hookup with her sister.

"Great day for a picnic."

Jaelyn jerked her head up and stared at the man in front of her. He was wearing a bulky jacket that snared her attention because the weather was too warm for the garment. But he wasn't sweating or even looking like he was suffering from the heat. The guy even had his hands pushed into his pockets and he looked straight at her with a focus that was eerie.

"Picnics are great." Jaelyn tried to sound calm but her voice was slightly higher pitched than normal.

His eyes swept her from head to toe in a manner that made the hair stand up on the back of her neck. The weirdest sensation twisted through her belly because when she took a moment to look into his eyes, there was something lurking there that doubled her apprehension.

Crazy eyes.

That was how her grandpa had jokingly referred to people who looked like this. That sort of glee that glowed even in the bright light of day and warned you that there was something inside them which wasn't quite sane.

"Jaelyn!" LeAnn said with a snort when she spied her

and then propped her hands on her hips. "Grandpapa wants you. He sent me looking for you."

Her sister was clearly annoyed by the request, but Jaelyn felt overjoyed to see her sibling, even if she was snarling at her.

Safety in numbers, she thought, except the guy was looking at LeAnn like a prime steak.

"Thanks, I'll be right there."

Jaelyn looked around but the weird guy was missing. She'd failed to notice him leaving and he'd done it silently. She scanned the area around her, somehow feeling like it was a good idea to keep tabs on him. Not knowing where he'd gone sent another tingle through her belly.

"Well . . . get going already before Grandpa thinks I didn't do what he sent me to do and thinks I don't hear what he grumbles about me beneath his breath. I like being a cheerleader, and making it pro isn't just shaking my butt. It takes serious training. I am starving right now while everyone around me is stuffed. But there are weigh-ins on Tuesday."

Jaelyn looked at her sister, but LeAnn only pulled her lipstick out of her pocket and set about touching up her lips. Raspberry gloss slid along her lips, renewing their perfect shape and glistening with the promise of passionate kisses.

"I'll be sure to let him know you found me, LeAnn."

Her sister paused and turned to look at her. A hint of a genuine smile curved her lips. There was also a glimmer of the memory of the girls who had once snuck into the kitchen for hot chocolate well past their bedtime.

"Cool."

LeAnn muttered the single word with a shrug of her shoulders. "He's my grandpa, too, and all. I'm just not very good at talking to him like you are. He doesn't like the same stuff I do."

There was a touch of vulnerability in her voice that hinted at a need for approval from their grandfather, but LeAnn shook it off and lifted one hand to wave her toward the family camp.

"I mean it; don't get him smoked with me. I can do that just fine on my own."

"I just noticed something, LeAnn."

Jaelyn watched her sister try to hide behind an annoyed expression. "You aren't as much of a bitch as you put on."

"Yeah, well, don't tell the other girls on the squad. They are pure bitch and they like to eat anyone not tough enough to face them down. Even if they all swear they are my dearest friends. They'd smile while I went down and toast my demise with a bottle of chilled wine."

LeAnn waved her off and looked back into the mirror while she picked at her hair. Jaelyn hesitated just a moment longer, watching the way her sister fluffed her hair. There was a skill in her hands that didn't come from being a nitwit. LeAnn spent hours polishing her skills, and it seemed only fair that she gained what she wanted for all her effort.

But why Bram?

Jaelyn bit her lower lip and started back across the park. Disgust blossomed inside her but it wasn't quite strong enough to drown the jealousy eating at her.

Oh yeah, it was the green-eyed monster of envy turning her disposition bitter. Bram had never been hers to lose. It was ridiculous to stew over it.

In fact, she needed to get a fucking grip.

And everyone thought she was the good little sister,

into family and all the things that made church ladies
smile with approval. The truth was, she was rotten at the
core because she was eyeing her sister's man and there
was nothing worse than poaching from your own blood.
History was littered with examples of how often jealousy
had ripped families to shreds. Shakespeare had made a
good living writing about it.

"Your grandfather is as formidable as I recall."

Jaelyn jumped, completely absorbed in her thoughts.
Bram was too close in front of her and she recoiled as
though the man could read her thoughts. Panic flashed
through her in a split second while she flung herself back,
away from his imposing body. She landed on the side of
her foot and felt her ankle taking her weight at an angle
that sent pain shooting up her leg. His hand shot out, his
fingers curling around her upper arm faster than anyone
should be able to react. With that single grip, he lifted her
up enough to keep her from truly spraining her ankle, and
set her straight.

"I didn't mean to startle you."

His voice was just as rich as a double espresso and
packed with the same amount of caffeine-fueled punch,
too. Her heart jumped, increasing its pace, while adrenaline started pumping into her bloodstream.

"I should have been looking where I was going," she
muttered.

Agreement flashed through his eyes, and with a hint
of personal knowledge that sent a chill down her spine.
His eyes were a summer blue. She'd never wanted to look
into a man's eyes like she did at that moment. It was a
hypnotic pull that kept her staring at him while she became strangely aware of his grip on her arm. She felt every
finger, where they began to close around her bicep, and the

heat of his flesh pressing against her own. It shook her. Without a doubt, she felt that single touch rippling down her body until her toes felt like they were actually curling. Her mouth even went dry. It was horrifying but it was also damn exciting.

Fucking, damn, hot, exciting.

"There you are, Bram." LeAnn shattered the connection and Jaelyn actually cringed as guilt threatened to gag her. She jerked her head to the side, severing her ability to keep staring into his eyes. She hated doing it and that only filled her with more scalding guilt.

She was a rat.

LeAnn moved around her and cozied up next to Bram, taking advantage of his raised arm and slipping beneath it. His eyes narrowed, drawing Jaelyn's gaze back to his face. His expression was tight, betraying the fact that he wasn't as happy to see LeAnn as she was to see him.

*You're just seeing what you want to see . . .*

LeAnn smiled at her but there was no missing the get-lost look in her eyes. She slid her hand along the length of Bram's arm, her fingers gently stroking the hard ridges of muscle that his rolled-up cuffs revealed. She didn't hurry, her touch a sensual caress that spoke of plenty of intimate knowledge. LeAnn captured his wrist and pulled it away from where his fingers were still wrapped around Jaelyn's bicep.

"I missed you so much, Bram."

LeAnn aimed her full attention up into Bram's face while she twisted and pressed her body against his.

Jaelyn jerked back and turned quickly to avoid seeing any more.

Jealous . . .

It was so stupid but she couldn't deny it. She scoffed at

herself as she forced her feet to move faster and take her away from the root of her dilemma. She didn't hear any footsteps behind her and that only sent a jolt of pain through her. Somehow, she'd failed to notice just how much she liked Bram Magnus. Countless conversations surfaced from her memory and she was filled with humiliation now that she noticed just how pathetically she'd been hanging on his every word.

Stupid. And the churning emotions twisting in her stomach were promising her the penalty for being so short-sighted was going to be steep.

Like climbing up the face of a rock wall.

But she was going to do it because there was no way she was going to pine for him.

Nope.

Bring on the blind dates, she was ready.

Gideon ground his teeth together. His feet were moving and he didn't bother to worry about where he was going.

He couldn't think.

Emotions and thoughts whirled inside his mind like a tornado, flinging ideas wildly. They were impulses that he had to fight against acting upon.

Which one?

He stopped and stared at the photograph. His cock hardened instantly now whenever he looked at the picture, and standing close enough to smell her skin had been the sweetest torture he'd ever experienced.

God, he wanted that pain again.

His cock was still rigid and throbbing. Looking up, he gained his bearings and headed toward the flat he'd just bought. Perched on top of a new building, the hallways still smelled of fresh paint.

Quiet and still, with the newest in soundproofing for his windows and walls. Exactly the place to bring his pussycat once he caught her. He was going to make her into a pet there, where no one would be the wiser.

Pushing in the door, he engaged the high-tech security system with a press of his thumb against the panel before shrugging out of his jacket. Sweeping the empty flat, he forced himself to dig up some patience.

He wasn't ready yet.

But he grinned when he looked at the bed he'd found a few days ago. Moving toward it, he reached out to grip the thick ironwork that made up the headboard. He gave it a jerk and it held firm. Now that was quality. Sure it cost a bundle but now that he was stateside, money would be the advantage he'd lacked in Afghanistan.

He'd watched that picnic long enough to know a gold digger when he saw one. Bram Magnus was about to get a front-seat view to his girl walking away from him.

His cock ached. Releasing the iron, he slid his hand down and opened his fly. His swollen cock made use of the freedom instantly, poking out toward the bed.

He was going to fuck her here.

He would enjoy the sight of her spreading herself out for him while the glory boys had nothing in their beds but the seconds. Prime ass like the one at the park always went to the guy with money.

Gideon had the money.

Gideon looked at the picture again, holding it in his left hand while his right one handled his erection. He gripped his swollen flesh, working it back and forth while he stared at the picture. In the park, she'd been even more of a succulent morsel than she was on paper. He was going to just watch her first, maybe use a dildo on her just so he could enjoy watching her without the interference of feeling his cock burning inside her snatch.

Excitement made his breathing rough and his hand moved faster. Lust fueled his motions and his balls tightened until they couldn't contain their load anymore. Spurts of cum shot out onto the sheets that covered the bed, his fingers crumpling one corner of the picture as pleasure filled him until he cussed.

The hand with the picture landed on the bed, supporting him as satisfaction raced through the meat of his cock and he shuddered with it. The afternoon sun made the cum glitter and he laughed.

Pushing his cock back into his pants, he closed the buttons before replacing the picture in his shirt pocket.

He couldn't wait to see her again.

In fact, he wasn't going to wait. He was going to follow them home and discover what address to begin sending flowers to.

Cleaning up after a picnic was exhausting.

Which was sort of welcome, because Jaelyn needed to keep her mind off the fact that her sister was with Bram.

Seriously, she needed to drop her fascination with him. Like . . . now.

The house grew quiet, but sleep felt a million miles away. She was a bundle of twitching nerve endings that didn't seem to realize nothing wonderful was going to happen.

Live in the moment . . . before it was gone.

Yeah, she'd done that and wasn't sorry.

LeAnn had disappeared and it didn't take any more details to surmise just what she and Bram—her boyfriend—were up to. The relationship worked for them.

Which just meant she needed to get on with finding her own man.

Headlights danced across the kitchen window along with the beat of a stereo turned up too loud for closed windows to filter out completely. The base beat pounded through the glass a few moments before the car turned off and she heard LeAnn close the door with more force than normal. Her sister looked furious, her lips set into a snarl as she stomped down the driveway and yanked the front door open.

"What's this?" Milton sat up, glaring at his front door as it slammed shut. He wiped a hand across his face and shook his head. "What's eating you, girl? It's nearly midnight. Too late for slamming doors."

LeAnn froze, looking as if she'd forgotten there were other people living in the house. For a moment her face retained its furious expression but she soon banished it.

"Sorry, Grandpa, I lost track of the time."

Her sister offered her grandfather a look that almost appeared sincere, but when she noticed Jaelyn watching from the kitchen doorway, her face tightened instantly. "Can't really blame me. Bram has that sort of effect on a girl."

"LeAnn?"

Her sister turned her back on her and disappeared into the hallway. A second later there was a dull thud as her door shut.

Milton muttered something Jaelyn couldn't hear before going down the hallway toward his bedroom.

Grabbing the trash, Jaelyn headed for the side door and the trash cans that were waiting out on the curb for pickup in the morning.

"You really shouldn't be out this time of night, even if you think you live in a good neighborhood."

Jaelyn jumped and the trash bag went smashing into the concrete of the driveway. A word rolled out of her mouth that sent one corner of Bram's lips up.

He was leaning against the tree that shaded the front yard. The trunk was thick enough to hide his body, and somehow she got the idea he'd chosen the spot exactly for that reason. It was the darkest shadow in the yard because of the glow from the front porch light.

It was also the same spot they'd connected in.

So long ago.

Her cheeks stung but LeAnn's words where still bouncing around inside Jaelyn's head.

Bram emerged from the shadows.

He moved with a silent purpose that was slightly unnerving. It raised the hair on the back of her neck because seeing it drove home just how lax everyone around her was. He lifted the lid on the large trash can for her but she didn't drop the bag into it because her mind suddenly latched on to the fact that she hadn't heard his steps. She looked down and his feet were still laced up in black boots that looked ready for an inspection.

He plucked the bag out of her distracted hold and tossed it into the can while she pulled in a startled breath.

"Glad you came out, it saves me the trouble of texting you at an inappropriate time." His lips twitched as though he was pleased to see her. "We were interrupted today." His voice was deep and husky, awaking every daydream she'd indulged in. His head angled back so he could look directly at her, and in spite of the darkness, she felt his gaze settle on her.

Like he was hungry.

*So was she . . .*

"We were? It looked like you were happy to reconnect with LeAnn."

She watched him shake his head and something rippled through the air between them.

Jaelyn could have sworn she felt the heat rising off him.

Or maybe it was moving between them, like some live current.

He stepped forward and she caught a look at his face. The muscles along his jaw were tight but there was something in his eyes that hinted at longing.

"I had some details which needed clearing up with her." His voice was low and deep and it sent a quiver through her belly. Excitement curled into a ball and burned there because that tone was better than any daydream; it was ten thousand times better.

"What details?"

She shouldn't have asked. Her brain was making way too much of the opportunity to contemplate what her options were if Bram had broken up with LeAnn.

"Making sure she knew we were finished," he confirmed in a solid tone. "I came to see you today."

*Oh man . . . opportunity was calling her name . . .*

Her world tilted off center again. Hunger busted through the barrier she'd sealed it behind, clawing its way through her core. Every logical conversation she'd had with herself melted like a cube of sugar under a faucet, leaving her with nothing but the man in front of her and how much she didn't care about what anyone else thought.

Just the fact that he'd said he'd come to see her . . .

But reality was a vicious bitch who showed up right on cue to crush her budding fantasy with a reality check.

The look of fury on LeAnn's face as she'd come in floated through Jaelyn's mind.

She shook her head. "You're on the rebound."

Honestly, she was trying to convince herself as much as him. His eyes narrowed but Jaelyn shook her head again.

"I saw LeAnn when she came in." Jaelyn didn't give him a chance to argue. "So, we're not talking tonight."

It was logical.

It made sense.

It was safer.

And it sucked.

But she watched his face, saw the way he contemplated her words. There was resistance in his eyes, yet it melted under the cold hard facts. He nodded and she turned around.

Rabbit to burrow . . .

God, how she hated that visual!

The only thing that made her keep walking was the fact that she was pretty sure she would hate herself even more if she gave in and came back out to talk to him.

Because they wouldn't be talking long.

Nope. Bram wanted something different and so did she.

It would be a hell of a ride, she didn't doubt it. He'd deliver on the toe-curling experience she's dreamed of, for sure.

But she'd be selling out on her dreams.

So she locked the door.

He wanted to go after her.

The impulse was stronger than he expected and the truth was, Bram was sort of tickled to feel the intensity.

A man's thinking could get twisted up while he was deployed. But the urge to get close to Jaelyn was stronger than ever.

She had more sense than he did.

Even if he'd seen her fighting the force that was trying to draw them closer together.

His phone vibrated. He looked at his dad's number and decided fate was reinforcing Jaelyn's rational choice.

It would be better. He wanted to do things right, be worthy of her.

Not that he had a clue how to go about it.

"Bram," came the voice over the phone when he answered the call.

Bram knew the tone his father was using. It was the one every child on the face of the earth recognized. There was parental authority in it but what made the spine stiffen but it was more than tone, it was also the fact that Bram was old enough to recall just how many times his father had been right to kick his tail.

"Bram, I try hard to let you be your own man because I know it's important to you to be more than the colonel's son."

"Something I appreciate, Dad," Bram answered. "What's on your mind?"

"You mean besides the fact that you didn't come to see me or your sister before heading out to California?"

"I'm old enough to remind you of how lonely being deployed makes a person."

There was a snort on the other end of the line. "That crack didn't win you any points. You came through DC and didn't stop to see me."

Bram grinned. "You're locked in your classified lab . . ."

"I would have come out," Bryan said. "That cheerleader is not the love of your life. Don't expect me to be any too happy to know she ranked higher than me."

"I'm not here to see LeAnn." Bram cut to the admissions. "It's her sister I came looking for."

"Son—" his father began.

"I know," Bram said, cutting him off. "It's not the most advisable situation. But LeAnn was fooling around on me and I started something with Jaelyn. As stupid as it was, I can't seem to shake it. They're night and day, Dad."

There was a long pause. "I'd argue with you but I know that tone you're using."

It was a relief to hear his father say it.

But it also tightened his insides because he knew without a doubt he had something bad for Jaelyn and he had no reason to expect her to welcome him when he'd been stupid enough to fool around with her sister.

It wouldn't be the first time he challenged the odds, either.

"Bram, you aren't going to want to hear this, but you're going to." His father began to lay out his pearls of wisdom. "I hear something in your tone I never have before. But you've chosen a very dangerous path with Hale and his team. I know you crave it, you come by the instinct from me. Your mother couldn't live with it. She doesn't even send you a birthday card because of how bad my life scared her. Beth doesn't want to risk knowing you and your sister because my work might translate into someone seeking retribution through you two. I didn't tell her before we got married who I was, because I wanted her too bad. It blew up in my face three years later and you don't have a mother because of my mistake."

It was a topic his father rarely discussed. The fact that

Bram's mother had left them, unable to deal with her ex-husband, even though it meant she would never get to see her children. She'd cut all ties, marrying again and never looking back. Bram only knew what she looked like from a picture album stored among his father's things.

"Keep it in mind, son," Bryan said, finishing up. "And you'd better get your tail out here to see me before you disappear with Kagan's teams of Shadow Ops."

"Yes, sir."

"Magnus out."

Bram looked toward the house.

He could walk away.

Maybe the correct word was "should" walk away.

The moment the thought crossed his mind he knew he didn't have the strength to do it. There was something drawing him toward Jaelyn. It was so strong, so intense, part of him felt like it would be impossible to forgive himself for throwing in the towel when all he'd done was write letters.

Face-to-face.

That was the way it needed to be. If she told him to go, he would.

*I came to see you . . .*

Jaelyn chewed on her lower lip and headed for a shower. In spite of the fact that she'd dragged herself out of bed before dawn, she was now wide awake with her brain running in circles.

*We were interrupted today.*

A shiver went down her spine as she recalled the way the man looked into her eyes. It was beyond intense and just the memory of it made the hair on her neck stand up.

But a second before she turned on the light in the bathroom, she caught the hint of a shadow beyond the window. She blinked and the guy was still there, watching LeAnn through her bedroom window.

"What the hell?"

Her grandfather roared from the hallway. Jaelyn spun around but her grandfather was already yanking the back door open.

"Grandpa!"

Her grandfather charged at the man, yelling words she hadn't known he knew. The man turned around and lunged at the old man. There was a sickening crunch as his fists collided with her grandfather's head.

"Stop!" It was a feeble attempt to protect her kin. Jaelyn raced forward as her grandfather fell. LeAnn let out a scream and kept screaming as she watched through the bedroom window.

Jaelyn ended up in the dirt, feeling the skin on her hands being scraped away as the shadow shoved her out of the way. He ran toward the back of the house. A second later, Bram skidded around the front of the house. He covered the distance in a heartbeat, hitting his knee next to her.

"That . . . that way . . ."

She was panting but managed to point toward the backyard.

Bram pushed off his knee in a fluid motion, the light from the streetlamp flashing off a gun in his hand. But the sound of a car starting and tearing through the alley filled the night. Bram didn't let it stop him—he climbed the fence and fired off a shot at the car.

Jaelyn reached for her grandfather. He was stiff and lying on the ground.

* * *

"Damned civilian law enforcement."

Her grandfather didn't care for the paramedic who tried to keep him on the gurney. "It's just a knock on the head. I've had worse."

"Grandpa," Jaelyn said as she pressed him back with a firm hand. "Your heart isn't handling it well. You need to see a doctor."

"Ha!" Her grandfather snapped but stayed put. "You mean these medics want to wring some profit out of being called here tonight."

"Mr. Sondors, I really think it's a good idea for you to agree to transport."

A second cop added his similar opinion. There were half a dozen police cars scattered on the front lawn.

"Only if you tell your fellow officers to stop giving Bram there a hard time. Just because he had a gun. You all act like a man doesn't have the right to run a Peeping Tom off his property."

"More than a Peeping Tom," Jaelyn added. Her grandfather's face was turning purple, his right eye already swollen shut.

"My point exactly!" he pointed a finger at the cop trying to give him advice. "And look at the way your buddies are acting. That young man was there when I needed him. Who knows what might have happened to my granddaughters if he'd gotten into the house."

Jaelyn stole a glance over at where Bram was facing down four burly officers. They all had their hands on the butts of their sidearms. He had his back against a squad car but he still didn't look pinned. There was something in his stance that warned her he would take them all down if he needed to.

"I'm not going anywhere until I talk to that boy."

The cop grumbled but ambled away. He talked to the officer in front of Bram for a moment. The man finally nodded. Bram brushed past them without a single glance. Her grandfather lifted his hand and beckoned to him.

"Mr. Sondors." Bram hit his knee next to the gurney.

"Tell him to go to the hospital," Jaelyn said. "He's being stubborn."

Bram considered her grandfather for a long moment. "Might be best."

Her grandfather nodded at last. Relief spread through her.

"So long as you promise me you'll look after my girls. Can't stand the thought of them here with that peeper loose."

"I'm not going anywhere," Bram said as he looked back at her and she felt the full force of his hard gaze. "You have my word on that."

"Well, I am," Jaelyn informed them both before she climbed right into the back of the ambulance and sat down.

Her grandfather reached out and grasped Bram's forearm. "Stay with LeAnn. I know she's . . ." He waved his hand in the air.

"She's your granddaughter," Bram finished.

The paramedics were pushing the gurney toward the open doors and lifting it up. There was a clatter as the wheels and supports folded up. It was too noisy for further conversation but Bram sent Jaelyn a look that was full of promise.

Gideon was shaking. There was a potent combination of rage and frustration swirling around inside him. He gripped handfuls of his hair as he tried to control his thoughts and regain control.

"Now that . . . is a fine looking pair of tits."

Gideon jumped, turning around to find a man leaning against a tree and smiling at him like he hadn't just said the word "tits."

"Nice ass, too," he added, before he offered his hand. "Sullivan's the name, Ricky is what my ma called me."

"How do you know what I was doing?" Gideon demanded.

Ricky took a drag off the cigarette in his hand and offered it across the space between them. Gideon gave in and took it, inhaling deeply so that the tip glowed red.

"I saw you follow them in the park," he said, chuckling. "But only because I was doing the same. You've got good taste, my man."

Gideon laughed in response. Ricky shook his head when he tried to hand the cigarette back and pulled another one from his shirt pocket. He took a moment to light it and draw a lungful of smoke that he let tickle his nose before he blew it out in a long, milky stream. "I'd sure like to fuck one of them."

"Yeah," Gideon remarked, shifting as his cock hardened. "It's not going to happen. Chicks like that always go for the uniform guys."

"I'm more of a take-it sort of guy," Ricky said. "Don't fucking care what anyone thinks of me, either."

Gideon perked up, watching Ricky draw off the cigarette, waiting to hear what he'd say next.

"I mean, life's gotten too damned polite if you ask me . . ." He blew smoke out again. "Today's bitches won't admit it, but they like a man who takes command."

Gideon nodded, his eyes bright.

Ricky shook the cigarette at him. "All she needs is the chance to feel you jerking her hair."

Ricky lifted the cigarette to his lips and drew in a breath. Sure, smoking was slowly killing him, that just made life more intense because he was aware of it slipping away. A concept Bram Magnus had introduced him to recently.

Bram and his team of Shadow Ops that was.

It was going to be a personal favor to track them down and get back in with Tyler Martin. At least until Ricky killed the man for double-crossing him. No one pulled one over on a Sullivan and now that he'd found Bram Magnus's soft spot, Ricky had the opening he needed to extract his revenge.

Bram's little cheerleader was popular on social media. They liked getting shots of Bram when he was with her, too, which was how Ricky had tracked Bram down.

Gideon would make the perfect resource. A nice pigeon to take the dirt when it splattered. Damn but lady luck was paying up in spades today. The guy was almost too easy to work over. But then again, life had been a bitch to him lately. It was time for him to get his due.

Time warped inside a hospital.

Jaelyn rubbed her eyes and sat up as she tried to find a clock. The room her grandfather was in was cast in darkness, but there was still plenty of light spilling under the drawn curtain from the open door to the hallway.

An orderly had brought in a cot for her and she'd collapsed on it at some point just before dawn while her grandfather was still grumbling over the doctor's insistence that he remain for observation.

She sat up, looking toward the bed but her grandfather

was still sleeping. She picked up her shoes and tiptoed into the hallway on sock-clad feet to keep from waking him.

She fished through her purse for enough coins to buy a cup of coffee from a vending machine. The scent made her wrinkle her nose but beggars couldn't be choosers. She wandered outside to add a little fresh air to the taste of the machine coffee in an effort to find a silver lining.

The coffee still sucked but Jaelyn smiled because her grandfather was doing well and honestly, she'd drink sucky coffee in exchange for not having him truly injured.

"Jaelyn Sondors?"

The coffee went flying but the guy in front of her didn't seem too worried about it. In fact, she detected a tiny flicker of amusement in his eyes before he was flashing some laminated card in her face.

"Bram Magnus sent me to pick you up."

There was a teasing hint of Irish brogue in his tone and when he smiled, his face was really sort of cute, if she didn't notice the pink patches from healing wounds.

"This way . . ." He opened the back door of a sedan that was double-parked.

"Sorry, I'm not leaving." Jaelyn turned and left. Her temper was sizzling.

She skidded to a stop just inside the hospital doors, fumbling in her purse for her cell phone.

But then she stopped.

Yeah, Bram had nerve. But he was also fresh from a military deployment, so attending to details likely just came second nature to him. And he had promised her grandfather.

She needed to let it slide.

It was the right thing to do.

She dropped her phone back in her purse and followed the signs toward the cafeteria.

Less sucky coffee would help.

"Your plan crashed and burned."

Ricky turned the wheel and headed away from the hospital. "You need to enjoy playing the game a little. If you just want your cock drained, I know a place to take your money for the ride of your life."

Gideon watched him for a moment before looking out at the road in front of them. "I think the other one is his girl. The cheerleader."

Sullivan didn't agree but he also knew that Bram was sitting on LeAnn, which meant she was important to him. Either one, it didn't matter to him. What he wanted was a way to strike back at the members of the Shadow Ops team that had taken down the Raven.

Not that Ricky cared a bit about Marc Grog, who had used the underworld name of the Raven. Nope, Ricky hadn't shed a tear over the guy who was gutted by Saxon Hale and his team.

What Ricky cared about was that Carl Davis and Tyler Martin had decided to tie up Ricky like a loose end, after they'd hired him to track down Ginger Boyce.

They'd failed, or at least Tyler Martin had, because Carl Davis was running for president of the United States and Tyler was the guy taking care of all the dirty work. Like making sure it never came to light that Carl Davis had been dealing with Marc Grog.

That was where Ginger Boyce had come in. She'd seen Marc murder someone and Saxon Hale had been close enough to extract her while she was still alive. In a way, it was fun to see how a team of Shadow Ops had gotten the jump on men like Carl Davis and Tyler Martin. Ricky liked a good fight more than anything else and watching the good guys take on the elite of Washington was proving to be pretty cool.

At least until it had landed him in a Mexican jail.

Now it was time for payback and Bram Magnus was exposed, so that was where Ricky planned to start. Besides, Ricky would bet Tyler Martin was going to make a try for Saxon Hale's team. Bram Magnus was the only member crossing into the open. It was their weak spot. Tyler would be along to exploit it.

So he'd put up with Gideon while he waited for Tyler to pop his head up.

Gideon was pathetic. Lusting after Bram's girl when Gideon had a nice plump bonus from his service in hostile territory.

That was another sort of opportunity, the money-making kind. Gideon had cash and Ricky was going to make sure to take advantage of that as well. Just as soon as he finished paying Tyler Martin back, it was going to be time to retire. Maybe head back to Russia where he could open a fight club. He had the funds. But a Sullivan never let anyone pull one over on him.

As far as honor went, it was his only creed.

"I thought you worked from a home office."

Jaelyn wasn't used to being the second one up in the morning. Bram watched her take in his presence before he reached over and pulled the coffeepot off the machine and poured her a cup.

"Your grandfather offered the garage loft to me," he said by way of explanation.

"Right," she said as she took a sip of the java. "I should have changed the sheets."

Bram offered her a shrug but pointed at her suit. It was a little unnerving the way he noticed details about her.

And hot.

*Now don't go down that thought path . . .*

"I telecommute a lot but there are times my employer likes to see me," she said.

"We still haven't talked."

Damn but she liked the sound of his voice, especially when it had a tone of determination.

*Yeah, like wine. And you know what's going to happen if you let him intoxicate you . . .*

*Yep she did . . . and the idea was growing on her.*

She was drinking coffee to avoid answering him and it suddenly bothered her a whole lot.

She wasn't going to be a chicken. Jaelyn lowered her mug and looked Bram straight in the eye.

"Maybe it's best we don't have that particular conversation."

There, she'd said the right thing.

The sensible thing.

*It sucked.*

Her cell phone started chiming, the morning beginning with a bang. Yeah, reality was cold and hard, and he was something else.

Something that belonged in the midnight hours when practicality didn't have to be listened to.


"You do know your stuff."

Ricky offered the compliment to Gideon as he fast-forwarded through the surveillance footage their little camera had taken throughout the night of the Sondors home.

"Shit, you can get those little cameras at Costco these days," Gideon said. "Putting location beacons on the cars, that was a little more tricky."

"But worth it," Ricky crowed. "Now we can get on with nabbing your pet."

"But . . . which one?" Gideon was rubbing a hand over his head. "We still don't know . . ."

Ricky shrugged. "We just need to test out which one Bram goes after."

Gideon looked at him with bright eyes. It was almost too easy to manipulate the guy. Like showing a dog a treat and making him sit before you tossed it to him.

"Come on," Ricky said with a grin. "I've got an idea. Bring your toolbox, I'm going to need you to kill a surveillance system."

The rat race . . .

Jaelyn left the boardroom on steps that sounded sturdy. Her feet ached and her smile felt frozen in place but there was also a sense of satisfaction filling her. She slid into an elevator alone, because being a remote employee meant the days she did report in were longer, since her employer made sure they were still getting their money's worth.

It was worth it.

Even the stillness of the parking structure didn't bother her. The regular office personal had departed at five, a good two hours ago. It didn't concern her because she didn't have to report back in at eight in the morning.

Besides, it wasn't like she was parked in a seedy part of town.

Being an accountant was mundane, but companies needed good people who could keep the books straight. Lucrative companies. The modern age meant she could compile all those reports from any computer, including the one in her home office. It was a job that met all the criteria of being successful in the adult world.

So why did she feel like she was waiting for her life to begin?

Was that the source of her fascination with Bram?

It was a fair enough question. Jaelyn slid behind the wheel of her car and turned the key.

But nothing happened.

A little tingle of dread went through her as she looked at the switch for the headlights.

Nope, they were off.

She tried the key again but there wasn't even a little click-click-click to tell her anything was responding. A tap on the emergency roadside assistance button failed to bring her any response, either.

She pulled her cell phone from her purse but the garage was blocking her signal. With a grumble, Jaelyn opened the door and got out, heading toward the outer edge where she might be able to get a signal.

The sound of her dress shoes echoed through the empty space, bothering her a lot more than it had when she'd arrived.

Amazing how vulnerable she felt.

It was just a dead battery. No need to get jumpy.

But it was still strange the way her body grew tense, all because she knew her car wasn't working. It was almost as if she was tapping into some sort of hidden survival instincts lurking in her DNA. Her senses were heightened, her heart beating just a little faster.

She jerked her head around at the sound of a motor. A quick look at her phone showed her the thing was still searching for a signal. The car came into sight at the edge of the ramp, turning down the lane and coming toward her.

Overreacting or not, she ducked into the stairwell, jumping down the flight with little tapping sounds from her heels before she came out on the floor below. Her phone rewarded her with a connection and she punched the call button.

But the problem with business centers was that there were very few people left around at the end of the day. The sun was setting as she walked along the well-kept walkways and listened to the phone buzz.

"Jaelyn?" her grandfather answered. "What's wrong?"

"Nothing," she replied. "Just have a dead car, so I'll be late."

"Sun's already going down."

"I know. I'll be fine."

There was a muffled comment on the other side of the conversation.

"Really, I'm just going to call a tow truck to give me a jump start. Don't worry."

"Bram says he knows who to send over."

"Um . . . really, I can handle this," Jaelyn replied.

"Already done." Bram's voice came over the line. "There's a coffee shop a block away from your location, wait there."

"Ah . . . how do you know where I am?"

There was a slight pause. "All phones have location chips in them these days."

"Right." Honestly, she needed the help but there was still something unnerving about the way he operated on a different level from the rest of the civilian world.

Of course, that was it in a nutshell. Bram wasn't a civilian. Off duty, sure enough, but there was part of him
that would always be something different.

"Thanks."

She cut the line, feeling like she was clinging to him.
Part of her wanted to be braver, more confident.

More worthy . . .

*Yeah, that's going to get you into a world of trouble.*

The thing was, she had a sinking suspicion she'd love
every second of it.

"You let her get away," Gideon griped.

Ricky looked across the front seat of the car. "Thought
you wanted to know for sure which one was his girlfriend?" He turned the steering wheel and continued out
of the garage. "Personally, I don't care. Both of them look
like juicy fucks."

"I want to know . . ."

Ricky wheeled into a parking place on the floor above
where Jaelyn's car was. "Let's see what happens."

Gideon swept his finger across the tablet he was holding and typed in some numbers. A moment later, the security cameras from the garage turned back on, giving
them a live feed. Gideon scrolled through the images until
he had one of the cameras near Jaelyn's car.

The guy was smart.

Ricky admired the way he knew his way around security
tech. It made it so much easier to track Bram Magnus.

It didn't really matter which one the guy was bang-
ing. Being sisters, he'd come looking if one of them went
missing.

At least, that's where Ricky was placing his bet. Gideon
was getting on his nerves with his obsession but Ricky

was going to wait the guy out. The prize was worth the fight.

And a Sullivan never quit.


"Nothing wrong with the battery."

Jaelyn watched as the tow truck driver tried to jump-start her car.

"Or the cables."

The guy arrived in a truck that sparkled and looked like it could handle pulling a car out of an avalanche. He was going through the engine with a flashlight and a look on his face that told her he knew his business very well.

"How many miles on her?"

"Thirty-two thousand," Jaelyn answered.

The guy made a sound under his breath as he continued to look.

Another vehicle came up the ramp, its engine growing louder as it came into sight. Bram pulled up next to her, sweeping her from head to toe before he looked at her car. He was driving a truck with a shell on it and a full-size spare tire secured to the side of it.

Of course he was. She looked at the truck, realizing it suited Bram perfectly with its "take on the worst nature might throw at it" demeanor.

"You didn't need to drive out here."

Bram surprised her by grinning. "Your grandfather would have come if I didn't."

Jaelyn felt her lips twitching. Bram sent her a knowing look.

"Okay, you've got me in a box with that reasoning."

She conceded the point before Bram went and shook hands with the tow truck driver.

"Doesn't make any sense," the driver said as he looked into the engine compartment again.

Bram stopped and pointed a flashlight at the driver-side window, right at the weather seal.

"Think someone used a Slim Jim on it?" the driver asked.

"Wouldn't be this dead if someone hadn't tampered with it," Bram responded.

"Come on," Jaelyn said. "No one . . . tampered with my car."

Bram looked up at her and she caught sight of the man who had chased a prowler around their house. He was all business, determination blazing in his eyes.

"Someone was on your property and now your car is suddenly dead without reasonable explanation . . ." Bram laid out what he saw. "I don't believe in coincidences. Especially when they keep happening."

He turned to the tow truck guy. "You have a secure impound yard?"

"Of course."

Bram pulled out his wallet and withdrew a credit card. "Tow it. We'll deal with it tomorrow."

The man was already reaching for his clipboard, swiping the card through a portable machine, before Jaelyn had the chance to intercede.

Bram sent her a look. "There's no point in arguing."

"Maybe I don't want you to feel like you have to take care of me."

It was the truth and yet, very exposing.

There was too much noise from the truck as the driver hooked up her car and pulled it up onto the bed of the truck. Which gave Jaelyn too much time to notice the way Bram looked at her. There was an intensity in his blue eyes that made her insides quiver. No one had ever made her believe she was quite so important before. The tow truck guy gave a quick toot on his horn before he pulled away, leaving her feeling like she was alone with a tiger.

Thing was, she liked the idea a whole lot.

"Why are you so determined to talk to me?"

Bram stepped closer. "Why are you so worried about being alone with me?"

Now there was a question.

It was tempting and razor edged. Impulses were bubbling up from cracks inside her she hadn't even realized were there. It was like he freed some part of her that she'd never even known about before.

"Because I can't seem to keep my hands off you when we're alone," she answered ruefully.

As far as wise things to say went, it was about as far from the mark as it got.

But it was oh so very honest.

She watched the way Bram's eyes glittered with victory. His lips thinned with hunger as he stepped closer.

"If I scare you, baby . . . say so, and I'll leave you be."

It was a challenge, one her body leaped to in response. Damn if he wasn't the bull she wanted to wave the red flag in front of.

"You know you don't scare me, Bram, that's the problem. You make me want to throw a gauntlet down just to make sure you know how much I refuse to be scared by you."

His eyes narrowed. It was part warning and part declaration. He reached for her but honestly, she'd dared him to do it.

He curled his hand around her nape, holding her with a grip that stopped just shy of pain. Instead, it sent a tingle down her spine as she absorbed his strength on a cellular level.

He loomed over her, titling his head so he could claim her mouth. If it was a kiss, she'd never been kissed before. This was different. Far removed from what she'd experienced before.

It was hungry.

And primal.

He took her mouth with a motion that twisted her insides with anticipation over just what he might do if he got his hands on the rest of her.

And it wasn't one-sided.

No, she reached for him, flattening her hands on his chest, rubbing over the muscles she'd only been able to look at before. Her heart was thumping like a jackhammer, sending her blood pulsing through her so all she longed for was to strip down.

Right after she clawed his clothing to shreds.

"Damn it . . . ," he said with a growl, his mouth an inch above her own. "I shouldn't have started this here . . ."

"Now who's chicken?"

God, she was a piece of work. When had she become a hussy?

*When you kissed Bram . . .*

There was a spot-on truth if ever she'd heard one. He made a sound under his breath as the grip on her nape tightened.

Bram's lips twitched, curving into a little smile that sent a shiver down her spine. It wasn't a congenial expression, not by a long shot.

Nope, this was a warning, one she felt curling her toes. He was such a pure man-animal. Maybe it had been im-

TAKE TO THE LIMIT 71

pulsive to kiss him but she was a hell of a long way from repentant.

"Inside . . ." He was pulling away, leaving her feeling his retreat keenly. There was a chirp before he was pulling the back door of his truck open. Inside, there was a black lining on the bed to protect it from dents and rolled up bedding.

Of course he was prepared.

He flattened his hands on either side of her as she ended up leaning against the side of the truck. The sheer intensity of his presence both delighted her and sent her reeling. It was like someone had turned up the volume on her senses to the top of the scale, making her aware that she'd been existing in a world of whispers until that moment.

Now, the thunder was loud enough to shake her core.

"Or you can get in the front seat and I'll drive you home."

His tone was soft and full of challenge. Hell, the guy was being aggressive and calling her bluff.

Uncivilized?

Savage?

A threat to her independent woman?

Truthfully, she wasn't really sure what exactly it was but she sure as shit knew what she wanted from him. And with him so close, the scent of his skin being drawn in with every breath, intoxicating her, there was no filter left.

He wasn't the only one who could be bold . . .

She reached up and pulled him down so that she could rise up onto her toes and kiss him.

Like she'd never have another chance to taste him.

She'd surprised him.

She felt his body tense, the muscles on the back of his neck tightening as she pressed her mouth firmly to his. She'd felt like his presence was intense, but it was nothing compared to the jolt that went through her when their flesh connected. She was reeling and absolutely thrilled to her core.

Nothing mattered except the taste of him and getting more of it. Her only fear was that he'd pull away.

Bram didn't disappoint her.

One moment, she was suspended in contemplation of him rejecting her, and in the next, he was wrapping her into his embrace, binding her against the hard body she'd been unable to forget.

"God . . . Jaelyn . . ." He buried his face in her hair, inhaling deeply. "I dreamed about the way you smell."

*She'd dreamed about him alright, too . . .*

So much so, she was impatient to get back in contact with his skin. She dug her hands into the soft jersey of his black T-shirt and pulled it up, out of his waistband.

"Christ—" He jerked back from her, drawing in a ragged breath.

His rejection was the one thing she feared and it left her horrified.

Bram captured her wrist, his fingers closing around it in a grip that was firm and just as solid as he was. He pulled her behind him into the truck. The shell rose up above the cab of the vehicle making it rather spacious inside. Bram released her and turned to pull the door shut. It left them in semidarkness as she watched him grab the sleeping bag and toss it down to cover the bed.

Bram hooked her around the waist and pulled her against him a moment later.

"Hummm . . ." It was really more of a purr than a word.

Just a sound that reflected how much she enjoyed the way he claimed her.

It was a no-holds-barred sort of thing. Bram held her head tightly, his lips pressing hers apart as he teased her lower lip with the tip of his tongue. Encased in the privacy of the truck bed, her impulses flared into flames.

He made her frantic, or maybe "demanding" was a better word. Jaelyn grabbed for the loosened edge of his shirt, her fingers fumbling as she tried to shove the garment up and over his head.

He drew back so that he could rip the shirt over his head. For one spectacular moment, she got a glimpse of his chiseled chest. In the next, she was chucking her own shirt over her shoulder and absorbing the way his lips curved.

It was very male.

And very satisfied.

She reached behind her to unhook her bra.

"No." It was a command, soft, yet hard edged. Her fingers froze as she felt her eyes widen, suddenly worried that he was going to reject her.

She was pretty sure it would crush her.

Bram waved his finger back and forth. "Not . . . so . . . fast."

She caught a hint of need in his tone and watched his expression reveal something she'd never expected him to allow her to see.

It was the raw hunger of a man who had been serving his country. Doing the right thing, while keeping his soul in chains so he might be called honorable. It surely left him feeling like he'd been deprived of the things everyone else enjoyed due to his diligence.

Well, she'd be happy to fulfill his needs.

"Just . . . a little . . . slower, Jaelyn."

She brought her arms around her body and crossed them over her chest, trailing her fingers over the swells of her breasts. His gaze focused on her hands, his lips parting in hunger.

She'd never imagined she had the power to mesmerize him.

And she realized it was a privilege.

She opened up her arms as she reached her shoulders, teasing the straps of her bra for a moment before she turned around and opened the waist band on her skirt. The sound of the zipper filled the space as she pushed it down her legs followed by her nylons. The night air was cool against her newly bared skin and she let out a little sound of enjoyment because she was so heated.

Her breath caught as she heard Bram shucking his pants as well. Anticipation tightened in her gut, heightening her perception yet again. They were so close together but she would have sworn she heard him coming for her, felt her skin tingling as his body heat reached across the space between them to tease her.

Awaken her.

"Perfect . . ." His voice sounded raspy next to her ear as he cupped her shoulders. "So very . . . perfect."

He found the clip in her hair and opened it. The soft strands of her hair fell down to cover her neck and shoulders. He shifted, sweeping his hand beneath it as he stroked her neck, his breath teasing her bare skin.

"I promised myself . . ." He swept her bra straps over her shoulders. ". . . that I wouldn't rush you . . ."

Her breasts were heavy, making her bra sag now that it wasn't held on her shoulders. Bram worked the hooks free in seconds but she turned around and crossed her arms over her chest as her brain insisted on thinking about what he'd said.

"You mean . . . you thought about . . . me?"

It had been a legitimate question, one she really wanted to know the answer to. At least that was until she caught sight of him.

It was a sin to cover his body with clothing.

Her mouth went dry and her need to know his motivations shriveled up in the face of just how cut and hard he was.

Raw.

The concept of man-animal had never been more fitting. It left her with nothing but cravings and he was exactly what she wanted to feast on.

"Every day . . ." He bit out the words. She got the feeling she was missing something, it was flickering there in his eyes but he was moving closer and her priorities were shifting.

Reaching for him was more important than conversation. Her bra fell when she unlocked her arms, slithering down her body to leave her breasts free. He let out a groan as he cupped them, his gaze lowering to them as he brushed her nipples with his thumbs.

"I want to play with these . . ." He leaned over and captured one hard point between his lips.

She gasped, arching back as a jolt of pleasure went down her back. It hit her right in the clitoris, making the tiny bundle of nerve endings a mass of demanding sensors.

Bram eased her back, until they were lying on the sleeping bag.

She rolled toward him, frantic to slide her hands along his arms and chest. She opened her thighs, clamping them around his lean hips as he threaded his hand through her hair to capture her and pin her in place for his kiss.

His mouth devoured hers and her appetite was raging just as fiercely. She needed to meet him, passion for passion, be more than just taken by him. It seemed impossible to touch him enough. She was stroking him, kissing him back, running her hands along his sides and along the edges of his hip before she closed her fingers around his ridged length.

"Don't do that." He growled at her, shifting his weight so she lost her hold on his cock.

"The hell I won't," she declared as she rolled over toward him.

"I like your spunk, Jaelyn . . ."

A moment later, he was rolling and pinning her once against to the surface of the bed, each of her wrists clamped above her head in his hands.

"I want to make sure you know how much I enjoy the way you challenge me . . ."

It was an abrupt power shift. One that sent an odd little feeling of excitement through her. He didn't miss it either, stilling above her, his grip secure but not biting.

He was watching her, gauging her reaction. Arousal went snaking through her, stunning her with how sharp it was because it conflicted with her logical thinking brain.

But it made sense, in a very strange way. He was a man-animal and she liked him that way.

"Fuck me."

It was blunt.

A hell of a long way from how she'd ever spoken to him before. It was her turn to gauge his reaction and it didn't take long. His lips thinned, his grip on her wrists tightening.

"Jaelyn . . ." There was a warning in his tone, one that pissed her off.

"If I wanted a nice guy . . . I wouldn't have kissed you."

She'd never been so honest, not even with herself. It didn't fit with the image of her life, the way her grandfather compared her to LeAnn.

*But it felt so right!*

To be wrong, or naughty, or maybe just true to her feelings.

"Or pulled your shirt off," she added. "I like you without clothing, Bram. Without . . . politeness . . ."

His lips parted into a grin that was anything but nice. It was menacing and all bad boy, man-animal. It triggered a jolt of need that felt like it shook her to the core. His cock was against her thigh and she was certain she felt it jerk.

That just made her wetter.

He shifted, withdrawing for a moment. She heard the sound of a foil packet being ripped open before he sheathed his length in a condom. And then he was coming back to her, covering her, lifting himself enough so his cock settled between her spread thighs, the head of it nudging the folds of her sex.

He lowered his head so his mouth hovered over hers. "Fuck?" His breath sent a shiver across the delicate surface of her lips. "Yeah . . . I want to do that to you, baby . . ."

He pressed forward, her body opening to accept his girth. But she was tight, and he stopped.

"You said you were waiting . . ."

"Because the last time I had sex . . . it wasn't worth the effort . . . ," she answered. "I want you."

His face tightened. There was a flare of enjoyment in

his eyes as he pressed forward again. Her body gave way, taking his length.

"I want to do other things, too . . ." He pulled free and she whimpered, unable to contain the needy little sound.

"Like claim you . . . ," he whispered as he slid back into her. This time, he penetrated easier, her body taking him as she lifted her hips. But he didn't press much deeper. Instead, he gave her only another inch of his flesh and then he held her in place as he watched her whither.

He made good on his words, working his hips in slow thrusts that left her covered in a thin sheet of perspiration as she waited for him to satisfy the needs twisting in her core. Time slowed down, leaving her aware of every motion, every millimeter he penetrated, and how long he made her wait for satisfaction.

And he was making her wait, watching her, judging how close she was to the edge.

"I hate you so much right now." She growled at him, twisting her wrists in a bid for freedom.

He leaned over and bit her softly on the side of her neck. The tiny pain combined with the craving to have him deeply seated inside her, making her more insane than she already was.

"You enjoy the fact that I don't play nice . . . said so yourself."

It was the truth. She locked gazes with him. "And you like that best about me."

Enjoyment flashed in his eyes. There was a hint of vulnerability there, too, but she was too far past thinking to dwell on. All that mattered was the fact that she could see his resolve crumbling. Watched it falling away to be replaced with raw hunger.

The mood shifted between them, ripping away the last

shreds of control. It left them both at the mercy of their cravings, desires they strove to feed, moving together as pleasure twisted deeper, intensifying, and finally blinding her as it flashed through her in a burst that shattered absolutely everything in her world.

It was gut-wrenching and mind-numbing, reducing her to a panting heap that had no strength left.

But she didn't need any. No, Bram pulled her close, warming her when her skin chilled, lulling her to sleep with the sound of his heart.

"Told you she was the one," Ricky muttered as he drew a drag off his cigarette.

Gideon was holding the tablet so tightly, his fingertips were white. He was watching the way the truck rocked back and forth.

"I want to kill him."

Ricky offered the cigarette across the front seat of the car. "And waste the chance to let him know you have his little bitch spread out in your bed? Thought you wanted to have fun with him. Dead men don't suffer."

Gideon turned his bright eyes toward Ricky. There was the unmistakable look of insanity in his gaze. The glint of obsession. Some guys needed a target to deal with the stress of being in a killing zone. The military had a fancy term for it: post-traumatic stress disorder.

Ricky just knew what it looked like.

"How are we going to get her?" Gideon demanded.

"Now that part," Ricky said as he dropped his smoke out the open window and turned the key in the ignition, "we need to be careful about. Because we'll only get one shot now that the captain saw you watching through the windows. He'll be on guard."

"He's not as smart as me."

Ricky drove toward the exit. "I noticed. Why do you think I keep telling you we'll get her? We just have to be patient and make sure we set it up just right. You got everything you need to keep her?"

"Yeah," Gideon muttered, looking back at the tablet. "I'm ready."

Ricky headed away from the parking structure because Gideon might be ready but there was no way Bram Magnus would be lax enough to let his guard down tonight. They needed a different setting, some place where their prey was alone and out of Bram's sight.

The moment would come.

And he'd be ready when it did.

Jaelyn was lying on him.

Bram woke up, another car engine breaking through his slumber. He heard it leave and part of his brain wanted to think about just why there was another car in the garage this time of night, but the feeling of Jaelyn resting on his chest was far too distracting.

He stroked her hair back from her face with gentle fingers, still absorbing the fact that she was really there.

He'd dreamed about her so often, it wouldn't have surprised him to wake up and discover it was all another fabrication of his subconscious mind.

She was real.

He caught the sound of her breathing, and the gentle thumping of her heart against his side.

There were twenty other little things he noticed just then, tiny details of her person, from the way her eyelashes rested on her cheeks to the scent of her skin and the ache in his balls.

Release was always intense after deployment.

But he knew this was something different.

It scared the shit out of him.

Which only made him grin because somewhere during the time he'd spent with Saxon Hale and his Shadow Ops team, he'd stopped being afraid. The thrill of the chase had become his drug of choice and like any addict, he'd craved it enough to discard concern over any repercussions that might result from chasing what he wanted.

Now?

He found himself thinking about things every good guy was supposed to want. Like deep emotions and family ties.

But he was stuck on the realities of what his sister, Zoe, had endured because of their father's position. Her best friend hadn't escaped, either.

"Is it time to get back to the real world?"

"I guess you're right," she mumbled. "Can't sleep here."

Bram stiffened, his arms tightening around her as she spoke and as her words sunk into his brain. Jaelyn lifted her head, stroking his chest a final time before she sat up.

"We could," he answered. "But only if you want to explain things to your grandfather."

He was testing her. She didn't miss it, either, worrying her lower lip while putting her bra on.

"I don't lie to my grandpa," she said at last. "And I also don't mess with his ideas of what the world should be like."

She turned away, rummaging around in the space for her clothing. He should say something.

He wanted to.

But he hadn't earned the right to ask her for any sort of commitment.

All he'd done was lose his head and grab her the moment he'd gotten her out of sight of her family. It wasn't that he regretted it. No, he'd wanted her too damned much.

But she deserved more.

And somehow, he was going to give it to her.

LeAnn wanted to be pissed.

But her temper deserted her, leaving her standing in the hallway, the sight of Jaelyn creeping into the house branded in her mind. It combined with the way Bram watched Jaelyn disappear, standing in the driveway for a long moment, his body tight.

She knew the look on him. Well, on any man really. It was desire. What stuck was the fact that Jaelyn's hair had been mussed, her lips swollen, and she'd headed toward her room like it was the last thing she wanted to do.

Bram really had come back for Jaelyn.

LeAnn should have been able to take shelter in a storm of righteous prissiness over her sister's betrayal. Instead, she ended up taking a hard hit from her conscience.

She'd cheated on him.

The best guy she'd ever dated.

Actually . . . the best *man*. She'd blundered big-time in not realizing the potential Bram brought to a relationship. Sure, he'd been as interested in a hookup as she was, but there was a core of integrity in him that she really should have taken time to think about trying to touch.

Gramps was right. She was an idiot.

Bram stood for a long time in the driveway. At last he turned and headed for the garage and the loft apartment.

That stung, too. He wasn't leaving.

He'd always left after getting a fix from her.

It had just been sex.

LeAnn was forced to face that fact, feeling trapped by the circumstances of her making. But even accepting blame didn't change the way her feelings were threatening to rip her in two. Like a concrete block was pressing down on her chest, making her struggle to draw a breath. Hot tears stung her eyes as they spilled down her cheeks.

LeAnn reached up, catching some of them on her fingertips and carrying them down so she could stare at them.

She never cried.

Bram was worth it though.

It wasn't that she thought she had any chance of regaining him. No, she realized with a sick twisting of her belly that she'd dashed her chances with him and there was even some part of her that wouldn't take him back now that he was with Jaelyn.

Jaelyn deserved a guy like him.

As for herself? Well, she looked out into the night and realized she had everything she thought she wanted and nothing that really meant anything to her.

Crying wouldn't solve anything and it wasn't until she made it into her room that she made herself stand in one place and wipe her eyes on her sleeve.

There.

One thing accomplished. Now to straighten out her thinking.

She needed to find a direction in her life because it dawned on her, she had everything she wanted and happiness wasn't anywhere in sight. The reason was simple, she didn't like herself.

Well, that was going to have to change.

\* \* \*

Morning wasn't kind.

Jaelyn rummaged through the cabinet, looking for the jumbo coffee mug someone had gifted her grandfather with at some point. She didn't care if it would likely go cold before she consumed half of it.

The idea was what counted.

She needed to know she had reinforcements on her side against the flood of reality coming at her with the rising sun. Her stuffed email box represented a good place to take shelter, too.

"I'm going down to deal with your car."

Jaelyn spun around, only this time, there was a glint of approval in Bram's eyes for how jumpy she was.

"Stay on guard while I'm gone. Inside would be best. Don't open the door."

"Excuse me?" she asked as her brain played catch-up. She'd been stuck on where they'd ended up the night before, but now his words had recent events flooding back. "I doubt my car and the prowler are connected."

Bram folded his arms across his chest. "Never trust a coincidence."

"I agree," Milton Sondors said, joining the conversation. "I made sure both my girls had new cars so they wouldn't be left stranded. Something's not adding up."

Bram liked what her grandfather said, and Milton approved of Bram's thought process. Jaelyn found herself fending off a little tingle of dread.

But she shoved it aside, refusing to let circumstances scare her. Lord knew, she had enough concrete facts to undermine her peace of mind.

"Jaelyn?"

Bram wasn't willing to let her go without solid agreement on her part.

"I'm going to the office," she muttered. Meeting his gaze was a major miscalculation on her part.

Her composure crumbled like sand beneath her feet as a wave rushed over them. In a second, she was floundering, looking into his blue eyes, and facing the man she had no resistance to.

At least his expression tightened, proving she wasn't the only one feeling the . . . well . . . the pull between them.

"I'll keep an eye on my girls," Milton said.

Jaelyn turned and hurried toward her office as her cheeks stung with a blush. Her grandfather might be old but he wasn't stupid.

At least it felt like he could see everything she'd given in to with Bram, like it was written on her face. It wasn't that she regretted it. No, she just felt like she was floundering as she tried to stand up on her surfboard and ride the wave. She wanted to be confident enough to do it.

Life on the other hand seemed to have other ideas about how much it was going to jerk her around.

Well, she'd wanted to live in the moment. It would seem the moment was going to deliver a kick-ass ride.

All in all, she wasn't complaining.

Just trying to catch her breath so she didn't pass out.

Staying busy was the only way to keep sane.

*Chicken . . .*

Jaelyn accepted her self-criticism and kept right on moving toward the garage.

Sure, she was trying to escape the house and the fact that her grandfather was watching her.

Bram's warning or his intuition?

She wasn't sure, but by evening, she grabbed a set of

clean sheets and went toward the loft as an excuse to find a moment of privacy that didn't include hiding in the bathroom.

There was a warm breeze blowing, hinting at summer heat waves as it blew through the new green growth on the trees. It made the leaves rustle, releasing the scent of fresh new life.

The bed in the loft apartment made her stop. She caught the scent of Bram's skin coming from it. Frustration nipped at her because she really needed to get a grip on herself. She'd found the toe-curling experience she'd craved but that was no reason to become obsessed.

"I guess you think this loft qualifies as part of the house."

Jaelyn jumped, the sheets she'd carried up the stairs went spilling to the floor. The only morsel of dignity she managed to hold on to came from the fact that she didn't shriek.

"Could you stop sneaking up on me?"

Bram offered her an expression that made it clear he had no mercy for her. "What if it hadn't been me who followed you up here?"

He shut the heavy exterior door and it closed with a very solid sound. "No one would hear you scream, Jaelyn."

*He'd made her scream alright . . .*

She picked up the sheets and carried them to the bedside table and then pulled the coverlet free as her damned cheeks started to heat.

"So . . . what's the verdict on my car?"

"The computer was offline."

Jaelyn looked back at him. "That's weird."

Bram moved up on the other side of the bed and had

her fixed with a hard look while he helped pulled the fitted sheet over the edge of the mattress.

"It's suspicious," he said.

"I'm sure it happens . . . a lot."

One of his dark eyebrows rose. "The chief mechanic at the dealership claimed he'd never seen it before. He'll know more once he brings it back online, if he can recover the system that is."

That tingle of dread went down her spine again and this time, it was a true shiver.

"Glad to see you taking it seriously now."

Jaelyn stopped and faced off with him. "I'm not going to let a couple of weird happenings turn me into a chicken."

His lips twitched. She watched the way a glint entered his eyes. "Yeah, you've told me before that you aren't afraid."

He'd stepped around the bed. She felt his approach as much as saw it. Her damned blood was starting to boil, or something. All she really knew was her thinking abilities were being smoked by the proximity of one Bram Magnus.

"Stop."

He didn't care for her order. The way his expression tightened and the fact that he kept coming just sent her over the edge into that place where her good sense had no voice and her emotions ran wild.

"You come one step closer, Bram, and I will forget all about having a conversation with you."

She could tell he liked that.

Well, it was an admission.

One which should have mortified her, except for the very real fact that she was once more entering a zone where nothing mattered except getting her hands on him.

Moments had a terrible way of ending. It seemed so much better to grab what came close enough for her to reach so she didn't end up knowing she'd missed her chance.

"I have trouble remaining objective when I'm close to you as well," he said as he backed off, but his lips curved into a very male satisfied grin that was a little too smug for her comfort level. "You know I have a valid reason to warn you to be cautious."

"This isn't a war zone."

"Which just makes it more important to take the matter seriously," he said.

"Oh, I take you very seriously."

And she still wasn't truly sorry she'd taken advantage of the moment the night before. Truth was, she doubted she ever would be.

Nope.

"I noticed."

His tone was raspy, as though she was hearing his emotions bleeding through. He presented such a picture of strength and pure confidence, she just couldn't quite believe it though.

He shook his head softly. "You drew me back here, Jaelyn."

Bram reached for her. For a moment, she just stood there, feeling like time had frozen as she soaked up the strength of his presence. Seriously, it was like some sort of power boast.

"I'm not planning on leaving until I discover just why."

It was a promise.

A solemn one.

A moment later, Bram slipped his hand beneath her hair and clasped her nape.

She gasped, locking gazes with him as he pulled her against his frame with a solid arm across her waist. The look in his eyes was just as hard as the body she was bound to.

"Defeat isn't something I accept without a whole hell of a lot more fight."

He slid his hand down until he was cupping one side of her bottom. Another breathy sound escaped from her as it felt like she was melting against him. Every curve of her body suddenly seemed created for the sole purpose of being pressed against his hard body.

"Tell me you want me to let you go," he said as his grip tightened on her butt, sending a zip of excitement through her system. "Tell me you'd rather sleep in righteous purity instead of letting me peel off your clothes so I can stroke every last inch of you . . ."

She bared her teeth at him. Curling her fingers into talons against his chest. "I'm the one who didn't get into the front seat last night. Remember that?"

"All . . . day . . . long, baby."

His gaze glowed with something she couldn't quite define. The reason was simple, it wasn't something that translated into spoken language. No, what it was, was pure and undiluted need. The kind no one faked. Instead, you did your best to make sure you didn't get rolled by the wave as it crashed.

Even then, the ride was worth the bruises.

She gripped his shirt and pulled it, stretching the jersey fabric as his belt resisted. His lips curled with smug satisfaction a second before he was giving her enough space to yank his shirt free. It went sailing onto the floor with his help, leaving her soaking in the details of his bare chest.

The man was pure intoxication. She moved back toward him, still incapable of resisting the pull between them.

He scooped her off her feet, cradling her in arms that shouldn't have been so strong. LeAnn was the lightweight, the girl who could fit into a size zero. Not her.

"You're going to throw your back out."

He was turning and lowering her to the bed. She ended up sitting on its edge as he pressed his hands into the mattress on either side of her thighs. His face was hovering just a bare inch from her lips.

"I'm going to give it my best try, baby."

His meaning was clear and it sent a bolt of heat through her. The loft was sporting a lingering chill because there was no point in heating it when no one was in residence. The look in Bram's eyes made Jaelyn long to strip off her clothing because she was rapidly becoming too damned hot.

"But first things . . . first . . ."

There was a wicked gleam in his eyes and a raspy note in his voice that made her catch her lower lip between her teeth.

"I'm going to taste you, baby . . ."

"Wait . . . ah . . . don't . . ."

Bram had her jeans opened before he grunted and fixed her with a hard look. "Why not?"

He was holding back his urge. It was raw, captivating her with its intensity. It was like seeing two sides of him, one was the man who had answered her grandfather with a sincere "Yes, sir" and the other made her shiver because it was the part of him she yearned to connect with no matter how uncivilized it might be.

"Stop thinking, Jaelyn."

He bent down and clasped her shoe with one big hand.

A moment later the cool air touched her sock-clad heel as she heard the sound of the shoe hitting the floor.

"Stop worrying and just let this happen . . ."

Her other shoe was gone and a moment later he was leaning over her, their faces inches apart once more. "Because I can't resist it any more than you can and there's one thing I figured out while I was overseas." He grasped her jeans and pulled them off her.

She ended up on her elbows, half prone across the bed as he stood over her, enjoying the sight.

"What?" she asked. "What did you figure out?"

"That I was a blasted fool for chasing your sister, and I'm going to make sure you know how much I want you."

Her breath was lodged in her throat, part of her soaking up his words like parched desert sand during a thunderstorm.

But Bram was making ready to unleash the lightning.

He caught her underwear and drew them down her legs before sinking to his knees and pressing her thighs wide.

She gasped. "Bram . . ."

He was already leaning over her open slit. "Told you . . . I'm going to taste you tonight . . ."

He was petting her bare mons. Teasing the sensitive skin where the hair was missing. Her heart was beating so hard, it felt like it might end up bruised against her breastbone.

Not that she cared.

No, she was too busy writhing as Bram teased her folds, his attention sinking down to her open sex.

"You smell hot, baby . . . really hot . . ."

Heat teased her cheeks as his breath hit the wet skin. He'd taken her to heights before but a new level of sensory overload hit her. Just the feeling of his breath against her folds made her wither. Her eyes felt like they rolled back into her head as her lids slid shut because her brain just couldn't handle anything else but the stimulus Bram was applying to her sex.

"But you can get hotter . . ."

He was trailing his fingers down the sides of her sex, stroking skin that was acutely sensitive. She was shivering, her clit throbbing with anticipation and Bram didn't disappoint her.

"Oh . . . Christ!"

Her voice hit the low ceiling as Bram closed his mouth around her clit. The sensation jolted her.

Bram chuckled softly and looked up. "We're going to move up here, baby, because I love to hear you squeal."

"Bram."

Her reprimand went unheeded as he returned to tormenting her clit. He sucked, tongued, and drove her nearly insane as each motion of his lips sent her closer and closer to the edge of climax.

She was straining up toward him, seeking out that last bit of pressure to ensure the bubble burst. Time became irrelevant. Once more she was a slave to her needs.

Bram seemed to know instinctively the exact combination to unlock inside her.

He teased the opening of her body, rimming her with the tip of his tongue before he was thrusting two thick fingers into her. Another sound crossed her lips that was somewhere between a growl and a moan.

So needy . . .

So damned . . . primitive . . .

She wanted him to claim her. Wanted to be his prize.

She wanted . . . to be his . . . and she wasn't going to be denied.

"Enough!"

Bram snorted, raising his face so that their gazes locked. There was a smug grin on his lips and an arrogant glitter in his eyes.

But those did nothing more than fuel her desire to demand him. "I can tease, too," she informed him as she struggled to sit up. Just enough so she could tug her shirt off and unhook her bra.

His expression tightened as she bared her breasts.

"I like your tits, Jae . . ." He rose up, granting her a glimpse of his chest before she heard him popping the button on his fly. His cock sprang into view the moment he had enough buttons worked lose. Red and swollen, her passage felt even more needy at the sight of it.

"I like your cock," she declared boldly.

He was shucking his pants and boots, pausing to sheathe his length in another condom, but she heard him chuckle before the bed was rocking as he crawled up to cover her.

"Sugar and spice . . ." He watched her as he settled over her, brushing back her hair from her face with tender little motions of his hands while she spread her thighs so that his cock might tease the wet opening of her body.

"I'm not everything nice . . ."

He pushed up, bracing himself on his knees as he pressed her legs wide with a large hand on the inside of her thighs.

"Depends on the definition of nice . . ." His tone was full of husky male enjoyment. He grasped his cock and drew the head through her open slit. "I think this is a really . . . nice . . . view of you, Jaelyn . . ."

His gaze rose up to her breasts before he was focused once again on her open slit. His breath was raspy as he drew his cock head up and down, spreading the wetness from her body onto it until it slid easily between her folds.

It was a torment.

One she both craved and hated.

She wanted more and yet, he was driving her hunger up with his teasing. And there was something else, a deeper enjoyment of knowing he wanted the encounter to last.

She witnessed the straining muscles cording along his throat as he held off driving into her. His jaw was tight while he teased her with another swipe through her slit. Jaelyn found herself fixated on his expression, wanting to see the moment when he lost control. Needing to know that he couldn't resist her any more than she could stop herself from reaching for him.

What did that make them?

She had no idea.

And none formed because he looked up, locking gazes with her. His eyes blazed with hunger. Hot, blunt, sexual need.

She didn't want it to make sense.

He pressed forward into her, watching her as she took his length. A sound hit the ceiling and she honestly wasn't sure if it was his or hers. All she knew was that she'd never understood the word "pleasure" until the night she'd connected with him. There was a whole different level of feeling when they were together.

And she'd have done anything at that moment to have him there with her.

"More . . . ," she said in a raspy voice. "Faster . . ."

He shook his head, grinding his teeth as he flattened his hands on her inner thighs to keep them wide. "I'm going to savor this time . . ." He pressed deep, a little wet sound teasing her ears with the penetration. "Going to watch you . . . come . . ."

She shook her head, but he slid his hand over and found her swollen clit. He rubbed it, pressing down with the pressure she'd needed before. Coupled with his cock lodged inside her, she jerked as climax ripped through her.

It was hard and sharp, tearing the urgency away but leaving her only partially satisfied.

"Nice . . . ," he said raspily, too smug for her pride.

The bed shook as she curled up. He wanted to keep her on her back but she locked her legs around him, threading her hands through his hair so she could press a kiss against his mouth.

It distracted him as he returned it in full measure, gripping her hair while his mouth took hers. She was throbbing with need, his cock driving her insane inside her passage.

But she didn't want to rush things, either.

Who knew when it would end?

He shifted around, sitting on the bed. She curled her knees beneath her and lifted off his cock.

His eyes glittered with anticipation.

"Ride me, baby . . ."

His hands settled on her hips, gripping them as she started. Her nipples were hard little nubs that rubbed against his chest hair while she rose and fell. His shoulders were the only solid thing to hold on to as the bed rocked hard and faster in reaction to their motions.

"Yeah . . . make me behave . . ." He leaned back until he was flat on the bed as she took command of the pace.

"I like you . . . bad . . ."

The need to climax was building in her again, but he opened his eyes and sent her a look that made her fight it off in favor of controlling their pace.

"I know the feeling . . ." he said.

A need flashed through his eyes a moment before he was rolling her over.

"Bram!" she said with a growl, but it was too late. He thrust hard and fast into her.

"I'm going to make you squeal, baby . . ."

"I won't . . . be . . . alone . . . ," she insisted as she lifted her hips to catch every thrust.

He sent her a look full of need. "No . . . you won't . . ."

He was on the edge, using every last bit of his self-control to hold back his own climax. He bared his teeth as he drove faster and harder into her body. The head of his cock was hitting her G-spot and his balls slapped against her when he penetrated completely.

She was twisting once more, caught in the grip of need so intense, drawing in a breath was too hard to manage. They were straining toward each other, intent on pulling one another into the vortex. The bed was shaking violently as it all burst inside her.

Jaelyn cried out, twisting and writhing in the bright burst of pleasure. It went deeper this time, wringing more sounds from her, but what she heard was the harsh grunt Bram released as his cock started to jerk and spurt inside her.

And then there was nothing, except the twisting motion of the vortex. It wrung them both, leaving them spent, but satisfied.

Two quivering masses of flesh, entwined as slumber dragged them down into oblivion.

As far as moments went, it was epic.

The breeze she'd notice when the sun was going down had turned into a full Santa Ana wind condition. The trees were being whipped around by the powerful gusts but that wasn't what woke Jaelyn.

There was a man in bed with her.

A naked one.

Jaelyn indulged in a long look at Bram before she plucked her clothing off the floor and shimmied into it. A second glance showed him still lying on his back, one forearm covering his eyes while his chest rose and fell in an even rhythm.

She turned the doorknob slowly, opening it just as carefully. But she froze halfway down the stairs, a frown on her face.

Why was she leaving?

Honestly, she wasn't sure.

But something on the lawn near the curb caught her attention. She blinked, trying to absorb just what it was. Shock had her moving forward, toward the person lying there. Maybe she should have been more on guard but the need to help was too strong. She moved forward, reaching out to shake the person.

White hot pain went smashing through her skull. Then she was oddly aware of it growing brighter and hotter before she felt like it exploded, leaving her sliding toward the ground in an unconscious heap.

\* \* \*

Too easy.

Ricky Sullivan scooped up his victim and watched the way her head lolled around. He shook her a few times, just to make sure she was out good. Gideon was casting them nervous looks from behind the wheel of the car they'd stolen.

Ricky dumped her into the backseat before slipping into the front one.

"Shouldn't you cover her up?" Gideon asked as he pulled away from the curb.

"Nope. Any cop who sees her will just think she's drunk," Ricky replied as he reached up to loosen his tie. "That's why I told you to dress nice. We look like great guys, no reason to pull us over."

"Unless this car is reported stolen." Gideon was gripping the steering wheel so tightly his knuckles were white.

"Not a chance," Ricky responded with a grin. "I gave the dude a full ounce of coke. He's partying hard right now."

"You should have let me kill him."

Ricky's grin faded. "Bodies attract attention ass-wipe. I thought you were overseas because you're some techie genius. Looks like your smarts don't carry over into the rest of your brain. Blood splatters in tiny fragments and can be smelled or detected. Don't kill unless you have to, and when you do, make it look like an accident."

"Is that why you know so much about messing with cars?"

Ricky grinned. It was a smug expression and he wasn't a bit ashamed of it.

Gideon snorted as he made the final turn into his private drive. "They hired me because they can't recruit my kind of brainpower. Maybe I don't know the hands-on stuff but I can deal with the cyberworld. These days, there are cameras everywhere, just waiting to tell everyone where you've been."

Sullivan was losing interest in the guy but forced himself to remember that he needed Gideon. "So you remembered to kill the security cameras?"

Gideon scoffed at him. "No shit. And for the record, since you think I don't see the obvious, killing the cameras would be a tip-off. I've got a nice replay from a couple of months ago playing in case anyone is actually doing their job."

Sullivan was out of the car and dragging Jaelyn from the backseat a moment later. Gideon's new building was perfect because the other flats weren't finished. The top floor had been the builder's priority. They made it there in swift time via a private elevator.

Ricky tossed her down onto the bed that Gideon had decked out for her, watching as Gideon locked a collar around her neck while his eyes glittered with anticipation.

He was a sick fuck.

But one Ricky needed to make Bram Magnus pull in his Shadow Ops buddies.

"You did it . . . ," Gideon whispered as he looked down on the sprawled form of his captive. "You really got her . . ."

Ricky walked out into the main living area. He stopped to select a very rare bottle of whiskey from the bar and poured himself a double before making his way to a huge leather sofa that looked out over the city. The sofa compressed as he lowered himself onto it, surrounding him with the scent of fresh leather.

Ricky lifted the whiskey up to banish that before taking a sip.

He didn't give a fuck for what Gideon might be doing, so long as Jaelyn stayed alive.

The whiskey burned a path down his throat and hit his belly with a punch that made him bare his teeth.

Gideon wouldn't kill her. Sullivan snickered as he sipped again. He might do a whole lot of other twisted shit to her but he wasn't going to deprive himself of his newly acquired pet.

Which was all the time Ricky needed for Bram Magnus to take the bait and bring in his buddies. It was the action that would bring Tyler Martin into the mix, too.

Ricky was looking forward to it.

# CHAPTER THREE

He was a creep.

Jaelyn did know a thing or two about men and the one standing at the foot of the bed fell into the category of creep. He wasn't a dick, or a douche, but an actual sick-in-the-head creep.

She had to swallow to keep from throwing up.

She remembered him from the picnic. Her insides heaving again as she realized her thought about him being crazy was spot on.

There was a chain draped over her shoulder that went to a collar locked around her neck. Her head was throbbing worse than it did when she had a hangover but what really scared her was the look in the guy's eyes.

He was obsessed with her.

It was a good and bad thing. On one hand, he just might kill her, but on the other, she knew his weak spot. She suddenly realized her grandfather was the best person in the world for making her earn a degree because what she'd learned in the psychology class she'd had to pass was suddenly rising up from her memory.

Like a lifeline punching through her rising panic.

Creeps needed their games. He'd only kill her if she stopped providing amusement.

Her belly twisted with nausea again but the need to survive rose above her horror. Bram wouldn't let the guy see him sweat.

*Make the guy think you're playing along . . .*

"So . . ." She shifted and fingered the chain. "Did I sleep through the party?"

Her clothing was still on but it felt like a thin barrier against the gleam in the guy's eyes.

Okay, and the chain on her neck that was attached to a bed, but she fought to control the urge to panic. She had the sinking suspicion he was looking forward to her hysterics.

Her captor wasn't expecting that comment. She watched his eyebrows lower as he leaned on the foot rail of the bed. It was made of iron and he curled his hands around it.

"Party is just starting," he said. "You're the guest of honor."

Her eyes widened in spite of her resolve. He grinned in response, watching her like a bug he was making ready to tear the legs off of. She lost control, rolling over and stumbling into the bathroom next to the bed to heave up her guts. When she was done, relief was there to comfort her. No, what she was left with was the feeling of the chain lying against her back. The damned collar was also made of links of metal, big thick ones that sunk into the fragile tissue of her neck just from their own weight.

And her tormentor was leaning in the doorway.

*Don't let him see you sweat . . .*

"Enjoy the show?" she asked as she rose and flushed the toilet.

There was a huge walk-in shower behind the vanity, with four sides of glass walls. The guy glanced toward it, making Jaelyn cringe because he really was looking forward to watching her.

So she'd better get it together because that was the only card she had to play.

Jaelyn was gone when he woke up. Bram wiped a hand across his face, slightly stunned by how deeply he'd slept.

It had been a really long time since he'd been so relaxed.

He found his pants and pulled them on before sitting on the end of the bed to push his feet into his boots.

She'd left.

He warned himself to not get too upset over it. Sure, he'd been set on winning her for months but she hadn't known that.

It would take time.

He left the loft and walked over to the house. The kitchen was empty, the coffeepot still cold. Bram looked at it. Jaelyn had primed it the night before, all it needed was the switch pushed.

The fact that it was cold chilled his blood.

He went down the hallway and rapped on her bedroom door a single time before he turned the doorknob and opened it.

The bed was still made.

But the door at the end of the hallway opened. Milton looked out at him, his forehead furrowed for a moment.

"Are there any other vehicles Jaelyn might have used to leave?"

Milton Sondors's eyebrows rose as a very faint word of profanity crossed his lips. But he shook his head as LeAnn opened her door and looked at Bram.

"What's wrong?" LeAnn asked.

"Your sister is missing."

Bram knew it. Felt it in his gut as he retraced his steps through the house and back to the stairs that lead up to the loft apartment. He knelt down, peering at the concrete of the driveway.

But the winds were still blowing, pushing the dirt around. He moved toward the grass, looking for tracks. Milton joined him, surprising Bram with how adept he appeared to be.

The signs were thin at best. He wanted to see tracks but had to stop himself from leaping to conclusions. Under the large tree that shaded the front yard he found his evidence though. The ground had been moist until the wind dried it out during the night.

There were clear prints in the dried dirt.

"Cops will try and tell us it's nothing," Milton muttered.

Bram straightened and Milton rose, too.

"They won't even take a report for twenty-four hours but I'm calling anyway," Bram informed him. "There's an evidence chain."

"Jaelyn is stronger than you think." LeAnn had followed them. Bram caught the tremble in her tone but she looked at him and sent him a surprisingly steady look. "That's why she slept with you last night. She's no wimp."

"My granddaughter is a lady," Milton muttered.

"Sorry, sir," Bram replied.

"If you are sorry," Milton informed him, "you're not the man I thought you were. Best sort of gal in the world

is a lady who knows exactly when to strip her gloves off."
He winked on his way back toward the house.

Milton went straight to a china cabinet and pulled open a
lower drawer.

"Grandpa," LeAnn said. "What are you looking for?"

Her grandfather plopped a case down on the kitchen
table before sitting and working the combination locks
on it.

There was a click and then her grandfather was opening the lid of the case to reveal his set of guns. "Every
now and then, a good man has to go to war LeAnn. You
and your sister are all I have left of my blood. All I have
left of my sweet Jeanie and your mother." He wrapped his
hands around one pistol and lifted it with a surprisingly
steady hand. "Bram understands what I mean."

Bram stood with his feet braced apart, his arms crossed
over his chest, and his chin tucked down as he looked at
her grandfather with a very critical eye.

"Yes, sir, I do," Bram said. "On both accounts."

"So," LeAnn began. "Since I don't see you in any hurry
to dial the cops, does that mean you have a different plan?"

Bram sent her a confident look. "I have resources."

"Good," her grandfather said. "What resources?"

Bram stiffened. Milton sent Bram a look LeAnn knew
as one no wise person toyed with.

"Ones I can't officially tell you about."

Her grandfather chuckled. "Those are the best sort, son.
Can't wait to meet them."

Her grandfather seemed content with the answer.
LeAnn found herself fighting to keep her jaw from
dropping. Shock zipped through her as she looked from
Bram to her grandfather.

Family was always number one with her grandfather. He didn't back down or settle for half explanations.

Today he did. One look at Bram and he was content. A tingle went down her spine because she realized she didn't really know Bram at all.

But Jaelyn captivated him. LeAnn decided she'd never been so happy to lose a boyfriend. She found herself pondering her grandfather's words. Cancer had taken her mother and her grandmother. Somehow, LeAnn had forgotten just how few members of their family were left. It really was all that mattered.

And she was going to start living like she cared.

"I'll . . . do something about breakfast, Grandpa."

Dare Servant was a desperate man.

Okay, maybe he was being a bit dramatic but he reached for his phone on the first ring because construction wasn't his idea of what a Shadow Ops agent should be doing with his time. Even if he understood the need for an off-the-grid command center.

"I need you."

Dare listened to Bram's voice and heard the seriousness in his tone.

"Bring me up to date."

Bram killed the call.

He'd stepped over the line. However, it wasn't bothering him too much. Something was shifting inside him. Maybe it was that last thing that he'd been wrestling with, about stepping all the way into the Shadow Ops world.

The final tie that he'd needed to sever completely before Kagan would welcome him on board with a badge.

The willing desire to pledge himself completely to the life of making sure no one could track him. His team would be his family. His badge, his identity.

Bram didn't lament it. Nothing mattered but getting the resources into play that would make recovering Jaelyn a possibility. The numbers were clear. The local police wouldn't even begin a missing person's investigation until the following day.

That was too long.

But Bram knew thugs.

He'd brushed elbows with the type of men who lived without consciences. To fight them, he had to be ruthless.

Whoever had taken Jaelyn was about to discover just how good he was at doing his worst.

"If you think . . ." Thais Sinclair must have held the copyright on husky feminine drawls because Dare felt the sound of her voice rippling across the nape of his neck.

She drifted in through the door, moving in a way that drew his attention, even though he knew full well nothing was ever going to happen between them. Of course that was what made her an asset to their Shadow Ops team.

Fine, it wasn't politically correct. Not in the least. But bad guys didn't tend to play by the rules, so if Dare wanted his team to gain the upper hand against the seedier elements at play in the world, he had to load the deck in his favor.

Thais Sinclair was dark and seductive. She knew her art well, her eyes slightly narrowing as she pinned him with her gaze. Thais didn't just stand, either—she flowed, coming to rest sometimes in a position that was far more elegant than just standing.

She took the concept of bombshell to the limit. Blowing away a man's ability to focus.

"If you think," she repeated, softly now that she was closer, "that you are leaving without me, well . . ."

She swept him from head to toe, leaving him caught between the need to rise to her challenge and the desire to just admit she was pushing his buttons perfectly.

"It's not an assignment," Dare responded. "Kagan might have something to say about it."

"It's Bram," Thais argued. "That makes it personal. And Kagan can say what he likes."

"You can both be sure Kagan will have his say," Saxon Hale said, interrupting them as he came into the room. Their team leader sent her a look that made Dare jealous because Saxon was immune to Thais.

His wife, Ginger, had somehow inoculated Saxon against the pull of their female team member.

"But don't think I don't know both of you are just using that call from Bram to get out of construction detail," Saxon said as he wiped the sweat from his forehead.

Thais lifted one shoulder in a delicate motion. "Your point in no way changes the fact that I believe Bram deserves support."

"What's going on with Bram?" Vitus Hale wasn't far behind his brother Saxon. He lowered a case onto the floor, raising a little puff of dust.

"His girlfriend has gone missing," Dare replied. "You know the local cops can't move on that for forty-eight and there is an evidence trail."

Then Dare said, "You told me to stick to Bram."

"So why are you still here?"

Saxon Hale was a good team leader. One of the best

because he did his job but he never forgot that his men were his best resources. Dare sent him a nod.

The site was an old missile silo. A huge metal-and-concrete-lined hole in the ground that they'd spent three months just pumping the accumulated rainwater out of. Their section leader, Kagan, wanted it transformed into a secret underground command center. Now that Saxon and Vitus were both married, they'd been posted to the location.

Dare felt like his blood was turning to syrup in his veins from lack of action. Settling down might be fine for the Hale brothers but he hadn't gone and let Cupid make a domesticated man out of him.

Dare cut Saxon a salute.

His team leader scoffed at him. "Don't piss off the local cops too much."

"That means we should wait at least two hours before finding her," Thais said.

Saxon shook his head. "If someone took her, kick their door in. Bram is a teammate. We take care of our own. Tell Bram he should have called sooner. If there's trouble, he needs to suspect it's coming for all of us. Protecting him is protecting us all."

Thais offered him a serious look.

"Right," Dare answered.

Dare turned and pointed toward the door. Thais was swift on the uptake, turning and exiting the room. They passed teams of construction workers, all of them looking more like former Special Forces, and the reason was, every last one of them had a security clearance. Some of them were working through PTSD, others had just never found the means to integrate back into the civilian population.

Dare avoided thinking too deeply about how alike he and the men he passed were. At the moment, his Shadow Ops badge was secured to his belt and he had a case. He didn't delve too deeply into why he needed a crime to make him feel alive. Better to focus on the fact that he knew how to succeed.

After all, there was a life hanging in the balance.

No agent spent too much time pondering where his future was going to be. That was a bad place to go when you accepted a badge from someone like Kagan, his section leader among the Shadow Ops teams. If you took too much time thinking about your odds of survival, it wasn't the badge to carry.

Yeah, it was a wiser bet to keep his thoughts on the fact that Kagan had seen his razor sharp potential.

Something he enjoyed pitting against the bad guys.

Kagan allowed him to see a very refined group of scumbags. The sort no civilian cop had a prayer of touching.

Dangerous?

Fuck yes.

But it kept him alive and the missile silo was cutting off the signal. Dare didn't ponder those facts too long. Nope, he set his personal sights on being honest about who he was with himself.

He liked the edge.

Craved the fight.

Dare didn't bother to linger on just what it said about him, only that there were times a man like him had a purpose. Sometimes it took someone willing to break the rules to set the world right.

Whoever had Jaelyn was about to come face-to-face with three members of a Shadow Ops team.

He felt sort of sorry for the dude.

* * *

He wanted to see her naked.

The gleam in the creep's eyes made Jaelyn want to barf all over again but she dug deep and thought of Bram.

No one saw him puking.

So she wasn't going to be a wimp.

"Do you want a shower?" her captor asked.

Jaelyn didn't rise to the bait. He was growing excited by something and it chilled her blood the way he licked his lips when he was looking at her.

"Got everything you need," Creepy said with a grin. "Body wash. Some of those special sponges to keep your skin soft . . ." He licked his lower lip.

"While you watch?" She couldn't keep the disgust from her tone.

"You're my pet." He stated this with a conviction that would have had her throwing up again if her stomach hadn't already been emptied.

"You creep!" She plucked the soap dispenser off the vanity and chucked it at him. Creepy hadn't anticipated an attack. Her missile landed against his chest, earning a grunt from him as he recoiled out of the doorway. She dug her fingernails into the sliding door but it wouldn't close completely with the chain running through it.

Creepy started laughing.

It was a blood-chilling sound that proved everything she'd already decided about him and her circumstances.

She was the bug.

"That bitch is going to drive me insane."

Tyler Martin took a look around the room before he answered Carl Davis. There was a clink of ice against crystal as the presidential hopeful made himself a drink at the in-room bar before turning around and facing him with Scotch in hand.

A hundred dollar pour if Tyler wasn't mistaken.

"I swear," Carl drew off a sip and his lips tightened with the bite. "Miranda Delacroix running for Congress is the worst thing that could have happened to my campaign."

"Far from it," Tyler Martin argued. "Use her. The woman is the pied piper when it comes to getting the voters to follow her."

"No kidding. I tried to marry her fucking daughter," Carl said with a grunt. "Did you forget that?"

Tyler Martin sent his boss a hard look. "Hardly. I cleaned up the mess that stunt left behind."

"I wouldn't take that from most men," Carl remarked as he went for another sip. "Actually, not a single other man."

But Tyler knew where the bodies were buried. In fact, he'd done some of the digging of those unmarked graves in the service of Carl's interests. They were bound together by spilled blood and as far as Tyler was concerned, Carl better not forget it.

Tyler had sold out his own men for the position as head of personal security for Carl Davis.

Tyler didn't lose any sleep over it. Saxon Hale and his Shadow Ops team were the sort of men who really couldn't expect anything else. They signed up for the deadly assignments and he wasn't going to shoulder any guilt over the fact that the Hale brothers did it because they thought they were making the world safe.

Their personal motivations were their own problem.

He'd embraced that valor shit, too. Once, long ago, before he'd come face-to-face with men like Carl Davis and seen up close and personal the way Carl and his cronies thought about the men of the Shadow Ops teams as expendable. Tossing out scraps known as medals and commendations to the men who served them out of loyalty.

Tyler wasn't taking that honor crap in exchange for the parts of his soul he'd sold any more. He was going to share the glory.

Carl flashed him a smile and turned around to pour a second drink. "Don't worry, Ty, I know your worth."

Carl set the drink down in front of Tyler and held his own up for a toast. "Together, we're going to the White House."

Tyler lifted the glass and touched it to Carl's. "Keep your eye on the big picture," Tyler said. "Miranda Delacroix is voter candy. Play nice when it counts."

"And you keep looking for her skeletons." Carl reached up and loosened his tie. "That's your job."

"She shot her own husband," Tyler replied. "Even if we can't use that because Jeb Ryland had his damned office sealed and the Hale brothers covered up the rest of it."

Carl tossed down more of the whiskey. "Kagan's teams know their shit."

"And everyone else's," Tyler reminded him. "My days among the Shadow Ops helped me learn a whole lot of interesting details that I'm willing to use in your favor. Kagan and the Hale brothers will happily dance on your grave because you don't measure up to their ideals of honor."

"The presidency isn't for the innocent," Carl remarked. "Miranda might be collecting supporters but she'll fall flat on her face when she moves into Capitol Hill and discovers no one wants to help her achieve her goals unless she gets down to horse trading."

Tyler didn't mention that Miranda was a Delacroix.

Carl knew it well. The Delacroix name was an old one in Washington. It was the sort of connection a man running for president was wise to have in his corner. Carl knew that fact, too, and had tried to work a deal to marry Miranda's only daughter, Damascus.

Vitus Hale had ruined that plan.

*Eye on the big picture.*

Tyler would be better off following his own advice. The Hale brothers were off the grid now, settled in with their wives and playing house. The best thing to do would be to leave them alone.

At least until after the election.

Tyler slowly grinned and enjoyed the whiskey.

He was savoring the fact that Carl had poured it for him, too.

Things were turning out just the way he'd hoped when he'd turned in his badge and signed on with Carl.

There was no going back.

And no forgetting to tie up loose ends like Hale's team.

No, not when Tyler had sold out fellow agents. Carl made it so Kagan couldn't touch him, or at least the section leader knew it wasn't a good idea to mess with the man who would have the power to shut down his teams. It was exactly the sort of power card Tyler needed to hide behind. Which meant he was going to have to placate Carl's need to know Miranda's secrets.

It was nothing personal.

Just his job.

But he did admit, he fucking loved his position. In fact, he'd kill to keep it.

* * *

Bram was in the kitchen doorway.

LeAnn was fussing with the coffeemaker, doing her best to look like she had a clue how to clean it and reset it.

Truth was, she was lost and really didn't need a witness to the fact that she'd done precious little when it came to helping take care of her grandfather. She was ashamed but she'd deal with it privately.

"You can't go to practice tonight."

Whatever LeAnn had thought Bram might say, that wasn't it. She turned and looked at him.

"Whoever took Jaelyn might have been looking for you," he explained. "Or Milton. Until I have more information, you both need to stay where I can protect you."

"Or they might have followed you."

LeAnn was suddenly stumbling into the dining room courtesy of Bram grabbing her wrist and pulling her past him. She caught herself and flipped around just in time to see Bram lowering the handgun he'd pointed at whoever was in the side door that connected to the kitchen.

"Not bad, Magnus," the newcomer responded from the doorway. "The girl is a little hopeless though."

"What in the hell is going on?" LeAnn demanded.

"Dare Servant is tempting me to give him an ass-kicking," Bram replied.

"Is that the thanks I get for responding to your plea for help?" Dare asked with fake innocence.

"Backup," Bram said. "And it was a little gift from me to you but hey, if you want to go back to remodeling . . . be my guest."

Dare Servant had midnight black hair and eyes. LeAnn wasn't a stranger to good-looking men, but he was a dark devil. He knew it, too, which just made him more intimidating.

He also had the devil's own arrogance. There wasn't a hint of shame in his expression. No, just a very pleased grin on his lips.

The guy was completely in his element.

"I'll give it to you, Bram, he looks like a hell of a great resource," LeAnn remarked.

"I rather prefer this one," Milton said from the hallway. "As far as people I'd like to see breaking into my home, you're almost welcome, young lady."

"Thais came along," Dare informed Bram.

"Saxon said to tell you," Thais said from the dining room, "you should have called sooner."

LeAnn looked toward the female agent and felt her confidence crumbling. It wasn't that LeAnn doubted her own beauty, it was the fact that Thais had a badge on. She was drop-dead gorgeous and yet, she'd earned something significant.

LeAnn really needed a reality check. "I don't care about missing practice. If they boot me, so what. Jaelyn is what matters."

Bram's eyes narrowed and he stepped back, all the time contemplating her with that keen stare of his.

The one that she was pretty sure enabled him to look straight into her mind.

"Let her go," Thais suggested. "Let's see if anyone is watching."

"Too risky," Bram said.

Dare contemplated LeAnn for a moment. "The risk would be worth the possible gain. It's a lot easier to catch someone taking another shot than sifting through evidence."

"I'm in," LeAnn declared.

"You don't know what you're talking about," Bram informed her.

"I'm getting that," LeAnn said. She looked back at Dare and Thais. "Yeah, which just makes me more positive of how much I'm in."

LeAnn went down the hall and closed the bathroom door behind her. Milton let out a low whistle. "Looks like I might have something to be grateful for when this is all over."

He looked at Bram. "I like your friends, son, but I'm getting an inkling that this might be more about you than my girls."

Milton turned and shuffled away toward the back patio. Bram had to hand it to the guy, he played the old geezer perfectly but there was more going on beneath the Grandpa exterior. Milton left so that Bram and his team could talk.

And Jaelyn wouldn't be the first innocent cut down as a result of Shadow Ops operations. He'd been a naive fool to return to the Sondors home. Tyler Martin wasn't the sort of man who missed details.

"You'd have her body if this was a case of retaliation," Dare said, reading Bram's thoughts.

"Unless he's planning on making her death a long one," Bram answered. "As a warning."

"Let's take the cheerleader out and see if anyone sniffs around her," Thais said, interrupting. "That will give us a clear indication as to the target."

Bram nodded but his gut told him Jaelyn was the target.

And he'd led whoever it was straight to her.

\* \* \*

Two days later, Jaelyn decided enduring stinking wasn't worth it. She didn't have any different parts than other women.

Creepy likely owned his share of memberships to porn sites.

Still, she waited until she heard him crossing the penthouse, his steps growing fainter. Her senses had tuned in to his movements.

Yeah, like a mouse listening for a hawk's wings.

Getting off the bed and keeping her chain from rattling took patience. She got her clothing off and there was no sound of approaching footsteps.

*Creepy wasn't as noble as a hawk . . .*

She smiled at the mental insult as she turned on the shower, stepping in while it was still cold in an effort to get her bath before she had company.

She closed her eyes and tried to imagine herself back in her own bathroom. At least the water from the shower was the same temperature.

"Turn around . . ."

Creepy's voice broke through her concentration. Every muscle she had drew tight, her fingernails sinking into the soap bar.

"I want to see your tits."

Her belly was empty but it still gave a heave.

*No! She wouldn't let him get under her skin. She was going to be the hawk, he was the rodent.*

He was just a creep.

She refused to care.

"Come on, bitch . . ."

The lessons from that psychology class were rising up from her memory again. A warning was zipping through her at the sound of Creepy's voice becoming strained.

*Play the game . . .*

Don't let him get bored. If he did, she was worthless to him.

Stay alive.

"Careful," Jaelyn said as she peeked over her shoulder, careful to hide her mouth while giving the guy a glimpse at her wide eyes with wet lashes. "I know how to be a bitch."

There was a flash of twisted anticipation in his eyes. Jaelyn swallowed, forcing the nausea down as she blinked at him and rubbed her shoulder with the pink fluffy shower mitt he'd brought her.

"But I don't like to be one . . . ," she cooed softly, working her eyelashes some more. "I think it's overrated . . . There's nothing wrong with being a good girl."

"Is that how Magnus likes you?"

Creepy's complexion darkened. Anger flickered in his eyes. "Doesn't matter. You're mine now."

He was working himself up into a rage.

Jaelyn reached for the shower gel, lifting it high and making a show of drizzling it onto the mitt. She felt his eyes on her, felt dirty just because she was performing for him.

*No! He's the creep.*

Right. The game was surviving. He'd been planning for her capture, so he was pretty committed. Pleading wasn't going to get him to rethink his morals.

The only thing it might result in was her getting strangled to hide the evidence.

She forced herself to cast him another long look over her shoulder while she washed her breasts.

He started breathing hard.

She was nothing but live-action porn to him. But it beat

being the skeleton in the shallow grave. When she was free, she could throw up as much as she wanted.

When she was free . . .

Jaelyn latched on to that thought and realized it was the most important goal she'd ever set for herself.

"I call my team in, Magnus."

Kagan, the Shadow Operations teams' section leader never raised his voice. He kept his tempo even and unhurried. In short, the man was confidence incarnate.

Bram kept his jaw shut because he knew the section leader wasn't finished yet.

There was a soft grunt from Kagan that barely came across the phone connection. "At least you're not stupid enough to argue about whether or not you're on my team."

"I picked up the phone," Bram answered. "Even if I don't officially have a badge."

"And yet, you didn't contact me before pulling in two of my agents."

"This is about me and my involvement with Saxon's team," Bram explained, recalling just why he liked working with Kagan and his Shadow Operations teams. "Dare understands what happens to me, bleeds in his direction. It's why Saxon Hale assigned him to watch my back a few months ago. I'm the dumb ass who came out here alone the second I got leave."

Kagan only worked with the elite and that meant knowing his men's soft spots.

Bram needed the best to find Jaelyn.

"So Servant was a little too happy to tell me," Kagan retorted. "He thinks you need backup."

"Can't blame him too much," Bram answered. "He

isn't the one who got married. Saxon Hale was. Dare isn't ready to play house with the other members of the team who have settled down."

"So you decided to throw him a bone?"

"I might have encouraged him to slip his leash," Bram admitted. "To keep his skills sharp."

Kagan grunted and the fact that it was a phone conversation allowed Bram to let his lips part in a grin.

Maybe it was more of a smirk but no one was looking.

"The local PD wasn't going to move on this. It's serious and might be linked to Tyler Martin or the Raven." Bram got back to the case. "I stepped into the open. Drew them here."

"You did," Kagan agreed.

"Whoever is behind this went after the woman I was with," Bram said. "The car was a test to see if I showed up."

There was a moment of silence as Kagan weighed the information. The section leader had a lot of experience when it came to deciding if intel was worth anything or not.

"You might be reaching with that conclusion," Kagan informed him. "They could have grabbed the girl in the open. Even if you're involved with the sister, you'd still be invested, and it still might be linked to the cheerleader. Those sorts of women attract stalkers. Not that I disagree on the point of Tyler Martin being a possible suspect. He'd use her to draw you into a kill zone, remember that. I will be very upset with you if you get killed."

"Yes, sir."

Kagan made a sound on the other end of the line. "Try to keep a low profile. If it isn't Martin, no need to attract his attention."

"Understood."

"And the badge is the seal of approval," Kagan said, surprising him. "You're doing your probation period."

The line disconnected. Kagan wasn't one for chitchat. Bram was left feeling a surge of self-achievement. Guilt was right on its heels though because Jaelyn was likely paying the price for his actions with the Shadow Ops teams.

That's what his gut told him.

Dare and Thais both took that moment to appear in separate doorways. What gained Bram's attentions was the fact that Mr. Sondors was only a couple of paces behind Dare.

"Boss man says to keep it quiet," Bram shared. "Doesn't want us attracting attention to this operation."

Dare cocked his head to one side in a no-shit posture.

Thais offered him a delicate shrug of her shoulders. From her, it might have been agreement or a declaration of just how much she was looking forward to Kagan trying to rein her in.

All that mattered was that he had resources. They were the best.

Bram just hoped it was good enough.

Jaelyn's life depended on their performance.


"Done already?" Sullivan asked.

Gideon didn't answer, just stalked to the bar and started tossing ice into a glass.

*Dumb shit.*

Sullivan lifted his glass to hide his smirk.

"There's no hurry," Gideon groused when he turned around, showing off a boner through his jeans.

Sullivan shrugged. "Whatever makes you happy, man."

Gideon was a long way from happy, though. He chugged the drink, sucking in a harsh breath when it stung his mouth and throat.

"Well, there isn't," Gideon declared. "Because she can't escape and you made sure there's no link to us by using that dude's car. So . . . I'm going to enjoy breaking her."

*Tough talk.*

Sullivan fought the urge to snicker at the guy.

Pathetic.

Gideon would shit himself if he had any idea Bram Magnus was linked up with a Shadow Ops team.

"I'm out of here." Sullivan dropped his glass on an end table and stood up.

Gideon fixed him with a look that betrayed how unstable his mental state was. "What do you mean?"

The guy was starting to reach across the bar to where he had a nine millimeter stashed.

One of many.

"I mean, I helped you with the bitch because I wanted to tap her pussy," Ricky elaborated.

"She's mine," Gideon said.

"No shit, I've got eyes in my head," Ricky said as he shrugged into his leather jacket. "So I'm leaving before you and I have hard feelings. I never let a cunt come between me and a friend. Going to go get some."

"Oh." Gideon stopped reaching and watched him with a grudging gratitude.

"I just need a fuck," Ricky offered. "No reason for that to cause friction between us. See ya."

"But you'll be back?"

Ricky stopped at the door. "Want me to watch you bone her?" He let out a snicker. "How about cum on her face? That would be hot."

Gideon's eyes were glowing but the edge of insanity was still there. "I want her to fuck me . . ."

Ricky grunted. "Yeah, well, I'll be back . . . *later*. Much later, dude, because that is going to take some time." He stopped halfway through the front door. "But like you said, time is on your side. Make her eat from your hand, like a damned cat."

Sullivan enjoyed the look that crossed Gideon's face before he left.

Sick fuck.

Gideon had some serious issues. Not that it mattered to Ricky. Nope. Not at all.

What mattered was Ricky had everything he needed to draw Bram and Saxon Hale's team into a trap. On his own, Bram wouldn't be able to find the clue Ricky had left him.

Naw, hospitals had super-tight security.

But a Shadow Ops agent would walk through that red tape.

Sullivan didn't get in the elevator. Instead, he headed down just two flights of stairs to one of the newly finished condos. He opened the door and took a moment to inspect his screens. Gideon's penthouse was displayed across ten different high-definition monitors. He took a moment to enjoy the sight of their bait.

He'd have liked to tap her.

But nothing was going to be sweeter than using her to lure in members of Saxon Hale's team.

Sure, Saxon might not come. Not at first anyway.

But this was just phase one. Sullivan wanted Tyler Martin, too.

And he was going to get his pound of flesh.

In spades.

It was the Sullivan way.

# CHAPTER FOUR

She'd never seen this side of Bram.

Although, LeAnn sort of decided that calling him Magnus fit better.

He was all business. The hard body was now sporting a chest harness and a very lethal-looking handgun.

The weapon wasn't what made her leery of him.

It was his expression.

There was a sharpness to his features that went all the way into his eyes. In short, she realized she was looking at a man who could kill if it were necessary.

And it was for her sister.

The surprising thing was, LeAnn was happy for Jaelyn. She deserved a guy like Bram.

Maybe someday, LeAnn might find one herself.

"LeAnn, wait in your room," Bram said.

She started to balk but Jaelyn's face flashed through her mind.

It was important to prioritize.

* * *

She pushed away from the doorway but indulged in a last look at the way Bram and his team were getting down to work.

He knew what he was doing.

LeAnn made it back to her bedroom and realized just how little she knew him.

Really knew him.

Christ, the guy knew special agents and was clearly one of their brethren.

Was she a fool for jumping him and wasting the opportunity to have a deeper relationship with him?

Fact was, he wasn't around a lot of the time.

And now LeAnn understood why.

At least, a little more of the reason.

It hurt.

Doubly so when she realized she'd shared very little of herself with him. Somewhere along her road toward her personal goals, she'd built a hard shell around herself, forgetting what her grandparents had taught her about what was truly important in life.

The people who loved you.

Like Jaelyn.

LeAnn closed her door with a solid motion. She'd sit in her room all day if that's what it took to get her sister back.

That was all that mattered.

Psychology class was replaying across her brain again.

*Personal connections make you human . . .*

That was one reason people were so willing to spend money and effort on their pets. The personal connection.

She needed to establish it with her captor.

The thought made her skin crawl.

She clamped her discipline down on the sensation. He was not going to get into her head. She refused to allow him to control her beyond what he might do physically.

And she would do whatever it took to gain her freedom.

She shuddered because the sex toys lined up on the top of the dresser made it clear what her captor had in mind.

Well, she'd deal with things as they came.

And if he was stupid enough to get his dick near her face, well, that would be his mistake.

He was cooking for her at the moment. Jaelyn caught the scent of eggs and ham. She drew in a deep breath, gathering her composure and her courage.

She would prevail.

He was crossing the penthouse now. She quelled the nausea trying to twist her insides. She needed to engage him.

"I don't know your name," she said when he appeared in the bedroom doorway.

Creepy was distracted by her remark. Jaelyn watched the way he both liked and was frustrated by it.

"You've brought me to your world," she said, digging deep for enough control to keep her voice smooth and sweet. "Seems I should know who you are."

"I am the master." He growled as his expression became guarded.

The tray he was holding shook, making the fine china dishes rattle. She was starving but still too nauseated by the insanity in his eyes to actually consider eating.

"And you," he snapped, "are going to eat from my hand because you're my pet."

There was another rattle as he dropped the tray on the padded bench that was sitting at the foot of the bed.

"Or starve." He finished up before he knocked off one

of the silver domes covering one of the plates so he could grab a piece of toast.

The scent of the food wafted to her and made her belly heave. The dishes rattled as she make a frantic exit from the bed, slipping on the floor and hitting her knee before she made it into the bathroom to dry heave. Jaelyn caught the muffled cussing from the bedroom. She'd have liked to say she didn't give a rat's ass about how Creepy felt but that wouldn't be very wise.

She had to do better!

Had to be stronger than her reactions!

She'd heard the second man's voice. Between the two of them, killing her and disposing of her body wouldn't prove too hard.

The tile floor was cold. Chilling her as she contemplated how hopeless her situation was.

No, she wasn't a quitter.

Right on the heels of that thought though came the very certain knowledge that there was no way Creepy was going to let her live once he was finished with her. Who knew how many other "pets" he'd had. She finished brushing her teeth and went to the doorway of the bedroom.

Creepy was gone and so was the food.

She was so hungry, it hurt. But what worried her the most was how weak she felt. She had a chill that felt bone-deep and her muscles were quivering.

She needed to eat in order to survive.

Or at least so she'd have the strength to try and escape. Jaelyn turned around and considered the bathroom. Creepy was stomping around the penthouse. She let the sound of his tirade help her find the courage to search the bathroom. Every cabinet and drawer. She crawled onto the floor, taking care to keep the chain from making too much noise.

But all she found was makeup and towels.

She stood up and contemplated her options. The spotless mirrors showed her how bedraggled she looked.

Well, no one picked up the stray cat.

As much as she detested the idea of preening for Creepy's benefit, playing his game was the only way to help herself stay alive.

Jaelyn opened the drawers again and pulled out a curling iron and brush. She knew how to preen. There had been years when she and LeAnn enjoyed doing makeovers together. She was going to make herself adorable.

And it wasn't for Creepy. No, it was for her. She was going to survive by making her captor want to tame her or at least let him think she'd decided to bend to his will.

She didn't really care how it sounded to anyone, only that she got results.

She had a hell of a lot of living left to do.


Fried chicken wasn't on her grandfather's diet.

LeAnn didn't care. The look he gave her as he claimed two fresh-from-the-skillet pieces was worth the transgression and it was one of the few things she remembered how to cook.

It was a good memory, one that included time spent in the kitchen with her grandmother, mother, and Jaelyn. It had been a long time ago, though, and there was a stack of pieces that were singed.

But her grandfather smiled like a boy on Christmas morning.

"It's oatmeal tomorrow morning," she warned him.

He offered her a two-finger salute before carrying off his steaming plate toward the dining room table.

She moved the skillet to a cold section of the range and made sure the gas was off.

"I pissed you off."

Bram spoke from the doorway behind her that connected the kitchen with the dining room.

"Being sent to my room is hardly a problem," she told him firmly.

One dark eyebrow rose. "You denying it got under your skin?"

She propped her hands onto her hips and sent him her best solid stare. "Sure am. I let it roll off my back because I could see you and your team were working the problem."

"I'm a member," he offered. "Not the team leader."

"He's the new kid." Dare Servant spoke from behind her.

"I can handle this," Bram shot back.

LeAnn ended up leaning against the sink as she took in the battle of wills going on.

One side of Dare's mouth rose into a smirk. He was wearing a chest harness as well but there was also a badge clipped onto his belt.

Dare chuckled, pulling her attention back to his face. He winked at her before reaching past her to pluck a piece of chicken off the plate she'd been piling it on.

"Nice observation skills," Dare muttered as he snagged a plate and used it for the chicken.

"Are you in charge?"

"He's lucky I called him," Bram answered her. "I saved him from being bored to death."

"No argument," Dare said as he scooped up a huge

helping of smashed potatoes. "Besides, I never argue with the cook."

Another wink and Dare was shooting Bram a smirk on his way through the doorway into the dining room.

The oven timer dinged. LeAnn opened the door and pulled a pan from the top rack.

"For Thais and me," she said in response to Bram's questioning look. "With her figure, she doesn't eat fried food."

"You don't have to cater to us."

LeAnn finished plating the food before casting Bram a look. "They're here to help my family. Sitting in my room isn't my idea of helping. I will do anything to see Jaelyn home. Know something? They bring in security experts to tell the cheerleader squad what sort of things happen to girls who don't watch what they're doing. It's all part of making sure the owners of the team aren't liable if we get kidnapped or assaulted. I know the odds of recovering Jaelyn alive."

She didn't wait for him to respond but carried the plate into the dining room. His friends had taken over the living room, turning it into a command center of some sort. There was a large white board up with a time line on it and surveillance pictures of Jaelyn as she left her office, the market, the gym. There were various shots of her car as she crossed town from traffic cameras and a listing of every call she'd taken on her cell in the last month.

Thais Sinclair was looking between two different monitors as she used a mouse. That didn't mean the female member of the team missed LeAnn coming toward her.

"Seriously?" Thais remarked as she caught sight of the healthy food. But she grinned and nodded. "Guess you have a little first-hand experience."

LeAnn gave her a low chuckle but there was something about the white board with its pictures that was demanding her attention.

The prowler incident was underlined. So was the night Jaelyn's car had been disabled. It was the picture of Bram's truck parked next to Jaelyn's car that refused to let LeAnn move.

"You went to see her that night . . ." LeAnn was thinking out loud. "You didn't just call a tow truck and get her an Uber ride home."

"No, I didn't," Bram confirmed. He was watching her, picking up the fact that she was thinking through details.

"Because you wouldn't take a chance on a stranger like that . . ." LeAnn shared a look with Bram.

He shook his head, giving her the male version of I-don't-want-to deal-with-your-hurt-feelings.

LeAnn knew it well and yet, she pushed it aside in favor of a memory that was trying to get her attention. Like it was mega important and she realized it really was.

"Grandpa . . . ," LeAnn said. "Didn't you say Jaelyn was talking about a car trying to pick her up at the hospital?"

Her grandfather was chewing but his eyebrows lowered.

Bram stepped into her path. He was all business again, his expression sending a chill down her back. "What car?"

LeAnn felt the mood in the room change. It was as sudden as a balloon popping. What had been light and playful was suddenly loud and painful.

"She said . . . the guy claimed you'd sent him."

She heard a fork clatter onto a plate and then Thais was typing at a frantic pace. Dare had abandoned his food as well, moving to stand behind Thais. They stared at the screen for a moment, both of them visibly reacting to whatever was being displayed. Bram brushed by her, intent on seeing it, too.

Dare looked up. "It's registered to a Gideon, who just happens to be a military contractor—"

"Fuck!" Bram exploded as he leaned down and looked intently at the screen.

When Bram raised his face, there was a hard look of resignation. One he aimed at Milton Sondors. Her grandfather lowered his piece of chicken and wiped his lips.

"Tell it to me straight, son."

"This guy was deployed with me," Bram said, his tone thick with disgust. "A little off, but I didn't think he was unhinged enough to pull something like this."

"It's better than Martin," Dare muttered.

Thais was clicking and moving the mouse. Seconds crawled by like hours as LeAnn watched the three agents try and pick up a trail.

*Find her . . .*

"Not by much," Bram replied. "The guy was obsessed with the fact that he wasn't getting as much attention from women as uniformed men did." He stiffened. "As I did."

Bram's tone was ice cold with self-loathing.

"But now we know who has her," Dare said. "And he doesn't have the training to hide deep enough."

"No, he doesn't," Bram confirmed.

The links of her chain were too thick to pry apart.

Jaelyn looked at the tweezers she'd found among the bathroom supplies and tried to fit one end of them into the lock that connected the chain to the iron bed frame.

"Are you ready to eat?"

She turned to face Creepy, gaining confidence or at

least enough poise to maintain her composure from the flash of surprise on his face. She knew what he was seeing.

The hair.

The makeup.

The way she'd put on one of the expensive sets of silk nighties he'd put in the closet.

Oh yes. Creepy was grinning like a fourteen-year-old boy who had just managed to sneak his first *Playboy* into his room.

Jaelyn latched on to the moment, letting it build up her confidence.

She could turn the tables on him.

Success meant life.

He rolled his lower lip in and when it came back out, it was shiny.

"I'm hungry . . ." she whispered as she moved slowly around the bed and perched herself on the padded bench at the foot. She patted it gently.

Creepy jumped and the tray went smashing onto the polished floor.

Jaelyn ducked her chin and looked up at him with big eyes.

"Fuck . . . ," he mumbled, looking at the mess but unable to keep his eyes off her. "Right . . . I'll . . . be back. Don't move."

"I'll be right here."

He nearly jumped as he turned and bounded out of the room. One thing about this penthouse was that you could hear everything. Jaelyn waited just a moment before she moved toward the mess on the floor. Her belly was rumbling, making low growling sounds. The scent of the food made her mouth water but she had other priorities.

She dug out two pieces of broken plate and held her

chain up so it didn't give her away while she was going into the bathroom to hide them. The silverware was tempting but she was afraid he'd notice.

She returned and scooped up the mess onto the tray, making it look like a mess.

"What are you doing?"

Creepy was back in the doorway. She lifted a shoulder and used a napkin to dab up some residue. "Just . . . cleaning up . . . I mean . . . my grandma raised me to be neat . . . a good girl."

She let fat tears roll down her cheeks. It was a risk. Some guys detested crying females.

Creepy was caught off guard. His eyes widened as he took the mess with him and disappeared.

Sullivan snickered and snorted beer.

He drug his forearm under his nose to wipe it away before peering back at his monitors.

Gideon was such a dumb ass. Fact smart, but street stupid. His new pet was playing him.

"It's personal," Bram argued. "Gideon was a little screwy on post but I didn't see any indication that he'd gone off the deep end."

But they had it now. The car was clearly registered to him and was brand-new. Bram leaned over, enhancing the footage to look at the driver. He had a hat pulled down low and the collar of his suit jacket turned up to help hide his face.

"Looks like he was expecting company, too," Thais remarked. "The female sort."

Thais had pulled up Gideon's bank records. A list of store transactions showed off body wash, lingerie, curling irons, and a dozen other bathroom items intended for the feminine customer.

"Do you know where she is?" Milton Sondors asked the question in a tone LeAnn had never heard her grandfather use. She'd have sworn he was thirty years younger and even glancing toward him didn't quite shatter that image.

Her grandfather was on his feet, looking ready to go to war.

Bram grunted as he stood. "I know where he took her."

Thais and Dare were suddenly in motion. For all that Thais was sultry and seduction incarnate, it didn't seem to stop her from grabbing a body armor vest and putting it on with all the same confidence Dare did.

"I'm coming with you," LeAnn's grandfather said.

Bram stepped up to her grandfather. "I need to handle it."

"I disagree, son. Whoever he is, this Gideon touched my family."

"He's my responsibility." Bram lowered his voice. "And I'm not going to let the local cops in. There is no way he's getting more rights than Jaelyn."

There was an ominous tone in his voice, one Thais punctuated with pushing a full cartridge into her handgun.

The sound was like a gavel pounding.

"Son—" Her grandfather wasn't planning on bending.

"Since we're not including the local PD," Dare added, "someone needs to man a position here. The guy knows where you live."

LeAnn realized she'd been holding her breath. She was relieved to have them working her grandfather out of his determination but didn't much care for being used as the reason.

Well . . . beggars couldn't be choosers.

Milton snorted. "You still think I'm some sort of fool," he said, pointing at Dare. "I taught both girls how to shoot before they needed bras because I know what sort of men inhabit this world."

"Wise of you," Thais purred as she reached behind her and plucked another gun off the table. It was still in a leather holster, the kind with a clip to be secured into a belt. "My personal rule is, don't shoot anyone the world will miss."

LeAnn caught the gun when Thais tossed it to her. "I'll keep that in mind."

Bram had turned to contemplate her. She pulled the gun, checked it with a sure hand, and pushed it back into the holster.

"Time is wasting," she said, looking past Bram to her grandfather. "Let them go. They look like they don't have as many rules to follow as the cops. It's sort of working for me."

Her grandfather drew in a stiff breath before he grunted and nodded. "Seems you have some good sense in that head after all, LeAnn."

"Thank you." Bram spoke softly.

"Don't think I didn't see your buddy Servant there reaching for his handcuffs," Milton exclaimed.

LeAnn turned wide eyes toward Dare. The agent lifted his hands into the air as though he had no idea what her grandfather was referring to.

"Be glad I need you, son," Milton warned him. "Because I don't much care for any insinuation that I've grown too feeble to see to my own family."

Dare gave it up and nodded once before all traces of playfulness evaporated from his face.

"I'll bring her back," Bram promised.

*Or die trying . . .*

LeAnn saw the unspoken words in the way his eyes narrowed. He was turning and moving toward the other end of the living room. It felt like time slowed down, giving her plenty of hour-long moments in which to memorize Bram putting his gear on.

So practiced . . .

So very much in his element.

Determination flared in his eyes and it was the last thing she saw before he was moving toward the door, his fellow agents falling into step.

The only thing left for her to do was pray.

Which to be honest, fucking sucked.


Creepy was doing dishes.

Jaelyn rushed into the bathroom but forbid herself to throw up. Her belly was just going to have to deal with the nausea she'd fought back with every bite he'd insisted on hand feeding her.

She grabbed the pieces of broken plate and used one to tap against the other, breaking off tiny bits until she had a grove on either side like an arrowhead.

The closet was full of lacy bits of lingerie. It made it simple to find a nightie that was more string than fabric. She tilted her head to the side and listened for the water again before sinking to her knees and using the tattered garment to tie her arrowhead to the end of the back-scrubbing brush.

It made a crude spear but Jaelyn smiled as she held it up. The sight of the chain connected to her collar just made her feel even more victorious.

She refused to be a victim.

"What are you doing?"

She jumped but tightened her hands on the spear.

"What are you doing?" Creepy demanded from the closet door.

He was coming toward her, his hands outstretched, while his face contorted with rage.

"Defending myself!" she cried out, screaming as she surged up and drove the spear into his unguarded belly.

He let out a scream that was as horrible as it was wonderful. There was a warm gush of blood, spilling over her hands as he recoiled. The broken plate sunk into his flesh but it took all of her strength. He recoiled, pulling off her weapon and stumbling back.

He looked down at the blood spilling from his body.

"Bitch!" he gasped. "I'll shoot you . . ."

The scent of fresh blood did something to her, made something snap inside her brain. She let out a roar and jumped after him. Creepy was staggering backward on uncertain feet, colliding with the wall while his face went a sickly gray. All the while he was trying to make it to the doorway, where he could leave her tethered while he retrieved a gun.

*Now . . . or never . . .*

Jaelyn leaped toward him. She jammed her weapon back into him with strength she hadn't known she possessed. This time, her spear penetrated deeper and she aimed up, toward his diaphragm. Creepy was reaching for her throat but there was a strange rattle as he tried to suck in breath. She watched him gasp like a fish.

"Gonna . . . kill . . . you . . . too . . ."

He came off the wall with a spurt of energy. She fell back, falling and hitting the floor with a smack. Pain surged through her body as she felt him grabbing her clothing.

She fought.

Fought like she'd never fought before in her life. Kicking and screaming as she struggled to make it across the floor of the bathroom.

Every second felt like it lasted an hour. All of her senses were keener, too. She felt her fingernails breaking as she clawed at the tile floor. Felt her knees bruising and scraping while she kicked at Creepy behind her. Every impact with him was solid and sent a jolt of pain through her entire body.

But she fought on.

"Freeze!"

Caught in the grip of her battle to survive, Jaelyn looked up in shock at the man coming through the doorway of the bathroom. Her lungs were burning, unable to keep up with the frantic pounding of her heart. She couldn't concentrate, couldn't seem to make herself understand what was happening. Her brain was locked into the struggle for survival.

Someone grabbed her by the back of her top and hauled her into the bedroom while someone else was stepping over her. She ended up looking at the man's boots while he shouted at Creepy.

Help . . . help had arrived.

In an instant, her body seemed to run out of fuel. She ended up in a heap on the floor of the bedroom. Every inch of her body hurting and pulsing and all the pain did was make her feel so very alive.

*Yeah . . . alive . . .*

She became strangely absorbed with the bright red

blood coating her fingers. She managed to roll to one side so she might lift her hand and stare at her fingers. The blood was pooling under her fingernails and running in little, thick drops down her wrist.

Blood from her kill . . .

"Clear!"

"Clear!"

Jaelyn jerked, realizing someone was crouched over her. She watched him lower his gun as he looked down at her.

Dark hair.

Blue eyes.

*Bram* . . .

"I've got you."

His voice was so welcome. Like a warm blanket on a cold night. Sinking into its fold was so tempting, and yet, the scent of the blood made her bare her teeth.

"I was doing just fine." She really had no idea why she felt the need to argue, only that the impulse was impossible to quell. Jaelyn lifted her hand, like some sort of declaration of her strength.

Bram shifted his attention to the blood, his lips curving just a tiny amount.

"Suspect is dead." Someone else came close enough for her to see. The badge clipped to his vest caught her attention.

Bram had the same body armor on. Clad in mostly black from head to toe, he looked dangerous and she realized she loved it.

Someone brought a key in to unlock the collar around her neck.

"I want to see him."

Bram's eyes narrowed. "He'll never bother you again."

Jaelyn struggled to stand. "*I want . . . to . . . see . . .*"

She wasn't going to wait for an answer, either. Jaelyn started toward the bathroom door, her legs shaking. But Bram gripped her arm and pulled her back. "It's not a pretty sight."

Jaelyn smiled. Most likely, she'd regret it later or at least realize it wasn't the brightest reaction to have let anyone see, but for the moment, impulses ruled her and she wanted to see with her own eyes.

"I'm the one who did the damage," she informed him.

"Let her see," a woman said.

Jaelyn turned to catch sight of a woman who had blended so easily with the two men, Jaelyn hadn't taken notice of her slighter frame. Whoever she was, the woman was the sort of pretty that fell into the category of beautiful.

"Sinclair." Bram turned and pegged her with a hard look.

"I want to see," Jaelyn repeated through clenched teeth.

Bram turned and caught her by her forearms. "Jaelyn—"

She shoved at him. "Stop trying to protect me."

He wasn't expecting that. She watched surprise register in his eyes before he was reluctantly moving out of her path.

Creepy was lying face down on the bathroom floor. A puddle of blood was seeping out of him. The dark-haired agent turned him over, revealing the wounds she'd made with her spear.

"Clever," Agent Sinclair said as she held up the spear. "Using what you had to work with."

"I killed him." She was shaking again, so damned cold and yet, victory was warming her like a double shot of whiskey. "Good."

Better than good really.

It was justice.

Ricky pointed his gun at the screen. "Got you . . ."

He watched the agents make their way up the stairs, their Shadow Ops badges clear enough even on the security cameras.

He'd fucking remember those badges for the rest of his life.

He reached for a cell phone and dialed 911.

"What is your emergency?"

"There are people . . . with guns!" Ricky did his best Southern drawl impersonation. "Kicking in the penthouse door! Bantam building, on Second Street . . . hurry up . . . I think someone is dying!"

Ricky lowered the phone and used a towel to wipe the case clean. The dispatcher was firing questions at him but he tossed the phone onto the desk before he wiped it down, too.

He needed to make enough noise so Bram Magnus couldn't disappear too easily.

Tyler Martin wouldn't pick up the scent otherwise.

Ricky grabbed his backpack and left the apartment, wiping fingerprints away as he went.

He shrugged into a construction vest and hard hat before hitting the hallways where the security cameras might be active. He made sure to stop along his way and check a few control panels.

He heard the first sirens when he hit the ground floor. A few workers looked up, curious as to what was happening.

Ricky walked by, through the parking garage and toward the lot where the construction crew was parking.

It was tempting to take a truck but he walked toward a gas station and around the corner until he spotted a cheap motel. The clerk took his cash and didn't bother to look twice at his ID.

Ricky slipped into the room, pulling out his burner phone to watch the show.

The resolution was crap but that didn't keep him from enjoying the way Bram and his teammates turned on their company.

The local cops had their weapons drawn . . . Bram's team wasn't giving up their guns, either.

It was fucking beautiful to watch.

Even better than his dreams of vengeance.

He kicked back on the motel bed and heard it groan beneath his weight.

"What I haven't heard you tell me is why you didn't call me and clue me in to what you were planning."

The local police sergeant wasn't happy.

Bram didn't much care. In fact, the only reason he was listening to the guy at all was because Kagan had asked him not to make waves.

"Someone better start explaining this mess," the guy continued. It wasn't that he was a jerk. No, he was attempting to control the situation, which was his job.

Problem was, Bram didn't give a shit. "It's a military matter."

The cop jerked. "The hell it is. This is my jurisdiction."

"Guess you should have taken the missing person report when you were called," Thais said.

"You have any idea how many people slip away from their families in this city?" the sergeant demanded.

"We had a clear evidence chain," Dare added.

The sergeant held up two fingers. "Two incidents, one being a dead car, isn't a chain."

"Coupled with a missing person, it's a chain." Thais was watching the cops keeping their sights on her as she moved forward.

"We don't hesitate when someone goes missing," Dare added.

"You don't seem to hesitate for anything, like the law," the sergeant bellowed. "You can't just blow in here with your guns out."

"He"—Bram said as he jerked his head toward Gideon's body—"became obsessed with striking out at me. Stole a picture of my girlfriend. Look around, he's been planning this. It's PTSD syndrome."

"You didn't know that when you came over here." The police officer cut through Bram's reasoning.

"We're licensed to carry firearms in every state." Bram spared the guy only a half glance. "Considering you didn't think it was worthy of taking a report, I'd say things worked out."

"There was no reason to believe she didn't take off on her own."

"Except for a prowler, who turned violent when confronted," Bram countered, laying down his reasoning.

"We take hundreds of trespassing reports a week in this city."

"This one came on the heels of a disappearance." Bram stood his ground as the cop tried to intimidate him.

"She wouldn't be the first girls her age to take off because their family doesn't approve of their choices."

"She's my girlfriend," Bram said as he stepped toward the guy.

"According to social media, the other sister is your girl-friend. Maybe that's why I thought this one took off after you started up on her sister. The press is going to have a field day with this mess."

Bram stiffened, Kagan's warning rising from his memory.

"I'm not going to the hospital," Jaelyn said, raising her voice.

"Then you're going downtown," the cop in front of him said as he turned his attention to Jaelyn.

"Why?" she said, facing off with him. Bram almost felt sorry for the guy but not enough to intervene. Jaelyn propped her hand onto her hip and narrowed her eyes. "He chained me to a fucking bed and watched me like a porn movie. In the shower, on the toilet. Told me all about his sick little fantasies. Insisted I was going to eat from his hand because I was his pet. Don't you dare tell me I don't have the right to defend myself against creeps like him. I'd kill him again."

Thais had given Jaelyn a jacket to cover the skimpy lin-gerie set she had on. She didn't much care that it was flapping open as she gave the cop a piece of her mind. Dare was watching with a bland expression Bram knew was just covering up his fellow agent's amusement.

Thais, on the other hand, did nothing to disguise how much she felt the cop was getting exactly what he de-served.

Bram's phone vibrated inside his vest. He pulled it out and only took a single glance to identify Kagan's number.

"You got your man," his section leader began.

"Yes."

Kagan grunted. "You're Magnus's spawn alright."

"Don't bring my dad or his rank into this," Bram replied.

"You learned how to hunt from your pappy, son," Kagan retorted. "Never doubt it."

Bram didn't. "Let's stick to the topic. Another thing I learned from my dad was not to hide behind him. There was no way I was going to turn over Jaelyn's location to the local law enforcement. Gideon followed me to her. It was personal."

"That's one of the traits I like about you," Kagan informed him. "Another is the fact that you finish what you start."

Bram had worked with Saxon Hale and Shadow Ops before. There was a reason they were mostly known by the rumors about them.

The reason was, Kagan and his team leaders didn't leave many clues behind to track them through. The horde of police in the room was a huge problem. It was a lot easier to have no witnesses than to tell people not to talk.

"I brought in resources, so it's my job to clear the deck?" Bram asked.

"Same thing I expect from any of my team members," Kagan confirmed. "You'll enjoy the part of telling the local cops."

"More than I should admit," Bram answered.

"Clean slate," Kagan said. "Leave no trace."

Bram tightened his hold on the phone. Kagan's meaning was crystal clear. With Kagan, it was more important to hear what he wasn't saying. If the press were sniffing around, there was no way the family could stay behind. Gideon might have followed him but Bram had brought in the team to deal with it.

So the team's safety had to be protected.

"Copy that," Bram replied. "I need resources."

"They'll be on scene shortly," Kagan confirmed. "I'll overlook the lapse this time. But don't be shy in the future, Magnus. There's too much chatter on the airways."

It was a reprimand Kagan wouldn't repeat. Bram killed the call and made a mental note to stop thinking like a civilian.

He'd made his choice and there was no going back.

"Sergeant." The police officer jerked his head around, responding to the authority in Bram's tone. "Get your men off site. Information blackout."

"Says who?"

Thais pulled a folded bundle of papers out of her vest and tossed them toward the guy. The sergeant caught them as the door of the penthouse was opened and Kagan's men started pouring in. They were all dressed in black, most of them wearing face shields to protect their identities. The only thing that was evident was the Shadow Ops badges on their belts.

"This is my jurisdiction," the sergeant insisted.

Bram stepped up to square off with the guy. "No, it isn't. Because this never happened. Handle your men or I will."

The cop was pissed but he shut his jaw, recognizing the determination in Bram and the fact that Bram was trying to let him maintain command of his own people.

"You're not the only man who's served his time." The cop sent Bram a look full of promise before he whistled and made a wrap-it-up gesture with his hand. His men were slow to respond, torn between a command from a man they were accustomed to answering to and the body lying on the floor.

The sergeant settled the matter by turning around and

clearing out of the penthouse. His men followed as Jaelyn gave a little grunt of approval. The clean-up team knew their job well, beginning the task of erasing every last bit of evidence from the scene. Jaelyn watched them take the chain and collar she'd been forced to wear and put it into a dark tub. She looked past it to where her captor was being rolled over and lifted into a body bag. The sound of the zipper was like nails grating on a chalkboard. She shuddered and clasped the jacket tightly against her body.

"If no one minds . . . I would really like to go home."

Gideon's penthouse was being cleared in record time.

Ricky snickered, enjoying the way the cops argued but ended up on the way down to their cars.

Fuck, there were a few things he could get to like about the Shadow Ops teams. It must be a blast to be one of their number.

That thought sobered him.

Tyler Martin had promised him a position that came with authority. There were always men who needed their dirty work done. Men running for president were often among their number. Carl Davis had Tyler Martin and Tyler had brought Ricky on board.

Right before dumping Ricky in a Mexican prison after it was all over.

Shit but he hated a man who welshed on his bargain. Maybe Ricky was a murdering son of a whore but hell, he keeps his word. And he didn't lie about what he was, unlike Tyler Martin in his suit and tie, standing there beside Carl Davis as they smiled and acted like great guys for the benefit of the cameras.

They were just as dirty as he was.

More so, because they were the ones who hired him.

In the end, he was just another man trying to survive, using the skills he had.

Gideon would never know what he'd been a part of. Ricky watched as his body was bagged and the blood cleaned up. The job wasn't finished until even the tile was jackhammered up and bagged. The penthouse was left with stripped dry wall and bare floors as every last bit of surface area was cleaned. The local cops wouldn't find a shred of blood left to support their claims of a murder happening.

Through it all, Bram Magnus kept watch.

And Sullivan watched him.

Soon, he'd lead Ricky right to the nest. That place where Saxon Hale and his team were dug in and calling home. Sure, Hale and his team hadn't double-crossed him but they'd been the reason Tyler Martin hamstrung him.

Ricky might not have a lot of virtues but no one crossed a Sullivan or got the best of one.

Jaelyn got out of the car the second she could and ran across the lawn of her grandfather's house.

"I can take the heat," Dare Servant said as he moved up beside Bram. "They can aim their frustration toward me."

Jaelyn nearly toppled her grandfather as she threw herself at him, locking her arms around him. LeAnn was only a half step away from them both. Bram could see her eyes shimmering with unshed tears.

"You don't have to be the bad guy," Dare continued. "Might be better all the way around if they think you're on their side."

Bram knew what his fellow agent was referring to. Behind the little group having a much deserved family

reunion was a house. One which had blossomed into a
home with the help of the family living inside its walls.
Honestly, he realized that was one of the reasons he'd
stuck around LeAnn so long. His own childhood was a
list of assignments as his father served his country.

There was part of him that understood why it hadn't
really bothered him to not have a badge yet. Dare was
ready to take the heat without flinching because it was part
of how the teams operated. LeAnn was a minor celebrity.
Her cheerleading team had leaked the information of her
sister being missing. They'd found Jaelyn but nothing
came without a price.

He'd used the team and had to cover their tracks.

"Anyone home?" Dare asked.

"Yes," Bram answered. "And no, I don't need you to
tell them. I made the call to bring you and Thais in, so
I'll be the one to drop the bomb on resettlement being a
necessity."

He'd be a fucking coward if he didn't.

"I'll check the details of our departure," Dare offered.
There wasn't a whole lot of empathy in his tone. It was
part of the job, part of making sure Shadow Ops teams
remained unknown.

Not that Bram expected anything else. No, Dare Servant was a seasoned agent. One who loved his job. Men
like Dare kept their attention on what mattered, which
was the mission objective.

They'd achieved that.

Jaelyn finished hugging her sister as her grandfather
ushered her through the front door. She looked toward
Bram, their gazes locking.

Damn if he didn't feel it as much as see it. She came

toward him, her eyes filling with uncertainty as he didn't relax.

Jaelyn didn't stop. She drew in a deep breath and kept coming.

"Thank you."

Her voice was full of relief and gratitude but what captivated him was the look in her eyes.

God, he wanted to be the man she saw him as.

"Thank you . . ." She turned and walked back toward the house.

Back toward the life he was going to have to tell her she had to leave.

"You know, Magnus, I like you and all," Dare began as he pulled his shades off and tucked them into a pocket on his vest. "But are you fucking blind? You were dating the cheerleader?"

"It wasn't dating. You think the life you've chosen mixes with a woman like Jaelyn?" Bram retorted. "I should have kept my hands off her. Gideon followed me here and it could have been worse. It could have been Tyler Martin."

"Another good reason why we have to clear this family out of here. Martin might catch wind of this and your connection." There was a ripping sound as Dare opened a pocket on his vest to pull out his cell phone. "Maybe you're heading down the same road Saxon and Vitus did. There's room at the nest for you and that little dove."

"Even if I was interested in playing house, I doubt Jaelyn will be very happy about having me once I tell her she's being relocated."

She'll be torn.

Deeply.

"And that it's because a guy in my circle followed me to her grandfather's doorstep."

Dare shook his head. "Not my area of expertise. I just know how to get the bad guy."

Jaelyn came into view through the kitchen window. She had no idea how dangerous it was to be seen.

*He craved her.*

Like a safe harbor.

All of the reasons why he shouldn't give into those needs were going across his brain. He recognized the logic, agreed with it even, and still rejected the idea of parting ways with Jaelyn.

Not that it was going to be entirely his call.

No.

In fact, she just might hate him when he dropped the bomb on her grandfather about having to relocate. The house Milton Sondors had bought for his bride and watched two generations of his family grow up in was no longer safe.

It would be easier if she hated him.

Bram felt his chest tighten.

Fuck.

Bram shook his head. "I brought it here. So I'll do the explaining."

Dare nodded. "I'll make the arrangements."


She was going to be alright.

Jaelyn repeated the words a few times and then ordered herself to stop hiding in the bathroom.

She looked at the familiar tile and towels. Nowhere near as expensive or posh as the ones in Gideon's penthouse.

But she preferred them so much more!

She dried off, feeling like her neck was going to snap because of how tense her muscles were.

Everyone was watching her.

*Waiting for her to lose it . . .*

Well, she had plans to disappoint them, but it was nothing personal.

Actually, it was deeply personal. In fact, Jaelyn was pretty sure she'd never wanted to prove something more than she did at that moment. Keeping her wits together was a point of pride.

Intensely deep and important.

*It was over.*

And there was no way she was going to let Creepy take up residence in her thoughts.

Jaelyn moved toward the kitchen and realized the silence wasn't in her head, it was in the house. She could hear the dishwasher chugging away while her grandfather sat at the dining room table.

"Grandpa?"

Milton Sondors jumped when she spoke to him. "I'm fine. Nothing to worry about."

He'd never looked so old.

Her hair was wet and she was starving but there was a stillness in the house that had her looking at the members of Bram's team.

*Bram . . .*

She was having trouble looking at him. He knew it, too. He was watching her from behind mirrored sunglasses, looking like it took a lot of effort for him to remain across the room from her.

Even behind shades, she got the feeling he saw more of her feelings than most people would. Did he know she was on edge? Of course he did. His lips were pressed into a hard line while she was hesitating in the hallway like some violated virgin.

*Well, Creepy hadn't gotten that far . . .*

So there was no reason to be so uneasy. Jaelyn straightened her spine and moved forward.

*If it didn't kill her . . . it made her stronger . . .*

Right.

"What's going on?" she asked of Bram.

She caught a twist of distaste crossing Bram's lips before he answered.

"Gideon wasn't the driver at the hospital. He's got an accomplice out there."

Jaelyn nodded. "I heard the other guy, but never saw him."

A chill went down her spine as a few key phrases rose from her memory like snakes in a swamp.

' *"I mean, I helped you with the bitch because I wanted to tap her pussy,"*

No, she refused to think about it.

But Bram noticed. His eyes flashed with knowledge as Jaelyn fought to control her emotions.

"You all need to be relocated and placed in new identities." He paused for a moment as his words cut her to the bone.

But at least it was a distraction. "Which means what?"

"Arrangements will be made to deliver your household goods to your new residence. We leave tomorrow. Agent Servant will have details shortly."

There was a click from behind her as Thais cleaned up her desk. The scent of Windex was in the air from the whiteboard they'd cleaned off. It was now blank, just like the house was slated to be.

"But . . . this is our home."

Her nightmare suddenly wasn't over.

"Home is where family is," Milton offered.

But her grandfather's tone was hollow, like he'd just been gutted. In fact, time was frozen while Jaelyn tried to absorb what Bram had just told her.

How in the hell did she deal with knowing they'd lost everything?

"I need your identification," Bram continued without a hitch. "Credit cards, medical, anything with your names on it."

Her grandfather stood up and pulled his wallet from his pocket. Her heart was accelerating, the sight of him tossing the worn leather billfold across the table so that it landed close to Bram was just too much.

"Its fine, Jaelyn, getting you back . . . is all that matters."

Milton was cooing. Using that tone of voice you used with a toddler or someone about to dissolve into a puddle of tears and hysterics.

She just couldn't bear to be predictable on top of everything else.

Or maybe "weak" was a better word.

Bram was so steady, so able to roll with the punches.

She'd reached for that part of him and she wasn't going to be a wuss now.

LeAnn appeared, her purse in hand, and passed off her driver's license to Bram. Her sister offered her a sweet smile that made Jaelyn recoil.

She couldn't keep it together if everyone handled her like a fragile baby bird.

The silence was deafening.

There was an icy chill in the air, like Jaelyn could feel the life draining out of the house she'd called home her entire life.

"Jaelyn," her grandfather spoke up to fill the void. "Would you mind frying up some chicken-fried steak? With sausage gravy and biscuits. You make it just the way your grandmother did . . . every Saturday morning . . . before she got sick . . ."

It was something to do.

Jaelyn shot her grandfather a grateful look before she headed into the kitchen.

Yeah . . . something to do. Something normal.

Kagan liked to operate off the grid.

For a section leader of Shadow Operations teams, it was a very healthy approach to take with life. His duty was his home, the roof he slept under was irrelevant and changed often enough to help him continue to be unpredictable.

Tyler Martin had warned him that the world wasn't as big as it once was though, and had advised him that the ability to hide was becoming impossible in a world full of surveillance cameras and tracking beacons. Tyler had used those facts as an excuse to sell out the Shadow Ops teams in his bid to secure himself a place with Carl Davis. Tyler believed it, had sold his soul for security or what he believed would be his ticket to being untouchable.

One thing Tyler seemed to be right about was the fact that Kagan wasn't as anonymous as he liked to think. No, Colonel Bryan Magnus, father of one Bram Magnus, appeared in the doorway of Kagan's office without a single warning. He stopped only for a brief moment before he strode over to the desk Kagan was seated behind and sat down, his uniform hat balanced on his right thigh.

"I told your man he didn't need to tell you I was here," the colonel began.

"Are you here?"

The colonel shook his head. "Just about in the same way as you never sent one of your men into the bed of my daughter."

"The evidence was there," Kagan reminded him of the reason Mercer had been assigned to the case. "Clueing you in would have been discarding my objectivity. The best way to prove you innocent was to have a full investigation without your knowledge."

"Understandable."

The colonel was just as good at keeping his thoughts to himself as Kagan considered himself to be.

"What are you looking to me to provide?" Kagan asked.

"You seem to like having my son on your teams."

Kagan nodded. "You taught him well."

"I did," the colonel agreed. "Which is why he cracked that case he's on in record time."

Kagan was surprised, doubly so when the colonel read it off his face.

"I know because the local police are a little unhappy about how my son and your team members . . . didn't include them in the rescue of one Jaelyn Sondors, which resulted in the death of one perpetrator."

"According to my agents, the girl killed her captor, and they just happened to get there around the same time," Kagan said. "How'd that report make it onto your desk?"

"Simple," the colonel said. "A few of those civilian badge holders are also military reserve. They had Bram's information from the trespassing incident. And while I might respect my son enough to allow him to be his own man, there is no way I don't make very sure I know where he is and who might be interested in finding out who he reports to."

"Are you here to tell me not to offer Bram a badge?"

The colonel slowly grinned. "Bram respects me because I earned it from him by not micromanaging his life."

"Respect is best when it's earned," Kagan agreed. "Why are you here?"

"The guy who nabbed her was a civilian contractor on his last post. He snatched a picture from Bram and used it to identify his prey."

Kagan let out a low whistle. "Looks like I'm going to be glad I let Bram call in team resources."

It was a subtle hint that Kagan had already given out a favor to the Magnus family. The colonel only offered him a half grin.

"I need you to stash the family with your resources."

Kagan didn't ask the burning question of why. No, he rolled the request around his brain for a moment before the colonel's reasoning dawned on him.

"You're worried there might be other military personnel involved."

"It's a possibility I'm not willing to overlook." The colonel's tone hinted at how hard it was for him to ask for help. "If I deal with them or allow civilian witness protection to take them, the information might be tracked. Your system, now that's a different matter."

"You realize my teams aren't designed for witness relocation?" Kagan's question received a snort. "Best I can do is stuff them somewhere out of sight."

"I just need you to sit on them long enough for me to chase down any stray evidence trails. And I don't need my son balking at the order to do it because he's concerned with hurting feelings." The colonel relaxed a bit, leaning back in the chair. "Seems Bram is set on accepting a badge from you."

"And you think I'm getting ready to offer it?"

There was another snort from the colonel. "I might advise you to not try and bluff a man who's been at this game as long as you have, Kagan." He stood up and settled his hat on his head. "But the truth is, if you're too stupid to have Bram on your teams, you're the loser."

Kagan nodded. "Agreed."

The colonel offered him a salute. "I will be in touch."

Jaelyn woke up in a cold sweat.

She gasped and rolled out of the bed because for a moment, she thought she was back in the penthouse.

But there was no chain, no collar, and the open blinds let in enough light from the street lamp to show her the familiar furniture of her room.

Right.

She was fine.

F-I-N-E.

But she was shaking and the night air was chilling her since she was slick with perspiration.

She eased down the hallway toward the back of the house where a half bath was built for those coming out of the pool. She didn't need anyone to know she'd had a nightmare.

Big deal.

It would pass.

She wasn't going to the hospital and she didn't need a shrink.

A quick rinse and she found herself looking at the backyard pool. Man, it had been a long time since she'd used it.

The pool was clean and sparkling. As she caught the scent of chlorine, happy memories rose from her mind, days of summer fun and swimming past sundown when heat waves were baking southern California.

She walked along the edge of the pool, immersed in the memories. A deep shadow was cast by the workshop that formed a natural barrier between the pool and the neighbors' house.

She reached for the combination lock and grinned when it popped open after a moment of fiddling with the stiff numbers.

She reached up and pulled a cord hanging from an overhead light and heard it buzz as it illuminated the inside of the work shed.

Inside was a collection of boxes and an old friend.

Tears stung her eyes as she looked over at the tools for what had once been her dream.

Glassblowing.

Damn how she'd loved it. The heat, the challenge of pitting her artistic ability against gravity, and a globe of molten glass. Turning the rod and working to mold her vision into reality before the glass warmed up too much and shattered or just fell to the floor like honey because she wasn't skilled enough to keep turning the rod.

An entire hot shop was sitting in the shed, carefully covered to keep it from rust.

"Thanks, Gramps," she whispered lovingly as she pulled a box down and found a number of her creations.

Like frozen fireworks, the colors were perfect. Man, she'd have gained some serious skill if she'd stayed with it. The vase in her hands was leaning to one side, proving that while she had natural talent, skill came with practice.

Life had gotten in the way. Her mother had been diagnosed with cancer and Jaelyn had stored away her dreams of being an artist in favor of a job that came with benefits.

The tears dropped down her cheeks, pissing her off because she knew she was crying about Creepy and not her mother. He was sitting in the back of her thoughts like some sort of specter. On impulse, she turned and hurled the vase at the far wall. It exploded when it hit the solid brick, falling down like a flow of water.

Better . . .

In fact, she felt like she could breathe again.

She took a deep, cleansing breath and reached into the box again. This time she pulled out a bowl that had a crack in one side. Jaelyn put her whole body into the throw this time, loving the burn that went through her arm while the bowl shattered.

"Feel better yet?"

She jerked around, a vase in hand. Bram was in the doorway, contemplating her with his blue eyes. A jolt of awareness spiked through her, delighting her because it meant she was escaping the grip of the nightmare she'd endured.

But the look of concern on Bram's face made her defensive.

"I'm good. And I don't need anyone watching me." She fought to find a neutral tone. "Nothing personal."

His face had been an unreadable mask. It softened a bit with her apology. The problem was, what she saw was pity and she needed to stay away from that.

*Very . . . far . . . away . . .*

\* \* \*

Jaelyn sent another piece of glass toward the wall. It burst in a shower of particles that the light from the overhead shop lamp illuminated.

Annihilated.

She liked the idea, allowing the word to roll around her brain for a good long moment. It killed off some of her anger, leaving her with a general, all around feeling of being pissed enough to take life on.

"There is no shame in seeking help after something like this, Jaelyn."

"I'm fine . . ."

She took the time to enunciate each word, liking the feeling of them as they slid past her teeth. Satisfaction warmed her insides as she finished and didn't feel any need to apologize.

But Bram was still there.

The guy had presence, she'd have to give him points for it. Some people just did. Others tried to cultivate it and spent a lot of time chasing something they were never going to get a handle on.

Bram had the sort of stare you could feel. But it sent a chill down her spine now because she still felt like she needed to scrub Creepy's gaze off her skin.

*She didn't . . . fucking . . . care!*

"I am not going to just survive," Jaelyn said as she half-turned to catch Bram in her gaze. "I will *thrive* . . ."

She'd never been so convinced of anything in her life.

Or at least the need for it, and the knowledge that she would die if she didn't succeed. It was like she was lying in a coffin, the pile of dirt to cover it in sight at the top of the hole.

She either climbed out or waited to hear the shovelfuls

of dirt hitting the top of her coffin, sealing her inside where a nice, slow death awaited her.

Bram had one of those hard, unreadable expressions on his face. But his eyes narrowed and his lips turned just a touch white because he was pressing them together so tightly.

"I believe you."

She liked the sound of that. Confidence stirred inside her, helping her believe her own claims.

Jaelyn turned and went toward the door. Bram didn't move. She realized he'd been making sure to keep his distance from her.

*Fragile baby bird . . .*

She tightened her resolve and kept moving. Her insides twisted when she got close enough to touch him. It was the same intense reaction she'd been enduring before Creepy had taken her.

The impulse to scurry through the door was strong.

She quelled it. Desperately needing to master her emotions.

Bram was her lover.

The man she'd chosen. And she'd done well, too. He was waiting for her to heal.

No . . . not heal . . .

Get her feet under her.

That was better.

Things inside her tightened as she got closer to him. The sensation was acute, like it had been before. The difference was, she felt raw, like she had a sunburn. In time, it would heal.

Fuck that.

Creepy wasn't going to claim any more of her time.

Jaelyn stopped in front of Bram, forcing herself to stay there while her body felt like it was rioting.

He knew exactly what she was doing, too. Understanding was in his eyes and in the hard set of his jaw. He knew what it felt like to come home after war.

"I just need . . ." Words failed her and she let her voice trail off.

Bram's eyes narrowed. He shifted, lifting one hand off his bicep where he'd been gripping his sleeve.

She cringed.

It just happened, the impulse horrifying her because she couldn't quite hide it completely. Bram froze for a moment, watching her struggle to gain a grip. He didn't let her linger in the moment, though. He reached for her again, almost in the same breath, stretching out his hand to stroke her cheeks.

So simple.

Yet electrifying.

"Kick it in the teeth, baby . . ." His tone was deep and husky. Full of confidence in her ability to claim victory.

She wanted to be the person he thought she was.

"That's my plan."

Her cheek still registered his touch. She felt it all the way back to her room. When she did fall back into slumber, Bram was on her mind.

Baby birds grew fast.

# CHAPTER FIVE

"He's going to throw up on you."

Saxon Hale only sent his wife, Ginger, a smirk. "If he does, it's because he wants more breast time." Saxon looked up into the face of his son and grinned. "Just like his daddy . . ."

Ginger rolled her eyes before reclaiming her baby from her husband. "Keep your dirty jokes away from my baby."

"That won't help," Vitus Hale offered from where he was scraping his dinner plate. "You breed with a Hale, it's in the DNA."

"Ah . . ." Ginger sighed. "Such a romantic word . . . 'breed.'"

Saxon stood up and wrapped his arms around her from behind. "You loved every second of it," he said and grunted as she sent her elbow into his side.

"Don't you two have an office to get to?" Ginger asked him.

Saxon shrugged. "More of a hole in the ground at the moment. We might actually have an office by next year."

"She's going to say it's too high-class for the likes of us," Vitus informed his brother before he carried his plate to the sink and offered Ginger a two-finger salute.

Saxon's phone buzzed. He pulled it out of his pocket and flashed the incoming number toward Vitus. "Kagan knows we're slacking off . . ."

Vitus slowly smiled as he flipped the phone the bird. Saxon answered with a half snort.

"Morning, sir."

"Servant and Sinclair got their man and the local PD is pissed."

Kagan might have been reading off his grocery list for all the emotion he allowed to seep into his tone.

Saxon wasn't fooled by it, though. He knew his section leader enough to realize Kagan was a master of making sure no one knew what he was thinking.

"Should I expect them soon?"

"Yes," Kagan said as he let out a rare, frustrated sound that made Saxon frown. "They're bringing company."

"What sort?" Saxon's tone snapped Vitus's attention back toward him. There were few things that got under Saxon's skin and his brother knew whatever was bothering him was something to take very, very seriously.

"The girl and her family," Kagan said. "And before you start listing the reasons why it's such a bad idea, let me cut you off by telling you I agree."

Saxon took a moment before asking his next question.

"So why is Magnus bringing them to my location?"

Vitus stiffened, his expression drawing tight with disapproval. Saxon shared it. In a very personal way. His family was there and every person who knew about the location of the future command center was a potential leak.

"Because I also agree with Colonel Magnus," Kagan said.

"Bram went to his daddy?"

Vitus's eyes widened.

"No," Kagan retorted. "But just as you're digging in because of your parental instincts, the colonel came to me because the man who snatched the girl was on post with Bram. It was personal."

Saxon let out a low whistle. "That's bad."

"Exactly," Kagan said. "If the colonel allows them to go to witness protection . . ."

"It will leave a trail," Saxon finished for him. "One that could lead back to my location."

"Right," Kagan said. "Keep them there until I can find another solution to satisfy Colonel Magnus. Bram is a team member. We take care of our own."

Kagan ended the call because it wasn't a conversation. The only thing left to say was "Yes, sir," but that was something the badge on his belt implied, so it wasn't necessary to verbalize it.

Saxon still cussed even though he agreed.

Bram was a team member. Was the situation outside the Shadow Ops scope of operations?

Yes.

And that didn't mean shit.

Bram had put his life on the line for the team. They'd be there in his time of need.

Saxon understood but he definitely didn't like the situation. Behind him, his older son laughed, driving home how vital it was to maintain the security of his home. There had been a time when he didn't think he needed love and home.

Now, he was certain he couldn't live without it.

* * *

"We're going where?"

Dare sent Bram a raised eyebrow. "Looked to me like you would be pleased."

Bram wanted to cuss but the picture hanging on the wall in the dining room of Milton and Jeanie Sondors on their wedding day stopped him.

"I can't believe Saxon agreed," Bram said.

"My guess is, he'll have plenty to say about it," Thais said, joining the conversation.

"None of it will be pretty," Dare said. "Hale doesn't concern me as much as your attitude does. Didn't you start something with her?"

"That's none of your business." Bram was working on lacing up his boots.

"You invited us to this party," Dare replied. "But seriously, we take care of teammates. If one man went bad on your deployment, another might have been in on it."

Bram tightened his fingers into fists. It was first light and things were in motion. Black SUVs with tinted windows had rolled up the driveway, the men exiting them before the parking brakes were set. They knew their purpose, striding toward the house intent on removing every last trace of the family who had called it home.

There was a courtesy rap on the door before the leader of the group opened it and spied Bram.

"Care to explain the tension around here?"

Thais cast her newly arrived fellow agent Greer McRae an amused look.

"Emotional entanglements," she offered.

Greer titled his head slightly to one side and peered at her over the rim of his shades. "Figured that out on my own."

"Really?" Thais drawled out. "Impressive . . ."

Greer lifted his hands in mock surrender. "Been a while since I worked with you, Sinclair. Give me a break."

"Thais is rusty," Dare said as he came into the room. "Needs some fresh meat to sharpen her claws on. Nice of you to show up."

Thais Sinclair narrowed her eyes before she lifted one leg and landed a roundhouse kick on Dare's backside.

"Doesn't appear too rusty from my vantage point," Greer observed with a smile.

"I'd like to learn how to do that."

Jaelyn watched the effect her attempt to join the conversation had. The new agent didn't give her much hope. He had the same stance and unreadable mask on she'd come to think of as Dare's standard look.

Thais, on the other hand, contemplated her from behind what Jaelyn had learned was just as practiced an expression, even if it was a soft curving of her lips that made her look sweet.

"I might teach you," Thais offered. "Since it looks like we're going to have some time together."

"Can I get in on that lesson?"

LeAnn had appeared from her room. Jaelyn took a long look at her sister.

"I know, you haven't seen this side of me in a few years," LeAnn offered in explanation.

"Missed it," Milton Sondors declared from where he'd been listening in the kitchen. He shuffled over to the doorway and considered LeAnn from head to toe.

She wasn't sporting the over-the-top look Jaelyn had come to expect from her. Instead, there was only a light application of makeup on her face, and her hair was cute but lacking the over-blown-out appearance Jaelyn was used to.

It was a nice sight, but Jaelyn felt the tension in the room growing. If she'd ever wanted to know what standing on a bridge as it was getting ready to collapse felt like, today it did.

And all she could do was wait for the ground beneath her feet to vanish.

Well, she wasn't going to cry about it.

At least not in front of her grandfather.

"Ready?" Bram asked.

He meant it for all of them but he'd looked toward her grandfather.

"Always ready, son. So long as I have my girls, everything else will fall into place."

LeAnn left first. Jaelyn watched the way Bram and his teammates positioned themselves around them.

Like they were sheep . . .

She knew they didn't mean it harshly. Bram was waiting on her. He was patient and kind.

Yeah, and treating her like a baby bird . . .

"Time to get this wagon train rolling," Jaelyn said. She was ready to take her first step toward one of the waiting SUVs.

There was a carefree whistle from her grandfather as he poured coffee into a thermos and screwed on the lid.

"Grandpa, that's too much caffeine," she muttered as she plucked a travel bag off the counter.

Milton winked at her. "Never you mind about me. Today I'm taking care of you."

Jaelyn caught Bram's lips twitching. He'd moved up beside her.

"Don't encourage him," she mumbled.

Bram paused next to her, so close she caught the scent of his skin. It sent a ripple of sensation across her skin, raising goosebumps along her arms. Their gazes locked and her world shifted for a moment.

Later . . .

*Later . . . what?*

It was a good question. One that drove home how little power she had over her own destiny at the moment.

She really fucking hated it, too.

Milton was the last one out of the house. He made it only a few steps down the front walkway before he turned around and took in the sight of the place where he'd brought home his bride. Jaelyn knew he had a picture of them tucked into his wallet but at that moment, she was sure he was seeing his life with Jeanie playing across his mind.

When Milton made it to the SUV waiting to take them . . . well, away . . . it was LeAnn who put her hand over his. He smiled, patting her hand as he made some comment about it only being a house.

Jaelyn found herself far more absorbed with Bram.

Damn but she was a rotten granddaughter, too.

But the truth was, she wanted control of her life back. Bram was something she'd reached for.

Was that using him?

She didn't know and honestly wasn't in the mood to contemplate it. The reason was simple, thinking about him gave her something solid. It might all turn out to be a mirage later; still, she wasn't willing to rein her thoughts in.

One step at a time.

\* \* \*

He had to lay low.

And be patient.

Ricky quelled the urge to follow the black SUVs.

That would be expected.

So instead, he waited a bit before heading toward a section of town where he could find men who didn't have files. They were the sort looking for better lives, standing on the corners where construction foremen came to hire them for a quick, cash payday.

Ricky considered the men, singling out one who had a truck. It was a beat-up one, but solid at its core.

"I need a lift to Las Vegas," he began.

"That is a long way, my friend."

Ricky pulled a thick roll of cash from his pocket. "Four hours out and four back. Beats working outside in this sun."

The guy was hesitating, which was all the opportunity another man needed to step forward and offer to take the job.

Ricky grinned, climbing into the passenger seat of a beat-up minivan. He rolled the window down and looked forward to leaving the city and the multitude of surveillance cameras behind.

Open road suited him. As soon as he evened the score with Tyler Martin, he was going to get lost in Ireland.

But first, he was going to look up Brendon, an air-traffic controller he'd used for information in the past. Shadow Ops teams might have the authority to shuttle their travel records into a classified file, but air-traffic controllers had the magic keys or passcodes to look into those encrypted files. No one flew a plane over US ground without there being a flight plan filed somewhere.

Sure, Brendon might be pissed for the way Ricky had

left him the last time but that only added an element of challenge to getting what he wanted from him.

Ricky did admit to enjoying a game that didn't bore him.

"Trouble?"

Tyler Martin looked up as Carl Davis asked the question. Carl offered him a half smile and a mock toast with his Scotch glass.

"You gave yourself away there, Ty," he muttered jovially. "I don't see you show your reactions very often."

Carl came into the office and settled into the padded chair next to Tyler.

"So what has your attention?"

There were times Tyler Martin wanted to kill Carl Davis. The guy was a fat cat, raised on the hard labor of those who would never taste his decadent lifestyle. He was an example of how some things never changed. There had always been haves and have-nots.

It was a harsh truth that Tyler had embraced when he sold out Saxon Hale for a job as Carl Davis's head of security.

So he had to deal with the guy.

"Bram Magnus has someone hunting down his command officer."

Carl's grin melted off his face, leaving him staring at Tyler.

"Are the Hale brothers working with him?" Carl asked.

"No sign of them," Tyler replied. "But I'll bet he's in contact with them. Shadow teams stick close to one another for life."

Carl was tapping his fingernail against his glass. "You advised me to let my issues with them go."

"Saxon and Vitus have gone to ground somewhere," Tyler began. "Whatever Kagan has them doing, I want to know about it. We never know when that information might come in handy. It's a good bet Bram Magnus will return to wherever they are."

"Right." Carl stood and tossed the rest of his drink down his throat. "You're the best man for the job, Ty. Glad to have you on the team."

Team.

Tyler had once had a very different idea of what that meant. Long before he realized men like Carl Davis used men like Saxon Hale. Carl would hand out medals and awards and make speeches about valor and integrity.

Sure would. Tyler had seen it.

And then Carl would go into a closed door meeting and vote to erase a secret ops unit to keep the dirt from splattering.

He and Hale's team were different because Tyler had faced the facts and decided to make sure he had a spot on Carl's team. He'd already done the dirty work, now he wanted a slice of the big cake. The lifestyle Carl lived and Saxon Hale couldn't sell his Medal of Honor to buy.

But it wasn't personal.

Life was just full of tough choices.

He'd made his.


"This is a classified location. I am in command and you are no longer in the civilian world."

Saxon Hale wasn't very happy about them being there. The vibe coming off the man was unwelcoming to say the least. Beside him, Vitus Hale was eyeing them with just about the same level of frigidness.

"Stay behind the fence at all times."

Jaelyn contemplated the row of boulders that made up the fence. Huge pieces of rock with dirt clinging to them were arranged around a tiny vintage house. The house itself was cuteness incarnate because, in spite of its 1950s vibe, it was restored perfectly.

There wasn't a chip of paint missing from the wood edging and every window sparkled. It was a stark contrast to its surroundings. All around them, construction was happening. That part wasn't what made Jaelyn view the house as something dropped there by a twister . . . no, it was the huge camouflage netting strung up over the entire site. The sunlight filtered through in a speckling pattern that made it feel cool when it wasn't.

"Classified" was the word.

Beneath the canopy of netting, there were large construction trucks moving around. Machinery hummed and clanged while men in hard hats worked. They weren't like any construction personnel she'd seen in her life. There were no bright-colored safety vests and even their hard hats had dark green patterns on them that suited the forest around them.

"Magnus, show them their quarters."

Saxon Hale left them, with his brother in tow.

"That was the hard part," Bram offered as he pointed behind them. "Your quarters should be a little more welcoming."

Their quarters were a mobile home type of structure. It was sitting behind the house, in a huge automobile graveyard. Stretching out behind the little house was an acre or more of slowly rusting cars. Saplings grew right up through some of them, while in the distance, a weathered barn stood witness to it all. There was no sign of the road they'd come in on, just more cars and forest.

Jaelyn felt like a punch had been delivered to her opinion of Bram. Her entire concept of just who he was had changed completely. It was like having her rose-colored glasses ripped away. She realized she'd seen him through a very carefully constructed persona that he presented when he was in the civilian world.

Now?

Now there was a gun on his hip and he fit right in with Saxon Hale and his brother, Vitus, because as far as Jaelyn could see, she and her family were the only unarmed people on the site.

The thing was . . . she found it really sexy.

*Maybe you need that appointment with the shrink after all . . .*

Jaelyn smiled at her own thoughts. She didn't need to go pour out her feelings while lying on a padded sofa and listen to someone tell her why she felt like she did. Nope. It was pretty cut-and-dried. Bram curled her toes, and she liked it.

A lot.

Sure, it was extreme. But so was Bram. She watched the way he blended in with the other men on the site, so at home. Actually, more at ease than he'd ever been while at her grandfather's house.

In a way, she felt like she was getting a look at him for the first time.

"You'll each have some privacy."

Bram spoke again as he directed them to the structure. It sported three doors, equally placed along one side. He opened one and Milton peered inside.

"That sure is more welcoming than the last set of quarters I had here," Milton said.

"Grandpa?" Jaelyn said in surprise.

Bram's expression finally changed. "What do you mean?"

Her grandfather chuckled as he turned and looked off toward where the construction was going on. "Yep. Been a few years now."

"You were here?" Bram asked incredulously.

Milton Sondors sent him a smug look and a wink before he pushed his hands into his pockets and whistled cheerfully.

"Oh boy." LeAnn shook her head. "He's not going to tell you, Bram."

Bram looked at Jaelyn but she nodded. "This is Grandpa's 'refusing to talk about the elephant in the room' mode. He's a master of the art."

And Milton was enjoying himself hugely. He accepted the key Bram had used to open the door and tucked it into his shirt pocket before he ambled off, pausing to look at some of the cars rusting back into the earth.

"I'll be here," Bram said softly next to Jaelyn.

She reached out and took the key from his hand. Her heart was picking up its pace, her mental musings during their travel time extracting a toll now that she was face-to-face with the opportunity to act on her thoughts.

Rabbit?

Or was it just wiser to give herself a little more time?

She unlocked one of the other doors and pulled it open.

"Jaelyn—"

"I need to think."

She disappeared inside, the door closing behind her. The action took too much effort, leaving her facing a crashing wave of emotions. It hit her, making her feel pinned to the wall while she tried to sort images of Bram and Creepy into two different categories.

Fuck but emotions sucked.


Las Vegas . . .

Ricky listened to the sound of aircraft taking off as he waited for Brendon to finish his shift as an air-traffic controller. Ricky remembered things, details, like what car the guy drove. Ricky was leaning against it as he smoked. Footsteps echoed through the parking structure as someone came closer.

Brendon went still when he caught sight of Ricky.

"Surprised to see me?"

"I am," Brendon said.

There was a note of anger in his tone, one that tickled Ricky because the guy was nursing a grudge over the way Ricky had left him.

Cold.

Ricky did like a challenge. Didn't much matter if it was fighting or something more personal like with Brendon. Ricky liked to win and you couldn't swipe victory if your opponent rolled over like a pussy.

"So what do you want?" Brendon surprised him by not whining.

Ricky took a moment to take another puff on the cigarette. Brendon was watching him when he blew out a line of smoke. "Sorry man, did you want me to stick around and play house? Thought you were still in the closet, worried about losing your job to those homophobic pricks you answer to."

Brendon shook his head. "A text would have been nice."

Ricky shrugged. "I'm more of a hands-on type."

There was a double meaning in his words. Brendon's

color darkened. Ricky enjoyed seeing the contrast with his white dress shirt collar.

The guy was debating his options. Ricky took another drag on his cigarette as he watched the way Brendon wrestled with his conscience. Lust was drawing his features tight, though, telling Ricky everything he needed to know.

The guy wasn't going to turn him down.

No, he was just going to put up a good fight. So he could live with himself tomorrow.

Fine.

Great, actually.

Ricky admitted to liking the knowledge he was going to fuck with the guy's mind just as much as his body. It would make the victory sweeter, more complete. Why just win a game if you could also completely dominate your opponent?

"Car's this way," Brendon said at last.

LeAnn wasn't shy.

Nope, not a bit.

She looked around outside their quarters before boldly walking around the little fifties-era house. Most of the action seemed to be taking place well past the boulder fence Saxon Hale had warned them to stay behind.

LeAnn contemplated the hum coming from the site and stepped past the boundary line.

It didn't take very long for Bram to meet her in the expanse of the wild plot of ground overgrown with weeds and saplings between the house and the construction site.

"LeAnn," he said, growling at her.

She flashed him a smile. "I'm sort of liking this new chapter of our relationship. I don't have to care if you're ticked at me."

Her comment caught him off guard. His lips pressed into a hard line as he hooked his hands into the construction belt he was sporting.

"Sister of your girlfriend, it's working for me," LeAnn continued. "You're lucky to have me."

"Care to expand a bit?" he demanded. "Because from what I can see, you're already breaking rules set up to protect you. I don't need a headache."

"Well, you took my phone, so I couldn't send you a text," she informed him, then waved her hand in the air between them. "Let's get on topic. This isn't about me."

Bram looked at her over the top of his shades. It hit her in the middle of her heart. On one hand, she was more convinced than ever of how right she was to go looking for him, and on the other, she was, well, a tad jealous that he'd never looked at her the same way he looked at Jaelyn.

*Moving on . . .*

"You need to go be . . . there for Jaelyn."

His expression tightened. "What's wrong?"

"She didn't say anything, doesn't know I'm talking to you, and it had better stay that way." LeAnn sent him a dead serious look. "But the walls are thin in that mobile unit. She's been in the shower for the better part of an hour."

He contemplated her for about half a second before he was striding off toward the mobile housing unit.

She smiled and jumped when someone chuckled nearby. Dare Servant was contemplating her.

"You guys take the concept of team to the extreme," she muttered.

Dare offered her a single shoulder shrug. "You're not

doing too bad, either. Might have thought you'd be a little bitter over seeing Bram with your sister."

LeAnn only sent him a bored look back. "He was a friend with benefits. And that was exactly the way Bram wanted it, too. I'm no worse than he was for enjoying the arrangement."

"No argument," Dare replied, pointing her toward the boulder fence.

LeAnn went feeling like her spirit was lighter than it had been in a long time. Hooking up hadn't really satisfied her, even if she'd claimed it was all she wanted.

No, somehow, getting a spot on the squad had become more important than anything else in her life. Sure, there was a sense of achievement in knowing she'd set a goal and succeeded.

But at what cost?

She caught sight of her grandfather. He was heading back toward the housing unit from where he'd been walking through the rusting cars that decorated the back half of the lot.

She barely knew him these days.

Well, change had landed on them all.

She walked toward her grandfather, heading him off before he made it too close to the mobile housing unit.

Yeah, thin walls for sure.

"Jaelyn . . ."

Bram startled her. She jumped, her bare feet slipping on the floor of the shower. Bram reached out and caught her by the biceps, reintroducing her to the amazing amount of strength he had.

Something slithered through her insides in response.

A sensation that made her smile as well as frown.

How did she deal with it?

With . . . him?

Her body had ideas. Ones that bubbled up, covering the emotions which had sent her into the shower in the first place.

"Come on, baby . . . ," he said.

*No . . . cooed.*

"I am not fragile."

But she was nude while he was fully dressed. She shuddered, hating the way Creepy's face rose from her memory making her belly heave.

"Look at me, Jaelyn."

Authority edged his tone. She like it a lot better, too, opening her eyes and locking gazes with him. His blue eyes were full of desire. The sight made her gasp as her balance felt like it was shifting.

But that was the way Bram affected her.

"Come out, baby . . ."

Her fingers were wrinkled from how long she'd been in the water. There was still steam rising from the water falling steadily from the shower head but she didn't feel it anymore.

"Alright." She crossed in front of a mirror and caught sight of her red skin. The air was cold but she looked back and realized the water was turned to the top of the hot water setting. In fact, the change in temperature made her a little woozy. She faltered and a moment later, Bram scooped her off her feet.

He wrapped her in a towel at the same time, cradling her as he carried her toward the bed.

"I'm not fragile," she repeated when he sat her down.

"You're overheated," he commented as he pulled the towel away.

"Don't gripe at me about it," she argued, feeling a need to flare at him. No, it didn't make any sense, but nothing did at the moment. "It was just a shower."

"No, baby . . ." He pressed a latch and the buckle holding his tool belt on opened. He dropped it to the floor as he opened his chest harness next. "It was a lot more than that."

He'd hit the nail on the head. Tear stung her eyes and it pissed her off.

"I'm fine."

Bram pulled his shirt off in the next moment, making her forget just what else she'd been thinking of saying. He was reaching for his fly when she stopped him.

"Don't . . ."

"You've got a choice to make, baby . . . be bold or fragile . . . tell me which one you prefer . . ."

*Bold . . . definitely bold.*

She reached for him, hooking her hands into his fly and opening it. He made a sound of male approval before she was pushing the fabric down his hips so that his cock sprang free.

"Is that what you want, baby?" Bram asked as he cupped her chin and raised her face so that their eyes met. "Want to be in charge?"

Her lips had gone dry.

*He was so very right . . .*

And she was wrong to take out her frustrations on him.

She pulled her hands back, staring at him as she wrestled with the dilemma of her impulses.

Well, at least that was a very familiar quandary for her when it came to Bram Magnus.

Impulse against reasoning.

Bram cussed. "Don't stop now."

His tone had softened, frustrating her with how much her emotions were flip-flopping. God, she felt like a newly caught fish, unable to control anything as she died while fighting for her life.

*Fighting* . . . she liked the sound of that word.

"I'm waiting for you to take your boots off."

He froze, one side of his mouth twitching up. "Well . . . yes, ma'am."

Jaelyn moved away as Bram sat down to do as she'd said. He was wearing steel-toed work boots that were laced up over his ankles. She plucked the towel from the floor and rubbed it through her wet hair.

When Bram finished, he stood and shucked his pants, facing her in nothing but creamy skin and hard muscle.

"Let the towel go, baby . . . Don't let him make you hide from me."

Her mouth was dry with nervousness but the confidence in Bram's tone made her bold enough to release the terry cloth. The towel slithered down to land on her feet.

Bram nodded. "What do you want, Jaelyn?"

*To go back . . . to the way she'd felt before . . .*

That was the long and short of it really.

And the night before Creepy had come into her life, she'd followed her impulses into Bram's embrace.

*He knew it . . .*

"Take me to bed . . ." Her tone was husky. Once again, it took only moments for her impulses to flare to life. What had just been an inkling a few seconds ago was now a roaring need.

Bram lifted his hand and curled his finger at her.

Jaelyn felt her lips twitching.

He was daring her . . .

And she liked it so very much.

She went toward him, felt him sliding his hands along her cheeks, holding her head before he leaned down and sealed her mouth beneath his own.

She shivered.

Only now she was warming, her skin drying and feeling more sensitive than ever. Where his hands connected with her face, there was a surge of sensation, a new level of intensity.

All she wanted was more of it.

She moved forward, reaching for him, continuing until she was pressing herself against him. He slid one hand into her hair, maintaining his hold on her as he kissed her with a slowness that threatened to drive her insane.

And she didn't want him to stop, either.

But he was moving his lips across her cheek, hooking one arm across her lower back and bending her over it so that her breasts were thrust up high.

"I love these . . ." He claimed one nipple, making her gasp as his lips closed around the tender tip.

A jolt of desire was running from her nipple to her clit.

So intense.

*So needy . . .*

She could feel her body heating, sense the way the walls of her passage were relaxing. Fluid was easing down to coat the folds of her slit and all the while, she was so conscious of how hard he was.

She smoothed her hands over his chest, along his upper arms and then down, reaching for his length because thoughts had dissolved into cravings, leaving her nothing but a pile of impulses that all pointed toward getting him inside her.

*Be bold . . .*

It was more than a need, the idea was pulsing through her. She pushed him back, straightening. She heard him growl and it only tossed more fuel on the fire consuming her.

"Sit."

Her voice was strong and edged. Bram's expression was hungry. His lips curled back as he bared his teeth at her.

"I'm going to ride you, Bram . . ."

His eyes narrowed with her declaration. The arm around her waist tightening as he backed up until he hit the bed and sat down. He lifted her up, pleasure glittering in his eyes as she placed her knees on either side of his hips and felt the head of his cock slip into her wet slit.

"I'm going to be bold . . . ," she said.

He cupped her bottom, spreading her folds as she lowered herself. But his grip controlled the pace.

"Let me . . ."

"Shhh . . ." He whispered against her lips. "Savor the moment, baby . . . feel the connection . . ."

She felt it alight.

His cock was stretching her passage, opening her wide as she sank down all the way, and he kept her there while it felt like she was on the verge of tearing.

So full . . .

So . . . close . . .

It was the thing she needed, deep down inside where

emotions refused to be ruled by logic or sense. At her core, she was a creature that wanted to show him she could keep pace with him.

She rose up, and plunged down, groaning as his length slid into her. Her clit was a pulsing bundle of nerve endings, every little motion sending pleasure through her.

Bram was groaning, too, his chest heaving as he lost control, loosening his grip and thrusting up to meet every one of her downward plunges. They were striving toward each other and with each other as well, united in a common goal.

She felt the climax bursting inside her. Heard her own cries bouncing around the room. Bram opened his eyes, gripping her head so that her eyes popped open in that moment.

She was bare in that moment. More naked than she'd ever realized a person might be. Pleasure was exploding through her, twisting and wringing her like a toy.

And Bram witnessed her need.

His blue eyes were bright with hunger and desire. His cock was rock hard inside her, her body wetter than it had ever been. She was gasping for breath, losing her grip on reality, when he flipped her over and pounded into her.

He took her back to that boundary of pain. Where she wasn't sure she could take it or him or her need for what he was giving her. He spread her wide, pushing her thighs open as he rode her.

Something jerked inside her. The hot spurt of his release made her cry out and then she was writhing as another orgasm burst inside her. This one was deeper, harder, and sharper.

It made her groan. The sound mixing with Bram's grunts.

*Savage . . .*

They both were.

But it pleased her. When her brain was able to process a thought once more, Jaelyn found herself enjoying the way Bram was sprawled on the surface of the bed next to her, both of them too heated to touch more than fingertips.

*It was intimate.*

That moment when they were bared to the bone or maybe to the soul was more correct.

Just bare and satisfied and she drifted into sleep, her thoughts completely wiped clean at last.

"I haven't been fucked like that . . ." Brendon was fighting to stay conscious. ". . . since . . ."

"Since the last time I was here," Ricky finished for him.

Brendon nodded and then his eyes rolled up in his head. Ricky listened to the way his breathing deepened and slowed.

Nice. He didn't really want to knock the guy out again. After all, Brendon was turning out to be a nice little source of information.

The air-conditioning was pumping the small house full of cold air. It felt good on his skin after the workout he'd just given Brendon. Ricky tossed a blanket over the guy so he wouldn't wake up too soon and grabbed Brendon's cell phone on his way out of the bedroom.

Ricky snickered as he discovered the fact that Brendon hadn't even changed his access codes since the last time Ricky had used his flight-controller status to track down Saxon Hale and his team.

Nope, it was pathetically easy to get into the global system.

The Shadow Ops teams weren't above the need for flight plan records. It was a sweet little loophole in their cloak-and-dagger world. One he didn't want them to discover until he'd exploited it.

It sort of tickled him to know that someone would track it down, as part of the investigation into why he'd been able to take out a Shadow Ops team. Ricky wasn't going to lie, it would give him a nice little buzz to know he'd pulled off something future agents would be trained on how to avoid.

Change the world.

Something his father had always lived for. Looked like Ricky would actually do it.

He tossed the phone down, wiped the screen clean before dressing and heading out of the door. The Las Vegas sun was brutal, but Ricky started walking anyway. Calling a cab or using one of the other options for a ride would leave a trail. Instead, he grabbed a bottle of water from a gas station and looked at the map posted in the window to find a bus station.

Buses were still a great way to get places without being asked for identification. He hoped Saxon and his team enjoyed their last few days of life.

Because he was coming for them, and thanks to Brendon's access codes, he knew exactly where to find them.


She was sleeping soundly.

Bram indulged in a long look at Jaelyn.

He carefully picked up his boots and tool belt and crept toward the door.

The dark circles under her eyes told him how much she needed the rest.

She needed him, too.

*Right, you're just hoping she does . . .*

Or maybe it was just better to remind himself that Jaelyn needed to heal. He'd come in the night before to help her, and she didn't owe him squat.

It was his fault she had issues to deal with.

The best thing he could do was let her have enough space to sort out her thoughts.

That wasn't what he wanted.

No. What he wanted was something he was having trouble defining. Of course that was nothing new when it came to Jaelyn. He needed to check himself. Let her decide what she wanted to do.

Even if it felt like it was punching a hole through his gut.

The fifties-era house came complete with a little boy.

Jaelyn emerged from her so very sedate room to find him merrily on his way into the auto graveyard.

He couldn't have been more than two, and with the contentment of toddlerhood, his blue eyes sparkled with the need for adventure.

A quick check showed Jaelyn that no one was around and the child was rounding the corner.

Well, it was something to do.

*Besides, wonder where Bram is?*

She took off after him, earning a happy little giggle as he realized she was following. He picked up his feet faster, running away as he laughed, completely assured by his youth that no harm would come to him.

Jaelyn scooped him up just as he was heading full speed into foliage that was twice his height.

He let out a whoop of laughter while clapping his hands. "Again! Again!"

Jaelyn placed him on his feet but pointed in a different direction and let him go. He took off but looked behind him to make sure she was giving chase. Jaelyn wiggled her fingers at him before she did.

He laughed again, raising her spirts as she tossed him into the air after catching him. But when she set him down, Saxon Hale came into sight.

"Daddy!"

The toddler ran straight toward Saxon. Jaelyn watched the way his face transformed while he caught the child, lifting him up and holding him against his side.

When Saxon looked back toward her, his expression was tight.

"Thank you."

The morning sunlight flashed off a head of copper hair as a woman appeared. "Don't growl at her," the woman admonished him. "She just saved your bacon."

The woman held a baby that was sucking on its fist. "He was supposed to be watching Max while I fed the baby."

"No problem," Jaelyn replied. "I seem to have time on my hands."

The woman let out a groan. "Careful, I'm a woman on the edge. Talk like that and I am going to bawl like a demented fool until you take pity on me and save me from the realities of having two kids under two."

"Jaelyn can cook," Dare Servant said as he came around the house. He was dressed in jeans and a T-shirt, clearly ready to join the construction crew.

"Ginger, it would be best—"

"Hush." Ginger cut Saxon off as she moved over and

handed the baby to Jaelyn. She went back toward her husband and lifted Max out of his arms.

"They aren't going to be here long." Saxon got his thought out even as his wife faced him down.

"Have a good day at the office, dear." Ginger wiggled her fingers in a little wave that earned her a raised eyebrow from Saxon.

Dare was choking on his amusement. He slapped Saxon on the shoulder. "Come on, boss man. We have to go now if we're going to beat the traffic."

Saxon turned his attention toward Dare.

"Okay," Dare said as he lifted his hands in surrender. "Truth is, I just hate when you get kicked out and have to bunk in the barracks with us."

Saxon started to flip Dare the bird but a low clearing of the throat from his wife made him close his fist tight. He leaned down and kissed her but shot Jaelyn a hard look over her shoulder before he and Dare took off around the boulder fence.

"He shot you the look, didn't he?" Ginger asked when they were alone.

"It was sort of cute," Jaelyn replied as she moved toward the woman.

Ginger made a snorting sound but she ended up smiling. "He is sort of adorable." Max was wiggling. "Guess that's why I agreed to have his children. Come on in. I'm not too proud to admit I am dying for some female companionship."

"I expected your call before now, son," Colonel Bryan Magnus said.

Bram indulged himself with a roll of his eyes because his father couldn't see it. "Dad—"

"I know," Bryan said, cutting him off. "You don't like me dropping rank in the middle of your life, makes me proud of you to see you wanting to earn your own place."

"That isn't going to work this time, Dad," Bram grumbled. "The compliment distraction technique."

There was a crusty chuckle on the other end of the line.

"You've marooned a good family with this maneuver," Bram said.

Bryan Magnus wasn't repentant in the least. If anything, he was laughing harder. Bram felt the edges of the cell phone cutting into his fingers because he was gripping it so tightly.

"Now that they're here," Bram said, cutting through his father's mirth, "getting them settled is going to prove nearly impossible."

"Son. A Shadow Ops team specializes in the impossible."

His dad always did have a way of changing to suit the moment with whiplash speed.

"I am right," the colonel added. "You don't like it, but the only option for keeping them completely safe was to take them onto that compound. Anything else would have left a trail. A faint one, but tracks nonetheless. I'm not arrogant enough to think otherwise."

Bram bit back a word of profanity. He was pacing, something he only allowed himself to do because there was no one watching him.

"Besides, seems a closer look at just who Milton Sondors is has me thinking it just might have been meant to be."

"Meant to be?" Bram said with a growl. "Their life is shredded because of me. I should have listened to you and broken it off with LeAnn a long time ago."

"You went back for the other one, son."

His dad's tone had turned serious.

"I know," Bram responded. "And it was a slipup on my part. Jaelyn deserves a man who hasn't got the sort of dirt on his hands as I do. I'm suddenly very clear as to just why Kagan hasn't offered me a badge. I've been hugging the fence."

"Kagan makes sure his agents are fully seasoned before offering badges. You've proved your worth and I know he sees it. As for the girl, I think she's got a stiffer backbone than you give her credit for."

"Maybe I don't have the right to make her prove herself."

"That moment is long past, son." His father spoke softly.

It was.

Bram didn't vocalize his thought.

No, there was something very personal about his feelings for Jaelyn. His dad signed off, leaving him standing between Saxon Hale's house and the construction site. He caught a glimpse of Jaelyn moving around in the kitchen.

She'd needed him last night.

Problem was, he was pretty sure he'd needed her even more.

He should have taken a hint from Dare and Thais. Realized that he had to choose between Shadow Ops and a woman like Jaelyn.

It was simply the responsible thing to do.

Fuck, he hated being objective at times.

Today he felt like it would tear something inside him to turn away from Jaelyn.

She could still be free.

She deserved his best and there was no way he was going to give her any less. A life attached to his dangerous choices wasn't the best.

He wanted to give her more than a shackle to his side.

Somehow, he was going to have to find the strength to turn his back on her.

For her own good.


Everyone knew their place at the missile silo, or so it seemed to Jaelyn.

The men rose with the sun. Their conversation drifted on the morning breeze along with the scent of coffee. She caught sight of them in their green hard hats from the small kitchen window.

Cooking had been one of her joys.

Now? She tried to talk herself out of feeling angry over only having kitchen duty.

It wasn't working so well.

Even knowing Ginger appreciated the much-needed sleep, Jaelyn found the walls closing in on her.

The real problem was Bram.

She grunted as she leaned on the counter later in the day. Her hands were chapped from dish washing and she was flatly sick of being grateful for the small bottle of hand lotion she'd had in her purse.

Yes, the real issue was Bram.

He hadn't spoken to her.

It hurt. With all of the intensity her conscience had warned her it would. The problem was the last time he'd come to her.

And she was getting really tired of him casting looks her way, while remaining behind his stone-man expression.

*Like you can do much of anything about it . . .*

She didn't care for how right her inner voice was. In fact, it nudged her just a little further down the road she'd been on, leaving her facing the fact that she was pretty pissed.

Fine, he hadn't done anything she didn't want herself.

And that had nothing to do with how she felt.

Bram came into sight, looking toward her. The afternoon sun hit his shades and Jaelyn felt her temper sizzle.

She balled up the dish towel she'd been using and chucked it at the far side of the counter. It hit with a less than satisfying soft sound. Jaelyn didn't care, she was already heading toward the back door. The child lock gave her a moment's frustration before she was striding across the yard and out onto the open grounds.

Bram had started to turn back toward the silo. He flipped around, ripping his shades off as he frowned at her.

"You don't belong beyond the gate and you know it," he said when she breezed past the last boulder.

"Too bad."

Bram wasn't backing down. Not that Jaelyn cared. Once again, he inspired something inside her which totally ignored things like rules, composure, or politeness.

Nope. None of it mattered.

Only getting to him and taking what she wanted. Her breath was slightly agitated from the pace she'd set as she planted herself in front of him.

"You've been a lot of things, Bram Magnus, but I never thought of you as a chicken."

Her statement hit him. She caught the glitter of it in his eyes.

"Don't think you can sneak out of my bed and hide beyond a fence rule."

He was looming over her a half second later, the space between them closed so his words didn't carry. She heard the precision-sharp edge of his tone and didn't budge.

" 'Chicken' isn't the word, Jaelyn. It's 'bastard.' " He grabbed her upper arms when she started to recoil from the self-loathing in his eyes. "You were in a tailspin last night. I knew it, and I took advantage of you."

He held her still, watching the way his words soaked in.

"You should hate me," he said. "Despise me, because I brought Gideon to you."

Jaelyn flinched.

"Well, I don't."

And she was going to hold tight to that idea.

*Somehow . . .*

"You aren't responsible for what a crazy creep does."

She gained her release but stayed in place, unable to do anything that would separate them. He was like some sort of power source she needed to move forward. The only solid thing in her life.

"You're making excuses for me." His teeth were clenched and she realized it was with self-loathing. "Don't. I willingly joined a type of life that doesn't mix well with leaving any trace of personal interests. I let my guard down and you paid the price."

"I thought Gideon was a contractor on your last deployment."

Bram gave her a single nod. "He was. But it could have been worse. Much, much worse." He drew in a deep breath. "I'm sorry, Jaelyn."

"Shit happens."

His lips twitched. It tickled her to know he enjoyed her cussing.

*He liked her boldness . . .*

"Glad to know we're on the same page," he retorted. "Now get back to your restricted zone. It's going to be a few weeks before you can be resettled."

"We haven't talked about us yet," Jaelyn informed him.

"There's nothing to say," he said, cutting her off. "Gideon might have been linked to my last deployment, but it was just lucky for me he wasn't someone related to my work with Shadow Ops. There can't be any 'us.'"

He started to turn away from her and it felt like he was being ripped off of her. The sting was unbearable. She lunged after him, catching a handful of his shirt.

Something snapped inside him. He was turning, catching her wrist and twisting her arm up behind her back. It flattened her against his hard body, sending a thrill of anticipation through her, even as the flare of determination in his eyes chilled her blood.

"See me for what I am, Jaelyn," he said with a growl. "You deserve better."

"I want you."

She was hissing, feeling like the words were escaping instead of merely being spoken. That thing inside of her, the one he seemed to awaken, wasn't going to allow her to let him push her away.

"Because you're dealing with the mental trauma of being a captive."

He was tempering his tone now. It infuriated her because he was taking too much guilt on his shoulders. She let out a growl as she struggled. The burst of rage caught Bram by surprise. For a moment, his grip tightened painfully.

But he was spinning her loose a second later, cussing under his breath because he knew he'd hurt her.

"Don't you ever dismiss me as not being able to deal with what life throws at me," she said, snarling at him.

"I'm stepping up to take responsibility for my actions," he retorted.

Duty was more ingrained in him than any other man she'd ever met. It was what made Bram the pillar of strength she was drawn to. But it was also the immovable object he was placing between them.

"I don't want your pity," she said firmly, finally succeeding in forcing her feet to move.

Bram reached out and caught her upper arm. Once more she felt her insides tighten as he stepped up so close, she could smell his skin.

"I'm not a good guy," he said in a raspy voice. "Look at what I've done to your family."

He let out a grunt and released her. There was a glitter of self-loathing in his eyes.

A new pain snaked through her. It deflated her anger because now, she was mad on his behalf. "Yes, I know what you did, and it's time to stop crying over spilled milk. Time to build a new life. This looks like a great place for a glassblowing shop. LeAnn and I actually did it together."

He was recoiling from her, retreating, and she reached for him once more. He caught her hand, twisting her wrist over just enough so that her arm locked up and she was unable to move closer to him.

"Do you know how much I want to ask you to marry me? Right here, knowing I'm a bastard?" He released her hand and held his up in surrender. "It's all I can do to keep my distance so you can cut the tie between us and have a shot at . . . well, something more than what Ginger has. Circumstances conspired against her. I'm not going to be the one who forced you into a life of waiting on my life and hoping it doesn't rear its ugly head and kill you."

She heard the gravel crunching beneath his boots as he started to walk away. Time had slowed down, trapping her in that moment with all of the swirling emotions being near him unleashed. There was no comprehension beyond the sure knowledge that he meant what he said. He didn't feel worthy of her.

Which only made her absolutely certain he was.

"Yes."

Her voice carried.

She realized Saxon and Vitus were watching them, clearly there in case they needed to intervene.

"Yes . . . I will marry you," Jaelyn repeated loud and clear.

Bram had turned to look at her. He froze, his body stiff. It took only a moment before Saxon and Vitus heard her. The two agents drew up tighter as well, watching to see what Bram was going to do.

"You can't mean that."

The shock in Bram's voice made her smile. She crooked her finger at him and he came, looking just as desperate to be near her as she craved being next to him.

"Take a good look, Bram Magnus, do I look like I'm kidding?"

Bram searched her dark eyes. Damn if he didn't feel like he was being pulled into them by a mermaid. One of those insanely beautiful creatures who was actually far more fierce than her delicate exterior proclaimed.

That was Jaelyn, though.

Everything perfect and peaceful, yet beneath her surface was a woman of iron strength.

She reached up and grabbed a handful of his shirt and used it to pull him down. He sucked in his breath as she kissed him. He was so shocked, all he did was follow her lead, reeling from what she'd said and knowing she meant every word.

"See you after work, dear."

And just like that, she turned and headed back toward the house.

He felt like his knees were going to give way, which was fitting because she cut him to the core every time she came near.

Marry her?

He'd let his thoughts slip past his control. Used his "outside" voice and there was no taking it back now.

The truth was, he didn't want to.

Which left him in agony because the temptation to let her keep her word was almost too much for him.

Fuck.

His thoughts condensed into that single word, leaving him lost as to his next step.

Just . . . fuck.

"The church is fifteen miles down the road, son."

Bram looked up as Saxon whirled around. Milton Sondors was happily grinning at them and honestly, Bram had to hand it to the guy. He'd surprised them.

The term 'sly fox' came to mind and fit perfectly.

Milton was enjoying his victory, too. Bram realized, locked beneath the time-wrinkled skin was a man who had done a whole lot more than Bram gave him credit for. In fact, the guy could likely give Thais lessons on playing an assigned part. Milton was putting on a persona of the carefree old man and it blinded them all to just what was going on in his mind.

It seemed he'd discovered where Jaelyn got her tenacity, too.

"Mr. Sondors," Saxon said. "This is a classified location."

Milton let out a chuckle. "I've known that for a lot longer than you, son."

Dare emerged from around a huge pile of old machinery they'd pulled out of the silo control center, clearly enjoying the way Milton was calling Saxon "son."

"It's been a long time . . ." Milton was talking to what had once been a systems control panel. He reached out and fingered one of the buttons.

Something Bram's father had said suddenly rose from his memory.

*A closer look at just who Milton Sondors is has me thinking it just might have been meant to be.*

"Were you a Minute Man?" Bram asked incredulously.

Minute Men had staffed the silo in its days of operation. Servicemen who had been the last line of defense against a nuclear strike. They'd sat at their underground consoles and waited for orders to turn their launch keys and deploy the warhead that had once been located in the silo.

Milton was fingering the key slot in the console. He looked up at Bram, confidence shining in his eyes. "Well now, that would be classified information."

"Fuck me," Dare Servant muttered with a grin. "You play a little old man too damn well."

Milton nodded. "Shouldn't have to tell you boys that you didn't invent cloak and dagger games, neither did my generation. There was a World War Two bunker here before the silo." He shifted his attention to Bram. "I married my Jeanie in that church, so you'd best get down there and make an appointment. Seems my granddaughter is planning on holding you to your word. Don't let her sweet exterior fool you, son. Jaelyn is just like her grandmother." He made a punching motion. "Knows how to jab up under a man's ribs."

He looked over to where Saxon and Vitus were staring at him. "Might want to open the vent shaft. The air can get mighty stale down there."

Vitus looked back at the plans of the silo.

"Won't find it there, son," Milton informed them. He picked up a pencil and contemplated the blueprints for a long moment. "Should be about there." He made a little mark on the faded paper. "With all that water, bet the door is crusted over." He pointed into the distance. "Comes up over there by that group of Chevys, the fifty-two is over the grate."

Milton offered them a wink before he started back toward the area he was restricted to. He paused beside the wreckage of what had once been a chair. The red fabric was dulled by time and rotten. The crew had unceremoniously dropped it. He reached down and pulled it upright. For a long moment, he stared at it, before the sound of his customary whistle floated behind him as he traversed the space between the house and the silo entrance.

Vitus turned and started toward the cluster of trucks.

"That family is full of surprises," Saxon muttered before he was off following his brother.

Bram ended up watching Milton for a long moment. The old man seemed to know it, turning around and sending him a stern look. Milton lifted his hand and tapped the wedding band he still wore.

He wanted to say yes.

Felt the urge bubbling up from inside him like a spring someone had drilled a well down to reach. It was life giving but he just couldn't get past the idea of knowing he'd be the one receiving life while Jaelyn was being consumed.

A whistle came from the truck, Saxon was waving him over. It was a welcome distraction.

Except he didn't care for how much he knew he was avoiding the issue.

Jaelyn was watching the coffeepot.

It was empty.

Her grandfather came in, his whistling filling the little vintage kitchen as he grabbed a clean mug and made his way toward the coffeepot.

"Don't think you're going to get away with whatever you were doing out there."

Her grandfather turned and smiled at her.

"Nope," Jaelyn informed him. "You're going to sing . . . loud and clear."

Milton Sondors looked back at the empty coffeepot and opened a cabinet. There wasn't a can of grounds anywhere in sight, just the lingering scent of it.

"Just like Jeanie," he muttered. "You know when to take off the gloves."

Jaelyn fixed him with an expectant look. Her grandfather sat the mug down and wandered out the back door. She snorted with frustration and was pretty sure she heard him chuckling.

A moment later, he plucked a thermos off one of the boulders where he'd stashed it and twisted the silver cap off. He leaned back against one of the boulders as he poured a steaming stream of dark java into the cap and toasted her with it.

There was a soft sound of amusement from behind her.

"Your grandfather is a gem," Ginger said as she leaned in the doorway of the kitchen with her baby on her breast.

"Sometimes I agree," Jaelyn muttered as she dug out the coffee grounds she'd hidden and went to make a pot. "Other times, I want to strangle him."

"Well, he got those boys to look at something," Ginger said as she peered out the kitchen window. "Can't say I'm not enjoying the way Milton catches them off guard. It's been far too sedate around here." She looked at Jaelyn. "Don't get me wrong, after the way I first met Saxon, a little quiet was just what I craved, but now I'm bored."

Ginger grinned and wiggled her eyebrows. "So . . . since your grandfather won't sing and Bram is hiding from you . . ."

Jaelyn turned and looked at Ginger. "Yeah?"

Ginger swept her from head to toe. The baby hiccupped and she lifted him and put him against her shoulder as she patted his back. "Come on down to the bedroom. Let's see what we can find to entice Bram out of the dark end of the work yard."


They needed to talk.

Bram ducked under the water in the shower before it was hot because he needed to find Jaelyn before the sun went down.

They'd end up in bed if darkness was there to help them ignore reality.

*I will marry you . . .*

Her words were like balm for wounds he hadn't realized he was sporting across the surface of his soul.

They were the force drawing him to her. The magic of her embrace was a shield against the harsh edges of his life.

Which was why he stepped out of the shower and went looking for his clothing.

A few moments later, he was looking for Jaelyn and he realized, it was both the best and worst thing he might ever do.

And she didn't make it easy for him. The door of her quarters was locked but he used his key and poked his head inside after she failed to answer the bell.

There was nothing much in the room. A bed that was neatly made. On one side was a desk with a chair pushed in and on the other was a doorway to the narrow bathroom. On the wall that the door was in there was a closet. It honestly didn't look like she'd ever been inside it. The bed was made tightly enough to pass inspection.

Bram shut the door and went toward the house.

Saxon looked up when he knocked on the screen door. His team leader shook his head. "Left half an hour ago."

Bram stood between the house and the mobile quarters, picking up the faint sound of the shower running in LeAnn's unit. Milton had found a hammock strung up in the backyard between two huge trees. The sound of his snoring drifted on the evening breeze.

The sun was a glowing ball on the horizon. There was an ache forming inside him and he realized it was because he didn't know where she was. All of the logic and reasoning aside, it wrenched his gut to know she was out of reach.

The sensation made a moment last a whole hell of a fucking long time while he slowly scanned the area in back of the mobile quarters unit.

Jaelyn stepped into sight, like she'd felt him searching

for her. She moved into the doorway of the huge barn, giving him a glimpse of a dress that allowed him a mouth-watering view of her legs.

Her hair was down, brushed out from the ponytail she kept it in most of the time.

His fingers itched to comb through it.

She was waiting for him. Duty might have been the reason he went looking for her but in the end, he realized she was drawing him to her, just as she always had.

God help them both.

"Do I want to know why you're looking out there at Bram with a smirk on your lips?" Saxon Hale asked his wife.

Ginger turned around and sent him a glance that still made his collar feel too tight.

"You mean . . . this look?" she asked in a sultry tone.

Saxon nodded. "You've been around Thais too much."

"Hummm," Ginger responded. "Actually, you should be far more conscious of the fact that I have spent the week with Jaelyn."

"Why is that?" Saxon asked.

Ginger smiled brighter. "You're adorable when you're trying to protect me."

Saxon sent her a look she knew well. It was the one she'd seen a lot when they'd met, right after she'd stumbled on a murder in the French Quarter in New Orleans. Without him, she'd have been the second victim that day.

"I'm not so sure you should get too cozy with Bram's case subjects."

Ginger felt her smile fade a little. Her husband could roll into mission mode in a snap of the fingers.

"Jaelyn," Ginger said, enunciating very precisely, "has been a tremendous help."

"Gin, don't get used to her being around."

Her husband wasn't being hard-hearted. No, he was using his low tone, the one he reserved just for her when he was attempting to break something to her he thought she'd be upset over.

"That's going to sort of suck." Ginger was back to purring. "Because Max is worn out, Trevor is half asleep, and as for me . . . well, I'm not exhausted because of Jaelyn helping out."

Ginger pulled the clip out of her hair. It tumbled down around her shoulders in a messy bundle of curls that drew her husband's gaze.

"Bram's determined to see them free to resettle."

Ginger sent her husband a flutter of her eyelashes.

"Jaelyn strikes me as being up to the challenge of dealing with him."

Saxon frowned at her. "Are you playing matchmaker with my men?"

"I may have loaned her a dress," Ginger said as Saxon caught her up against his hard frame. "In the interest of taking shameless advantage of having the energy to remind you why marriage is bliss."

Her husband was stroking her back, his eyes narrowed as he let out a low growl of approval. "It is, baby."

Saxon leaned down and captured her mouth in a kiss. Her senses came to life, like a rosebush in spring. Logic didn't have much to say about the way they'd always taken to one another.

Bram really needed to accept that fact about love.

Bram was coming for her.

Jaelyn savored the tingle that went across her skin. The barn was a huge structure but when Bram entered the doorway, she felt like it shrank. He swept her from head to toe, hunger drawing his features tight as he took in the dress she'd borrowed from Ginger.

It was just a jersey one but it left her acutely aware of how easy it would be to wrap her thighs around his hips. His gaze lingered over her belly, freezing the breath in her chest as she recognized the flare of need in his eyes.

"You're playing with fire, Jaelyn."

She offered him a small smile. "That's the story of our relationship, Bram." She shifted away from him, unable to stand still. "I might get a tattoo with it."

"Don't . . . you . . . dare . . ." He'd started to give chase.

"Ink my skin?" she asked softly. "Or do something permanent to say I want to belong to you? Something you can't hide from?"

"You don't know me, Jaelyn . . ." he said, squaring off with her. "Not really."

She forced herself to face him, fighting back the urge to keep retreating. The light was fading, and she was backed into one of the corners.

*Into the shadows . . .*

"I know you make me feel things on a scale I've never encountered before." She offered him a shrug. "I told you I was looking for someone who would curl my toes. You do."

She could see he liked the sound of that.

And it frustrated him as well.

Jaelyn moved toward him, the lust shimmering in his eyes drawing her forward with that boldness he alone set loose.

"I know . . ." She reached out and flattened her hand on his chest, closing her eyes as their flesh connected and she felt the surge of intensity rise inside her. "I know

I'd still be only half alive if I hadn't kissed you that night."

His features were tight with need. "*Fuck . . .*" he mumbled under his breath.

"Yes," she whispered.

She watched his eyes flicker with desire.

"That's not what I meant," he said, forcing the words out. "I came out here to tell you to forget getting married. To me that is. I shouldn't have touched you, shouldn't have let you give me your trust."

"I kissed you," she said. "And I do not, will not ever regret it because even if you're gone, I will know I was woman enough to take the challenge you gave me."

Nope. She forbid herself to ever regret it.

*Live in the moment . . .*

Jaelyn pulled away from him. She felt it keenly, the separation, and so did he. Another muttered "Fuck" drifted through the barn.

"I kill."

His tone was hard and razor sharp. His expression was that one she'd only glimpsed a few times, when he'd been in the heat of the moment and focused on defending them.

"And I am not . . . sorry." He reached out and grasped her shoulder, holding her in a hard grip that drove home just how much control he'd always used when touching her.

"This hand is dirty, Jaelyn . . . do you get it?" He was holding his other hand out in front of her face, the fingers splayed wide. "Dirty with blood. You need a guy who's decent. One who will come home to you and not chase danger. Not leave you wondering if you're going to get a call from his team leader instead of a husband coming home. I'm not the right kind of man for you."

"And I'm not naive. Or some little innocent good girl who's never watched a dirty movie," she countered, pulling back. He released her, his features tight with frustration and lust.

"I'm not sorry, either," Jaelyn continued. "Not sorry I kissed you the moment I could. Not sorry one little bit either."

She fingered the hem of the dress and pulled it up, drawing the garment off her body.

"And I'm not sorry I left my underwear off because I wanted you to join me in here and feed the need you kindle inside me."

It was an ultimatum.

And a declaration.

"And I'm telling you . . . showing you . . . that you're my greatest weakness. And no matter what, Bram Magnus, I will not be scared of what life throws at me. You're trying to return me to a life I was dissatisfied with. That's not your fault. But our paths crossed. I'm going with it, Bram."

She was magnificent.

Something between a phoenix and a siren. Rising up from the ashes and calling to him with a song he knew was going to lead to his death.

But he was too damned enchanted to give a rat's ass.

Bram moved toward her, gathering her up and pushing her against the hood of a car. She made a soft little sound of female pleasure, her thighs spreading wide to make way for his hips. It let the scent of her warm center drift up to him.

Intoxicating him.

Hardening his cock as he reached down to stroke her slit.

"I want to hear you purr . . ."

His tone was harsh. More of an order. He touched her folds, drawing his fingertips lightly through the wetness seeping from her passage and felt the bonds of civilization breaking.

"I want to hear you be . . . rotten . . ."

She leaned back, pressing her hands onto the hood of the car, so her tits were thrust high.

"Suck my nipples," she said raspily. "Until they pucker."

"Where in the hell did you learn to talk like this, Jaelyn?"

He was reaching for her as he asked the question because it was more explanative. A confirmation of just how well she took him by surprise.

"I'm learning right now . . . from the way you respond," she replied. "As I told you, Bram, I like being honest with you."

He let out a groan as he wrapped an arm around her waist to support her and cupped one breast in his other hand.

"I love your tits, baby. Plump and sweet." He captured the nipple between his lips, licking the little nub as she let out a breathy little sound of delight.

It sent a twinge through his cock. The organ hardening even more as he teased her nipple into a peak and felt it draw into a pucker with his tongue.

Erotic wasn't a strong enough sentiment to describe it.

Euphoric maybe.

He didn't much care, so long as she let him sate his hunger on her flesh.

"The other one, Bram, don't leave it out . . ."

He lifted his head and looked into her eyes. There was a woman staring back at him. The one who had so brazenly challenged him to marry her. He knew for certain she had more strength than he'd ever suspected.

She reached out and stroked the front of his pants. "I want to touch you . . ."

It wasn't a request. No, she was demanding it and he ripped his fly open in obedience. His cock sprang free, eager for space.

And her touch.

"Nice," she said as she stroked it. All she did was tease him with her fingertip and his heart was thumping like a jackhammer, his balls tightening as he feared he'd lose his load right there.

That's what she did to him.

So uncontrollable.

So combustible.

But the scent of her heat told him he wasn't alone. He reached down and teased her slit.

"Yeah, nice and hot . . . ," he said raspily, rimming the opening to her body with one fingertip. He watched the way she stiffened, saw the way her nostrils flared as her need built. There was a desperate urge building inside him to make sure he wasn't alone in his addiction to her.

"But you could be hotter."

He found her little clit and rubbed it. She gasped, unconsciously trying to escape. He held her with one arm as he kept the pressure on.

"I'm going to make you come, Jaelyn," he whispered.

"Going to show you why you left your body bare . . . for me."

"Oh . . . Christ . . . ," she said as she groaned. "Harder . . . just . . . yes . . . *there*."

It was a breathless little admission, one that made his cock twitch to get inside her but it also fired his determination. She was growing wetter, her clit swelling into a hard little pearl as her skin turned ruby.

The cry she let out when she peaked startled some of the birds nesting above them. There was a flapping of feathered wings before they settled and all Bram heard was the little sounds she made.

That he'd made her make.

Base.

Savage maybe.

But honest.

She lifted her eyelids and locked gazes with him. His fingers were coated in her juices, her scent thick in the air.

"I'm going to fuck you, baby . . ."

She locked her legs around him, guiding him closer as she shivered. "You'd better."

He gripped his length, rubbing the head of his cock through her wet slit.

Once, twice . . . a third time.

As much as he wanted to plunge into her, the little sounds she made as his cock head slipped along her slit just captivated him. He wasn't a stranger to bed partners who enjoyed sex.

This was different.

There was something about the way she came to life in his embrace that made her more sincere. She made him believe she craved him and not just the release.

Intimacy.

It was more than a word, it was a concept. And Jaelyn seemed to hold the power to make him believe in it.

He craved it, too.

Pushing forward into her body with a hard motion.

"Yes . . ."

She was purring, her face a mask of delight.

*He liked knowing he made her look that way.*

It was base, just like the urges driving him. But it was all laced with something else, something that kept him watching her face as he moved. Whatever it was, it kept his pace even, maybe even slow as he became determined to savor the ride.

Savor the feeling of her thighs wrapped around him.

She was lifting up to take each thrust, the walls of her passage tight around his meat. His balls were tightening, the burning increasing as he fought back the moment of release.

*Not yet . . .*

Her satisfaction became a driving point of his own need. Her eyes were glittering with hunger, with the need to be driven over the edge.

"Harder . . ." she said, her voice raspy. "Stop being . . . a . . . nice guy."

"Jaelyn . . ." he warned.

"Harder!" she insisted.

Later he'd remember how much he wanted to make love to her. Now, there was only the way her voice sounded as she demanded freedom for the beast inside him.

It liked the sound of it, too, uncurling from that spot Bram kept it contained in. He worked his hips in a fast motion, enjoying the wet sounds her body made when his cock entered her.

It was fucking mind-blowing. The birds fluttered again

as he hit the point of release, growling out while Jaelyn gasped and sputtered. He lost his load inside her, straining against her in those final moments. Pleasure ripped into him, tearing everything else away, and dropping his ass in a pile of quivering limbs like some trophy she'd earned.

Fuck, he'd be lucky to be taken in by her.

So damned lucky.

# CHAPTER SIX

"Good morning."

Her grandfather was waiting for her the next morning. Milton was watching her door, aiming his gaze straight at her.

Jaelyn felt her cheeks heat as she drew in a deep breath and quelled the urge to melt back into her room.

*Not going to be a wuss . . . remember?*

"You think I'm acting like LeAnn." They were hard words to say. Jaelyn cringed but couldn't seem to stop herself.

She felt like confessing.

Bram was temptation and she couldn't seem to stop herself from sinning. In the bright light of day, and the direct stare of her grandfather, she lasted all of three minutes before she started babbling.

Her grandfather cleared his throat before settling himself against one of the huge boulders that formed the fence.

"I think that girl just might have gotten her head on straight at last." He drew in a breath. "Not that I wished something so harsh on any of us. Still, you have to admit LeAnn is a much better person to be around now."

Jaelyn searched for something nice to say but ended up offering her grandfather a shrug of her shoulders. "Sometimes life gives you the kick in the tail you need."

"Ha!" Her grandfather choked on a chuckle. "And I've got a few bruises to prove it myself." He winked. "Most of them were delivered by your grandma."

There was a groan and roar as one of the large construction trucks started to move. Conversation died until it was far enough into the distance for them to hear one another.

"I think you're more like Jeanie."

Her grandfather smiled, his eyes lit with the memory of his late wife. "She told me we were getting married, too."

"What?"

Milton shrugged and grinned. "I was a lot like Bram. Enamored with my uniform and top secret posting. Oh man, I was high on my position." Her grandfather paused to take a sip of his coffee. It didn't matter what time of day it was on the site, there was coffee brewing and that made Milton a very happy man. Jaelyn frowned at him, because his doctor had told her to limit his caffeine and he knew it.

Milton toasted her with his cup, a gleam in his eyes.

"Now things were a little different back when I was dating your grandmother. She was a flower child. In touch with her feminine spirit and damned were any who tried to rein her in. She got herself arrested for walking on the beach topless more than once. I swear she got off a couple of times because the cops just loved her so much."

Milton let out a low whistle. "I loved that rebel streak

in her. It was everything I wasn't and she enjoyed testing my resolve. Walked right up to me the first time I saw her and caught me looking at how thin her top was and asked if I wanted to make love . . . right there . . ."

"Get out," Jaelyn said. "Why am I only hearing about this now?"

"Because we were young and stupid before the Internet. I could say she decided you two needed a solid role model but the truth is, she didn't want my career to suffer. So as far as the rest of the base was concerned, she was straight and narrow. At least until the bedroom door was closed." Milton wiggled his eyebrows. "Jeanie hid the pictures in a shoebox, but you and LeAnn found it one day while playing hide and seek."

Jaelyn searched her memory. "I don't remember that."

"I do!" Her grandfather chuckled. "Jeanie threatened to crack my skull with the rolling pin over it." He had to stop talking because he was laughing so hard.

Milton winked. "She didn't think those pictures of her without a bra were appropriate for you girls while you were too young to not mention them to your schoolyard friends."

Jaelyn slowly sobered. "I think I need to keep my memories of Grandma being respectable."

"Why?" Milton demanded. "I see Bram isn't the only one who thinks his generation invented everything. Let me tell you, Jaelyn, your grandmother and I scared the birds in that old barn more than a few times."

Jaelyn felt her face go up in flames. Her grandfather sobered, sending her a serious look.

"You marry your young man, and don't let him be pig-headed about it. Men need a rolling pin applied to them sometimes. When I tell you you're more like Jeanie, that's what I mean. Not that you cook and clean and take care of me." He shook his head lovingly. "No, you are a woman in touch with her nature. Never forget what a blessing that is, young lady. Too many folks go through their whole lives never being comfortable in their skin."

There was a gleam in her grandfather's eyes that she hadn't seen very often. Jaelyn realized it was respect. He was talking to her like an adult, sharing wisdom with her but not as her grandparent. No, this was human to human, from a man who had learned from life experience.

"Thanks, Grandpa."

He nodded and started to stroll away, a happy whistle on his lips. In the distance, Jaelyn caught sight of Bram. He'd taken to wearing a gun openly. The distance was pretty far but she knew it was strapped to his thigh as he leaned over a work table Saxon and Vitus had plans rolled out on.

Well, maybe he had a gun, but she knew where Ginger kept the rolling pin.

And the lace stockings.

After all, there was more than one way to win a war.

"You're working too late, son."

Milton Sondors eyed Bram for a moment before he went over and shut the office door. He came back on the slower steps of an older man, even as there was something about his demeanor that made Bram feel like straightening his back.

"Time for you to go over and discuss details with my granddaughter about your wedding."

Milton settled down in a chair.

Bram was avoiding Jaelyn. Or perhaps it was a little more precise to say, he was trying to shield her from the way his composure shredded every time he got close to her.

"If you're sitting in here, driving your buddy insane because he has a pretty little wife waiting for him . . . well, I can see it's time for a few more pearls of wisdom, son," Milton explained.

"I'll give you the room," Saxon said.

"Stay right there," the old man instructed.

The layers of age on Milton seemed to grant him authority in spades. Saxon Hale, Shadow Ops team leader, shut his mouth and sat as instructed.

At least Bram realized he wasn't alone in being unable to dismiss Milton. The old man was striking Saxon the same way he had Bram. Milton was one of those men who didn't have to brag about his life accomplishments. No, there was just something about his demeanor a smart man recognized and respected.

"You're a damned lucky bastard," Milton began, "to have a gal like Jaelyn willing to wear your ring."

"I'm no good for her," Bram said. "You've lost everything because of me."

"Now that is where you're wrong, son."

There was something about the way Milton said the word "son" that made Bram feel about two inches tall.

"The only things a man ever owns are his faith and his word. If he's the sort who keeps his word, someday, he might . . ." Milton paused and sent them both a hard look. ". . . might just discover life's true riches are measured by a woman who will put up with him. A gal who will remember how he likes his coffee and notice when he's down to his last pair of clean shorts. That's called 'making a home.' It's not about the structure where it happens."

Milton shifted his attention to Saxon. "You know what I'm talking about. I see the way you look at that wife of yours."

Saxon drew in a deep breath. "I do."

"I know what Jaelyn is worthy of," Bram said softly. "I'm not up to that standard."

Milton only chuckled, which turned into a dry cough before he was slapping his knee. "We're men," he explained. "It's an ongoing battle against just how stupid we are at our cores."

Saxon let out a soft sound of amusement that had Milton pointing at him.

But Milton's face went dead serious a moment later. "We're dogs. Men, that is. Some a little closer to wolves than others . . . and it's a necessary thing. To be untamed, to have men who will charge into the fight while knowing they just might get ripped to pieces." He looked at Bram. "You think your hands are too dirty, that she can't accept you . . . only that's the part of you that you let the world see."

He'd nailed it. Bram was nodding and he realized Saxon was, too.

Milton's gaze shifted between the pair of them.

"Come on," Milton said. "I want to show you something out in the barn."

It had been twenty-four hours and Bram was still thinking about the way he and Jaelyn had been in the barn. Returning to the old structure with Milton was awkward to say the least, but Milton's surprising ability to spring things on them was growing on Bram.

As in, he really wanted to know what the guy was going to drop this time.

The barn was packed with cars. The ones lucky enough

to be inside were in far better condition than the ones out behind the house. Milton wove between them, seeming to know the way. He stopped next to one that had a tarp over it.

"Give that a pull for me," he said, directing Bram.

A tug on both ends loosened the tarp. It slithered off the car beneath it, revealing a vintage Volkswagen camper van.

"This was mine." Milton was rocking back onto his heels, staring at the faded yellow paint. "Never thought to see her again and that's a fact."

"You're full of surprises," Saxon muttered.

Milton sent Saxon a look. "You're the sort of man who's well acquainted with the reality of just how tangled up life can be. The moment you don't think something is going to come back around and surface in your kitchen is the exact time you get caught with your shorts down."

Bram opened his mouth but Milton held up a finger.

"I know you know it, son," he said in a low tone. "And I've heard you saying how that's the reason you don't want to take Jaelyn down that road by marrying her."

"Are you sure you need me here?"

Bram felt himself sending Saxon a raised eyebrow. His team leader was a former Navy SEAL and a Medal of Honor recipient who was at home living off the grid. He didn't ask for permission to leave the room. Or get rattled by very much.

Milton was living up to the feeling Bram had of him alright.

"You're here to help me kick some sense into this kid," Milton continued.

"Maybe I think he knows what he's talking about."

Milton turned his full attention onto Saxon. "How'd

you meet that pretty little lady who's having your children?"

"This isn't about me," Saxon declared.

Milton chuckled and shook his head. "Let me take a guess: you ran into her during a case and just couldn't resist. Bet you tried, though."

Saxon didn't answer. He clamped his jaw shut, earning a nod from Milton. "This wasn't the first location I was assigned to. Met my Jeanie out West, on the California coast line. God, but she loved the sun and waves."

He was lost in the memory for a moment.

"I bought the HoneyBee here"—he nodded toward the VW van—"so we could spend the summer parked a few steps from the sand and she could wear almost nothing."

Milton turned his attention back toward Bram. "I was expecting my application with the Minute Man program to come through in the fall of that year. Like you, I didn't see my career mixing with a girl like Jeanie. Wanted to shield her from the dangers I was looking forward to shouldering."

"Not to be insensitive, Milton, but the dangers are a little different."

Milton shook his head. There was a serious look on his face that Bram realized he'd only seen there when he had been going out the door after Jaelyn.

"The Cold War was just as bloody as any other, son, don't doubt it. Men disappeared and so did their wives, as the locations of these silos were hunted down. Body parts got mailed to men in order to get them to give up classified locations, men hunted men, and did their best to break them. I know there are truly evil men in this world."

"I'm glad you understand, Milton," Bram responded.

"Oh, I do," Milton continued. "I told Jeanie the same thing. Know what she did? Spent most of August and September sewing together a patchwork quilt. She got the scraps from some church and would sit out in the sand with a hand needle, just stitching." He made a scoffing sound. "Damn it was an ugly thing."

There was a long moment as Milton was lost in his memories once again.

"Well, son," he said, looking at Bram. "When the season changed and I had to set out for my deployment, Jeanie shook that quilt out over the bed right inside there and climbed into it, bare as could be, and made it clear she wasn't going to be scared off."

Milton grunted. "Jaelyn is just like Jeanie. Make the mistake of overlooking that and you'll regret it."

Was he selling her short?

God, he wanted to say yes.

The need to admit it was tearing up his insides. Just the thought seemed enough for him to make his way back toward where Jaelyn was. Milton wandered off, leaving Bram alone with his questions.

"I was pretty determined to cut Ginger loose. You were there. In New Orleans."

Bram looked over at Saxon. There was a rare, unguarded look on his face.

"Food for thought, Magnus. I'm glad things didn't turn out the way I thought they needed to."

His team leader took off for the back door of his house. There was a way Saxon looked when he was gazing at his wife.

Like she was the only water in miles of desert.

Like he looked at Jaelyn.

"Are you ready to come in, Bram?"

He thought she'd risen up from his thoughts because he was so deeply fixated on her.

Instead, he found Jaelyn watching him from the open door of her quarters. She had every reason to avoid him. He caught a hint of uncertainty in her eyes and realized that was his fault.

And it was unacceptable.

"Yes, I am, baby."

Her insides twisted as Bram came toward her. The curl of anticipation was one she enjoyed, knowing it was going to spark off a blaze of need.

Bram came through the door and shut it softly behind him.

The only light on in her quarters was the red glow coming from a small clock on the dresser. It seemed enough for him, though, as he reached out and stroked her face.

"I've never made love to you, Jaelyn."

Her breath caught as he traced her lips with one fingertip.

"I'm a bastard for that."

She might have responded but he was stroking her cheek and all she managed was to draw in a gasp.

"I've been told I'm a fast learner though."

He'd made it to her hair and slid his fingers into the strands before tightening his grasp. He controlled his grip, holding her hair tightly enough to make her his, and still spare her pain.

"Maybe you should give it a try," she said. "I'm a great study buddy."

He buried his face in her hair, inhaling as he bound her

against his body with his other hand. "I might need a lot of practice, Jaelyn."

"I sure hope so," she said. "What's the point of getting married otherwise?"

He quivered.

It was a declaration that cut her to the core and promised her a companion in her own need for him.

It was more than physical. There was so much about him that captured her attention so completely, right down to the smallest details.

Like the smell of his skin.

Or the sound of him breathing in the scent of her hair.

Their clothing was a barrier. Neither of them seemed willing to endure being separated by the layers of fabric. The sound of them stripping made her cheeks heat but not out of shame or some sense of awkwardness.

No, it was with anticipation.

She leaned over and ripped the bedding free, allowing the faint red glow to illuminate the white sheet.

He wrapped her in his arms the moment he was bare, leaning down to scoop her off her feet and cradle her against his chest.

His heart was thumping just as fast as hers.

They'd had each other before.

This was different.

Bram stroked her. Petting her as though he was trying to memorize her body. He lingered over her shoulders before slipping his hands down to cup her breasts.

"God, I love these . . ." He was cradling her mounds, gently squeezing them before he leaned down and licked one nipple.

She drew in a soft sound that had him lifting his head. In the low light, he was just a shadow.

"I like the sounds you make, too."

"That makes two of us," she answered as she teased the length of his cock.

He stayed on his side, allowing her to see his face as she drew her fingers across his length and rubbed the spot on the underside of the head.

His jaw was tight and the sound that rumbled through his chest was low and deep.

And perfect.

She wanted to go slow but realized she just didn't have the self-discipline to stay separated from him. She rolled over, pushing him onto his back so that she could straddle him.

"I don't want to rush, Jaelyn."

He'd caught her waist, holding her above him. His cock rose up between them, slipping into the fluid already coating her slit.

"I'm shameless when it comes to you."

He let out a groan and then she was free to sink down onto his cock.

"So . . . damned . . . rotten . . . ," Bram said.

She sheathed him. Leaning down to brace her hands on his shoulders before using her thighs to rise up all the way, until only the head of his member was still inside her.

She rose and lowered, the feeling of their flesh moving against each other amazing. "No one ever made me want to get naked with them before." She opened her eyes and settled on his cock, holding still as she locked gazes with him. "And there were offers, don't think there weren't."

He sat up, proving his strength as he rolled right over and pinned her onto the surface of the bed.

"You're mine, Jaelyn . . ." He thrust hard against her, sending a jolt of sensation through her insides.

"Mine . . ."

"Oh really?" she questioned before she lifted her leg and twisted it right over his head. She managed to climb to her knees before he was grasping her hips and thrusting back into her.

"Believe it, baby . . ." He grunted. "Now . . ." The bed hit the wall as he thrust into her once more. "Or later . . ." Another thump against the wall. "Let's debate it all night . . . it works for me."

And she'd be a liar if she claimed it was any different for her. The need and hunger were twisting through her. She was pushing back, arching to take his thrusts. The grip he had on her hips seemed to intensify the moment somehow, driving her excitement up another notch as she lost the ability to keep her lips sealed shut.

They were encased in the moment. Jaelyn had no idea how long it lasted, only that she didn't care.

No, there was only Bram and the fact that he was with her. If tomorrow she landed right back in the claws of despair, she wouldn't regret inviting him into her bed tonight.

It wasn't really a choice.

He was her addiction.


His balls ached.

It was a crass observation but true nonetheless. Bram shifted as Jaelyn moved. She was restless, turning away from him. He eased her back toward him.

He needed her against him.

And that was a first.

The ache in his balls was something he'd enjoyed feeling

before. To put it bluntly, he'd liked finding partners who would keep up with his appetite.

There had never been any holding afterward, though.

Now, he'd have shot the man who tried to separate him from Jaelyn.

He was in deep. His emotions overflowing the place he'd banished them to. It was no longer a matter of logical thinking. Analyzing the situation was useless.

There was only Jaelyn and the way she watered the dried-out parts of his soul.

An alarm was starting to chime.

Jaelyn groaned and cracked one eye.

"It is definitely a coffee sort of morning."

She opened her eyes as Bram spoke from the foot of the bed. He was tucking the laces of one boot in before he reached for his gun that was lying on the dresser. He checked it before securing it in the holster.

"See you after work, honey."

He winked at her while she was hugging a pillow against her chest and trying to jump-start her brain.

"Will I?"

It was more of a challenge than a question and she didn't regret her tone of voice. Bram stopped with his hand on the doorknob and turned to look back at her.

"You will," he assured her. "We have a wedding to plan."

The mobile unit wasn't as sturdy as a house. The wall shook as he opened and shut the door.

But Jaelyn felt like it was the foundation of her life that shuddered.

Did she know what she was doing?

Hell no.

Then again, there was an instinct at work. Something she'd never realized lived inside of her. Bram had awakened it.

So no, she wasn't exactly sure what she was doing but the best adventures were the ones that included surprises.

"We need to talk."

LeAnn had been waiting for him. Bram felt a twinge of heat creeping along his nape as he closed the door of Jaelyn's room behind him. While he'd been focused on what his actions had cost Jaelyn, he'd avoided the fact that LeAnn was suffering a loss as well.

"I owe you an apology. Gideon found the picture I had of you." Bram came down the steps and faced her. "I know better than to bring personal items with me on missions since I'd been working with a Shodow opps team. It was a fatal mistake. I know the squad was important to you."

She smiled. It wasn't the practiced one he knew so well. This was something different. The truth was, he'd been avoiding noticing just how changed LeAnn was. It was like her shell had cracked, allowing something to hatch that was overdue in emerging.

"That's not what I wanted to talk about." She was suddenly moving toward him and the mobile housing unit. "You doubt my sister."

"Not really."

She smiled at him. Bram ended up staring at her because there was more sincerity in the expression than he realized he'd ever seen from her before.

LeAnn shook her head. "It's my fault she didn't answer your letters."

She went past him and knocked on Jaelyn's door.

"Back already?" Jaelyn was speaking before she looked

to see who was on the other side of the door. Bram watched her slap a hand over her mouth as her cheeks darkened.

"I need to confess something," LeAnn began. "I'm a horrible sister."

She reached inside her sweatshirt jacket and pulled something out. "These are for you."

LeAnn held up something and waiting until Jaelyn took them from her. Bram stepped closer, looking over LeAnn's shoulder.

"What the fuck?" The words just got past his lips.

Jaelyn looked at him, then at the bundle in her hand as she tried to make sense of his exclamation.

"Yeah," LeAnn said as she came down the steps. "I'm that rotten. So let's call it even on the picture-and-Gideon thing. I think I got a dose of what was coming to me."

Bram caught her upper arm as she tried to take off.

"No one deserved what he did to your family."

She pulled away from him. "This isn't about me, it's about the fact that you don't trust my sister's feelings for you because I stole your letters."

"His what?" Jaelyn asked in a horrified whisper.

"Letters," LeAnn answered. "And I didn't do it out of love. I was jealous and being childishly vindictive. A real girlfriend wouldn't have done it, even if she was heartbroken. So, I'm sorry."

The shocked look on Jaelyn's face wasn't for her sister. She aimed it straight at Bram. LeAnn left, but honestly, Bram didn't notice just where she went.

No, his attention was on Jaelyn. She clutched the letters to her chest, like a treasure she was being reunited with.

"That's why . . ." she whispered, "why you're trying to talk me out of marrying you."

"Only part of the reason."

Jaelyn slowly smiled at him. "See you tonight . . . dear."

She winked at him before she pulled the door shut.

Damn if he didn't enjoy her sass.


He'd written her.

Jaelyn sat on her bed, spreading the letters out so that she might see every last one of them. Their smudged envelopes only endeared them to her more.

So many . . .

There were so many!

She fingered them, arranging them in order of postmark. Fat, hot tears dropped from her eyes as she stared at them while her heart felt like it was going to burst.

And then, it threatened to tear in half.

How could he have doubts?

The horrible truth dawned on her. Bram was everything she always thought of him.

The best.

And it was the reason he didn't want to commit to her. The letters in front of her proved he'd wanted everything she did.

Only that was before Gideon.

Before Bram thought he was putting her and her family in danger. She really was rotten because she wanted to tell him it didn't matter.

Bram was putting other people's safety before his own happiness.

She didn't even come close to measuring up to him.

Her door suddenly opened. Bram came in, the scent of coffee along with him.

"It's a coffee sort of morning," he said as he offered her one of the mugs he was holding.

"Sure is," she agreed.

The coffee was strong and hot. It burned past the bliss she'd woken up enjoying, leaving her staring at cold, hard reality.

"You're right," she said. Her damn voice was almost a squeak. That pissed her off because she wasn't going to cry over something that came so second nature to Bram.

He was better than her.

Better than she deserved.

"We can't get married."

There. The words were out. It hurt. So deeply and acutely, the only balm was the knowledge that she was doing something important for her grandfather.

"Why do you say that?" Bram demanded.

Jaelyn flipped around to stare at him. "Because you're right. I have to think about how my actions affect my family. Just like you are."

Bram was furious. She watched his temper heat up as he slammed the coffee mug down on the dresser. "You said you would marry me, Jaelyn."

"And you've told me again and again just what a bad idea it is."

He was shaking his head. "So now it bothers you what I do?"

"No." She was on her feet facing him down. "It sucks that my choices could hurt those I love. You're just looking out for LeAnn and Gramps. I'm a selfish bitch to not catch on to that. I wasn't listening, just reaching for what I wanted. Thinking only of myself."

She wiped her hand across her face, forbidding herself any further tears.

Adult choices meant adult responsibility.

"We can't get married."

* * *

"We sure as hell are."

Jaelyn turned on Bram. She was a mess of emotions and even knowing it, she couldn't stop herself from letting it all out.

"Oh, now you want to change your tune?"

"I changed it last night, baby," he informed her. "After your grandfather gave me a few pearls of wisdom."

"He doesn't understand the risk," Jaelyn said, looking back toward the letters.

Bram grunted. "I made that same mistake."

He was suddenly on his knees, his arms wrapped around her lower body.

"Nothing is certain, Jaelyn, except for the fact that I can't keep my distance from you." He released her but kept hold of her hand. "So take the leap and marry me."

He simply was her choice.

And the glitter in his eyes told her that she was his.

"Let's go see this church my grandfather thinks is good."

LeAnn turned and sent Dare Servant a hard look.

Most men recoiled under it or at least tried to soothe her temper.

Dare Servant came closer.

"I don't need company, thanks." She was getting better at tempering her tone. Or maybe just recognizing when she had slipped into bitch mode.

"Sure about that?" Dare inquired. He was wearing his shades, watching her from behind their mirrored surface.

"So?" LeAnn took a breath and dialed down her temper. "Like I said, karma came calling. I'm a big girl. Jaelyn needs more help than I do. I needed to come clean, so those letters wouldn't be a problem between them. It's time I started helping my family out."

"I have an idea about that."

LeAnn had intended to walk away. Okay, she had nowhere to go, had done more walking around the rusted-out shells of the automotive graveyard than her grandfather had. Dare's tone hooked her attention. Truth was, she was bored.

"This way." He jerked his head toward the off-limits area beyond the boulder fence.

The huge nets that were strung up over the area to hide the construction trucks from satellites made for a speckled shade. Dare kept going until they came to an area that had large shipping containers lined up. She'd watched forklifts emptying one the day before. The doors were still open.

"Back here."

Dare pulled a flashlight off a table and used it to illuminate the inside of the cargo container.

"Right there."

Dare shone the light on something black.

"Our hot shop!" LeAnn exclaimed.

Sitting in the container were the ovens that had once been her and Jaelyn's dream studio. She reached out and stroked one, the surface was coated with dust.

"Gramps got this for us," she whispered. "Must have cost him a small fortune, too. That was before Grandma got sick. Jaelyn went and got a job with benefits to ease the financial load on the family. She really loves spinning glass."

"I heard a rumor about it," Dare replied. "Really want to help your sister move forward? She needs to keep busy."

LeAnn smiled and she realized she was more genuinely happy than she had been in . . . well, a really long time.

Then reality intruded with a very large helping of facts. "Yes, I'd love to but the gas bill will be way out of my budget."

A hot shop could easily run a six-figure gas bill.

"Got a plan for that, too." Dare started walking toward the open doors of the container.

LeAnn followed him, relief bathing her when she made it beyond the steel walls.

"So, what's the idea?"

"We need a cover for this place and a glass studio, well, that's not a bad one. Milton will make a great little old man tinkering in his scrap pile, at least as far as the rest of the area is concerned. You'll be the struggling artist grandchildren he dotes on, feeding your hippie-era fantasy."

It was too good to be true.

Or at least, better than she deserved. Jaelyn was worthy alright. Her? Well, she needed to work on it.

"Are you shitting me?" LeAnn asked.

Dare wasn't put off by her mouth. His lips twitched, which she admitted she enjoyed knowing she'd caused.

"No, ma'am."

LeAnn slowly smiled. She realized Dare was watching her and looked away. "Thanks," she muttered but realized how flustered she was and forced herself to face him. "It would be really great to blow glass again, and Gramps loves this place."

"It was mostly Bram's idea."

LeAnn turned and walked away.

"It was yours," Thais said from the other side of the door. "The idea."

Dare shrugged. "Bram is a team member."

Thais nodded. "Team members are always supported. I know."

Thais was hiding her feelings, which suited Dare. He liked the professional wall between them. He also enjoyed knowing she'd have his back covered no matter what it required her to do.

Fine, he was no gentleman because the honest truth was, Thais did some of her assignments in bed.

So did he.

Shadow Ops wasn't for the weak or easily offended. Bram's own sister had been targeted by them and had an agent slipped into her bed. It was a proven method of loosening tongues and to his way of thinking, better than torture.

And he had no plans to retire anytime soon.

If ever.


"Sure you know what you're doing?" Dare asked as he slapped Bram on the shoulder.

"Clear as a bell," Bram shot back. "So dust off your civilian suit. This wedding is happening."

The church was small. It had a chill to it, the sort that lingered in stone buildings from centuries past. The pews were solid oak and the pipe organ ran on foot pedals.

"Jaelyn deserves a wedding." He kept his tone low because the acoustics in the place were amazing.

"Who am I to argue against a perfectly valid excuse to drink?" Dare replied. "On someone else's tab, that is. Hope you got a credit increase because I'm planning on ordering the expensive stuff."

"Careful," Bram warned. "My memory is pretty good, buddy. Your turn will come."

Dare sent him a raised eyebrow. "Know something? I took off to help you find Jaelyn because there was far too much settling down going on around me. Count me out of that one, buddy. You are welcome to the marital bliss."

Dare clamped his mouth shut when the reverend cleared his throat. The man was coming toward them to discuss details.

Milton stepped forward. "It's been a long time. Your father married me to my wife in this church way back in sixty-eight. You were fresh out of high school."

The reverend squinted at Milton through thick glasses before he patted the top of Milton's hand.

"My granddaughter is ready to make a happy man out of this fellow, with your help . . ."

It was a thing of beauty.

The way things came together when a man was smart and patient. Ricky peeked through a door, loving the old church so much, he could have kissed the floor.

Oh, that wasn't on account of any soft feelings he had for the spirituality of the place. No, it was because sound bounced between the stone walls, letting him hear every word of Bram Magnus's as he planned his private wedding.

And the door . . . it was solid wood, maybe a century old if it was a day. Which meant the doorjamb was loose, giving him a slot to peek through.

Saxon Hale's team was buried alright but there was one thing they'd overlooked, and that was how remote the location of their new nest was. With the help of the information Ricky had lifted from Brendon's flight controller access and thus had been in the area, just waiting for some of Saxon's men to cross his path. He'd known they were there by the number of flights landing at the small area airport.

Brendon was a prime resource. Ricky was sure glad he only had to fuck the guy to get what he wanted because that way, he could tap the source over and over anytime he needed to look at flight plans.

Now it was just a matter of blending in and waiting for Saxon's men to emerge.

They might know a lot about blending in but Ricky knew a whole hell of a lot about what trained men looked like. There was a way they carried themselves, a certain walk, the jacket, even in warm weather, that hid chest harnesses. The way they kept their eyes moving.

Yeah, he knew it because he behaved the same way.

A wedding.

It was going to be the perfect place to take them all out.

Perfect.

Damascus Ryland Hale looked up as Colonel Magnus came into her office. He wasn't in his uniform, which raised questions galore in her mind.

"Sir?"

She'd worked with the colonel long enough to know he'd get straight to the point of whatever had sent him looking for her.

"Pack a bag," he said with a jovialness she wasn't accustomed to hearing from her commanding officer in the classified lab she worked in.

Not that it was a complaint. She loved her job. Totally adored it. In fact, she'd gone to great lengths to hide her connection with the colonel until it was too late for her father to stop her.

Her father had plans for her that included a political marriage to enhance his own career.

"We're heading upstate, I told your husband I'd escort you this time," Colonel Magnus explained. "Bring a dress, seems we have a wedding to attend."

Damascus slowly smiled. The colonel offered her a raised eyebrow. "I think that smile is more for the fact that you're going to get to see that husband of yours."

Damascus shrugged as she signed off and locked her computer system. "The wedding will be great, too." The colonel grunted, making it her turn to send him a questioning look. "Aren't you happy to see your son tying the knot?"

"Truth is," the colonel said, offering her a rare explanation, "I'm beginning to think Hale is some sort of pied piper. Both my kids seem to have fallen under the spell of his team members."

"It's a good place to be," Damascus offered as she moved through a doorway into a passageway toward her quarters. She had to use her keycard to open secure airlock doors that were designed to keep the deadly diseases she worked with contained in the lab if there was ever a containment breach.

Her job was just as dangerous as her husband's, just on a different level. She dodged germs while Vitus dealt with bullets.

The colonel followed her. Damascus didn't let it bother her. She'd known the price of working in the lab was that personal freedom was limited. Not that Magnus abused his authority. He had the right to enter her quarters anytime he felt there might be a security risk. To date, this was his first visit.

"Can I invite my mother?"

The colonel was standing in the living room while Damascus rummaged through her closet.

"I imagine the congresswoman hopeful will enjoy a break from the press hounds. It will be a nice, private event."

Damascus sent him a smile before she picked up her cell phone and typed something. She pushed the send button before tossing it toward Magnus.

"You'll have to tell her where we're going."

It was a little bit funny, the fact that she didn't know where her husband lived. Or maybe where he worked was a better way to put it. Not that it truly bothered her. Vitus would find her. Just as he had when she'd been kidnapped years ago. Once a SEAL, always a SEAL. It was a tad unconventional but she admitted it gave her a little tickle to think about him emerging from the shadows to surprise her.

Damascus zipped up her bag and joined the colonel. "So, am I going to meet the infamous Harley? Maybe Bram's fiancée has a parrot."

"Are you going to get around to telling me you're pregnant?"

Colonel Magnus could always be counted on to make sure everyone knew he held all the information cards. Especially when she was letting it slip that Vitus had told her about the colonel's pet parrot.

"I just assumed you already knew . . . sir." She offered him a soft shrug. "I did take the test in the medical office. It's your command . . . right?"

He offered her a soft scoffing sound before he was lifting her bag off her shoulder.

"Yes, you will meet Harley and I'm going to shoot

Bram if he has somehow found a woman with a female parrot because the last thing I need are offspring from my baby bird. He's enough of a handful."

"You appear to have received some good news."

Dunn Bateson was a recluse. Miranda Delacroix wasn't surprised to find him all but hidden among the shrubbery at the afternoon reception she was attending. Her security escort was, though. She gave the man a quick wave of her hand to send him away.

"Replace him," Dunn instructed. "If I'd been set on killing you, it would be done."

"We're not someplace where that sort of thing could happen."

Dunn wasn't backing down. He sent her an even stare. "Your father used to look at me just that same way."

Miranda nodded and drew in a deep breath. She regained her poise and smiled. "I did receive good news. It seems there is a family wedding this week. My daughter will be there and maybe even my son might make it."

Dunn didn't react. He swept the people around them, the Washington crowd of hopefuls. Miranda was running for Congress and set to sweep the votes. The fact that she was going to claim her late husband's seat was just a personal little victory that very few people understood.

Dunn was one of them.

She was his mother. The woman who had been forced to give him up so her family could use her to further their political ambitions. His father hadn't been their choice for their daughter. And they had threatened to destroy his father if she didn't return to the fold.

But she'd risked her own good name to ensure he was

born when it would have gone so much easier for her if she'd allowed him never to be born.

For that reason he was devoted to her.

It was the only reason he was seen so much lately. He'd turned out to support her and her causes.

"I hope you get to see your son," he said at last.

Dunn reached out and shook her hand. She passed a small piece of paper to him and smiled as she walked off to finish with the afternoon's festivities.

Dunn waited until he was inside his car before looking at the address she'd slipped to him. He had countless tasks waiting for him, but nothing was more important than family. And the opportunity to freely acknowledge his mother was very rare.

He stroked the screen of his phone. A tap and his assistant came on the line.

"Cancel my appointments for the week. I'll be out of touch."

Ricky snickered.

In fact, he was starting to turn purple from holding his breath as he clamped his lips together tightly to keep from laughing like a lunatic.

It was just getting better and better . . .

Saxon Hale. Vitus Hale. Dare Servant. Thais Sinclair.

And now, the family was coming together for a wedding. Lady luck was paying up with interest.

That got him thinking. There was really only one thing he liked better than getting the jump on someone who had bested him.

Money.

The kind of cash that could see him living in style for the rest of his days.

Hell, that was the only reason he'd taken the job from Tyler Martin in the first place.

The guy had funds.

Of course, men in high public office didn't get there by playing nice and they all needed someone to mop up their messes. Voters had such a bleached-out vision of the people they elected. Personally, he had no qualms about covering shit up because he felt if someone was going to be stupid enough to let men like Carl Davis pull the wool over their eyes, well, they deserved what they got.

It wasn't his job to pop their fantasy bubbles.

But it was Tyler Martin's job to blow those spheres where make-believe men served with valor and honor and never boned their secretaries.

Ha! All a bloke had to do was look at the secretaries heading into the Capitol Building in the morning to see what prime grade of ass they were. That was where the truth hit the pavement and anyone could see it.

That brought him back to Tyler Martin.

Carl Davis paid him to keep blowing happiness bullshit bubbles.

Bubbles that Saxon Hale's team had the evidence to pop.

He reached over and tapped a number into his cell phone. His memory was razor sharp, always had been when it came to details and numbers. The line buzzed a couple of times.

"Who is this?" Tyler Martin asked.

"Someone you thought you buried." Ricky let his Irish out. "I think you forgot just how much help I can be to you. That's the only reason I can think of for you leaving me down south to rot."

"You assume I was never coming back for you."

Ricky grinned. He'd hand it to Tyler, the guy didn't let a fleck of emotion into his tone. Which was good, because it was going to allow Ricky the chance to roll the dice and make a grab for some of the cash Carl Davis was investing in his run for the White House.

"No need now," Ricky offered smoothly. "In fact, I've got a bit of something interesting happening right in front of my eyes. It's the sort of thing I think you'd be interested in."

"What might that be?"

"I know where Saxon Hale and his team are."

There was a long pause. "How much?"

"Depends on what you want done."

"I'll be in touch." Tyler said before the line went dead.

Jaelyn gently ran her finger across the registry book where her grandparents' names were signed.

"Wow . . ." she whispered, conscience of how sound traveled through the stone church. But she was in a back room, a refectory where the book was kept. There were four of them, one each for baptisms, confirmations, marriages, and funerals.

"I hope you understand why it has to be a small, private ceremony." Bram came up behind her, lightly resting his hand on her hip.

"It's going to be a privilege to sign this book," she said. "And the only people who are important in my life will be here. One of the realities of working contracts from a home office. I really don't have a lot of social contacts."

"You gave up your social life to take care of Milton," Bram said as he rubbed her back. "He knows it, too."

Jaelyn smiled and fluttered her eyelashes. "Grandpa and I have a system."

Bram snorted. "Okay. Copy that. I won't touch it with a ten-foot pole."

"You're so smart."

Bram had backed away with his hands up in surrender. His lips curled in a very smug grin. "Smart enough to get you into town to buy a ring before you change your mind."

"Grandma left me her band," Jaelyn said as she followed him and let him wrap his arms around her. "I know Grandpa would have put it in his travel bag. So I just need a dress."

She'd surprised him. Jaelyn enjoyed watching it flash through his eyes, felt the way his arms tightened around her.

Happy endings actually happened.

Even to someone like her.

"Tell me your price for dealing with Hale's team."

Ricky grinned, enjoying the sound of Tyler Martin's voice.

"Make a transfer and I'll call you back if it isn't enough."

There was a pause. "Fine. I want them dead. All of them."

"I'll need a passport, too," Ricky continued. "Planning to retire, back to the home country."

"I'll deal with that," Tyler said. "Just make sure you get them all. The deal is off if you fail."

Carl Davis finished waving to the press and ducked inside the open door of the jet he was using to fly on to his next campaign stop. Tyler made sure the door was shut before he headed into an office to make the transfer.

He didn't blink over the amount or the fact that he'd never be able to retrieve the money.

Saxon and Vitus Hale knew too much.

"Where is that going?"

Carl was in the doorway. He was smart, Tyler would give him that. He stepped further inside so that the door could close.

"My man has located Saxon Hale's new nest."

Carl's face lit. "And you're . . . doing what?"

Tyler finished typing in his passcodes and the account information lit the screen. "I'm going to clean up the mess."

Carl was looking at the screen and the amount Tyler typed in. "I thought you advised me to keep my eye on the big picture."

"Don't get cheap on me," Tyler advised. "The Hale brothers know too much about you. Add in the fact that Bram Magnus is there, getting married, and I bet we might be able to deal with Colonel Magnus as well."

Carl's eyes glowed with anticipation. Tyler hovered over the enter key for a moment. Carl nodded.

"Oversee the operation personally, Ty," Carl said. "I don't want anyone else involved."

"It will be my pleasure."

And it would be. Carl was ahead in the polls and everything Tyler had sacrificed for was about to come to fruition. He would be Carl Davis's head security man.

It was best to tie up any loose ends and Saxon Hale's team was a mighty big one. Tyler pushed a button on his phone.

"Tell the pilot to hold off on liftoff. I'm disembarking."

\* \* \*

"Jeanie would be real happy to see you choosing that ring."

Milton's eyes were glossy with unshed tears. He started to work his own band loose but Bram stopped him.

"I can't accept that, sir," he said. "Truth is, I feel like I'm cheating somehow by not buying Jaelyn her own ring."

The ring came free with a pop. "They went up to that church together the first time, so they're returning there the same way, son."

Milton held out the ring but Bram hesitated.

Milton set his wedding band down on the table with a firm look. "I should have taken it off years ago. I'd be proud to see you wear it."

He winked at Jaelyn and went straight for the coffee.

"Well . . ." Ginger Hale emerged from the bedroom. "As long as you're happy with vintage . . ."

There was a rustle of fabric as she lifted up a dress and laid it out on the dining room table.

Bram choked.

Making Ginger chuckle. "You bet I saved it, Magnus, and you have no idea how hard it was to get a hold of someone in Dunn Bateson's employ who would go retrieve it from that cabin. But it was my wedding dress after all."

The dress had a flared-out skirt that would fall just past her knees and a crossover top that would give a great view of her cleavage. It all came together in a tight little waist.

"Try it on," Ginger encouraged before she looked toward Bram. "Bye."

Bram rolled his eyes before heading toward the door. Ginger grinned. "Now we can have girl time."

Such an innocent statement for so important a subject. Jaelyn discovered herself drifting into a surreal state.

Was she looking down the barrel of a loaded gun that would go off in her face?

*Ha! That sums up your entire relationship with Bram . . .*

It did, which just made it so simple to keep moving toward the moment when she would marry Bram Magnus.

There were butterflies in her stomach and she realized the sensation was part of the punch the moment should deliver.

The size of the ceremony didn't matter, the dress Ginger offered was great. The fact that it was going to be a Wednesday wedding day only meant she didn't have to wait until Sunday to know Bram was hers.

Ginger made a low sound of admiration as she zipped the dress up.

"Now that will turn some heads."

But the only thing Jaelyn found herself longing for was for Bram to return her love.

"Are you sure you don't want your own ring?" Bram was leaning against the boulder fence, waiting for her. "You're having to compromise on everything."

"Not everything." She came closer and laid her hand on his chest. "You are perfect, Mr. Bram Magnus."

He liked what she said. Jaelyn watched enjoyment flash through his eyes.

"Honestly." She pulled the rings out of the little zippered pocket in her sweatshirt that she'd placed them in and looked at them. "I feel like I need at least a decade before I even start coming close to living up to the challenge of these rings." She looked up, locking gazes with him. "My grandparents were devoted to each other. I feel like I'm still trying to understand what makes that sort of lifelong relationship."

"And yet you're marrying me."

She shrugged. "I can't help myself."

He nodded slowly. Something moved between them, something deep and so strong, it sent tears into her eyes. She was more exposed in that moment than she'd ever been in her life, more open to having her heart smashed, and absolutely certain she would die if he didn't return her feelings.

That had to be love.

"I know the feeling, baby." His tone was edged in rough emotion. Like he was on the edge, that same place she was teetering.

He clasped the back of her neck, tilting his head to the side so he might press his lips against hers. She knew his kiss now, and yet this one was different. She felt the yearning in it. The seeking.

It was more intoxicating than ever, binding her to him in body as well as soul.

"Read the letters."

She was still drunk on his kiss when he pulled away.

"Where are you going?"

"We're getting married tomorrow," he offered. "I'm sleeping in the bunkhouse, to remind me how good I'm going to have it when you agree to be my wife. Read my letters, Jaelyn, you'll see that I came back for you."

*I came back for you . . .*

She wanted to believe that. It was like the feeling of being eight years old and waiting for Santa Claus. You never saw him, but the magic was there on Christmas morning. Long before expensive gifts were on her list, she'd rushed down the hallway to be delighted by a Barbie doll.

Tonight, what filled her heart with magic was the dusty paper, filled with the thoughts of a man who had kept her in his heart while in a war zone and never given up.

She sure as shit was going to marry him.

Ricky slid a fingertip across the screen of the phone he was using.

He let out a low whistle at the amount in the offshore account.

His mother had never had more than barely enough. He was going to go back to Ireland and buy a big house and fill it with sons to carry on the Sullivan name.

"Don't get too excited. You haven't finished the job yet."

Ricky jumped but Tyler Martin made sure he was far enough away. He waited for Ricky to identify him before moving closer.

"I expect my money's worth, Sullivan."

Ricky shrugged and dropped the phone into his pocket. "Going down tomorrow. You're getting a real deal on this job. Miranda Delacroix is here, too."

Tyler chuckled. "Line that bird up with the rest of the bodies and there will be some icing on the cake."

There was tension in the air.

Tyler had good instincts and his were telling him that Ricky was itching for some revenge.

Not that it was anything new. When a man played a high-stakes game, he didn't make many friends.

It was better that way.

Better for Ricky to see him as a threat. A man to worry about disappointing.

"I'll be watching," Tyler said.

"A second man would make a huge difference in how many bodies hit the floor."

Tyler had started to turn away. He looked back at Ricky. "I hired you because my face is known. But if you're saying you can't produce what you promised, I can get someone else in here who can."

"You wouldn't know where they were if it weren't for me."

Tyler only shrugged. "That's irrelevant now. Should have hidden your cell signal better."

Tyler melted into the darkness. He'd been in Washington too long. It felt good to stretch his legs. There was something about doing things himself that he was starved for. Dropping his weight on Ricky Sullivan had been pure joy.

It was going to feel ten times better when he left the Irish bastard's body at the crime scene to take the blame.

It was the last piece that needed to be in place before he took his very hard-earned place at the big table. Some would accuse him of selling his soul but he didn't see it that way. Hale's team was the last dangling string that might someday be found to uncover everything Tyler had done to buy his spot next to Carl Davis.

Sell out?

No, he'd made his way using the skills he had to gain what other men like Carl Davis had been born with at their fingertips.

Life wasn't fair, so there was no reason for him to be brainwashed into thinking he had to play by the rules.

In a way, he and Sullivan had a lot in common.

Tyler honestly didn't want to kill him. The guy was resourceful.

But that wasn't going to stop him.

Nope.

He was too close to tying up the loose ends.

And he had never been a quitter.

Ever.

"I thought you were going to bunk with your buddies."

Jaelyn had left only one of the bedside lamps on. Somehow, the letters were too intimate to read in bright light. Or maybe it was because she didn't want to share them.

"Lost my confidence," he said. "Decided I should reinforce my position by making you breathless with ecstasy."

She laughed.

He shrugged.

"Too cheesy?"

She held up her hand, intending to give him an iffy motion but she was shaking. A quiver was running along her limbs and he didn't miss it. She felt her cheeks heating with a blush, realizing it was another little tattletale reaction to him.

He strode forward, reaching out to stroke one hot cheek.

She shuddered.

Her eyes closed as all of the words she'd been reading suddenly manifested into physical form. Like the wall between her fantasy world and reality dissolved, allowing her to mingle with her dream lover.

*"Tonight . . . I'm going to be your lover, Jaelyn . . ."*

She lifted her eyelids, uncertain if he'd spoken or if she was hearing her own thoughts.

Not that it mattered.

Nope, not a bit.

She reached down and pulled her top off. Bram sucked in his breath, filling her with confidence. Watching him take her in was insanely hot. She got hung up on the way his eyes narrowed, her hands frozen on the hooks of her bra.

He locked gazes with her. It was as much physical as it was a mental connection.

"I love the way you strip down for me, baby . . ."

"Good," she said as she popped open her bra. "Because sometimes I wonder if there's something wrong with me."

He stood up and ripped his shirt off. "Because you feel like your clothing is impossible to endure?"

He lifted one foot and popped the lace on his boot. "I know the feeling." He placed the boot at the foot of the bed and worked the other one free from his foot. "You know I battle over whether or not it's a good thing."

"How can you doubt?" she asked. "When you wrote me all of these?"

His pants got tossed aside, leaving him bathed in the meager light, all of the perfection of his hard body for her to feast on.

"Right . . . wrong . . . nothing mattered but coming back for you, baby . . ."

"I love you . . ."

Oh God, she felt like she would just stop breathing if he didn't return the sentiment. Nothing short of that was enough.

He caught her up, binding her against his body, cupping her nape and holding her head steady so that their gazes locked.

"I'm fucking obsessed with you, Jaelyn. I don't know if that's love, I just know I've never felt like this before. It's a fact that I think it's beyond love." His eyes blazed with something so fierce, she shivered. "I wouldn't have written that many letters to your sister and that's a fact."

"Good."

Rotten? Maybe. She flat-out didn't care. He was hers. The letters were hers.

"Now kiss me, Bram Magnus, and stop making me wait on you."

He complied but it felt more like he was claiming her. Holding her nape as he covered her lips with his and took his time kissing her.

She was burning for him, needing more than just his kiss. Every inch of contact was balm for her starving senses.

He scooped her off her feet, cradling her for a long moment before lowering her to the bed.

"We're going to need a place of our own," he said as he laid her on the bed. "So I can let you make all the noise you want."

"I am not noisy," she argued.

Bram lifted an eyebrow, a wicked gleam entering his eyes.

"Let's put that to the test, shall we?"

He slid down her body, pressing her knees wide and settling over her spread sex.

"Bram . . ." She gasped when she realized how much volume there was in her tone, tightly clamping her jaw shut.

Bram teased her mons, stroking the smooth skin. He looked up her body, locking gazes with her before he plunged his finger into her cleft.

She squeaked.

And gripped the bedding.

"Payback is a bitch . . . ," she warned him.

He winked at her. "I hope so."

She glared at him but her pique died as he spread her folds and licked her clit.

The intensity was off the scale, taking her so close to the limit of her tolerance, she let out another startled sound that she smothered beneath her wrist.

Bram chuckled before teasing her opening with a fingertip, rimming her with it while her passage ached for penetration.

But she didn't want him to rush it. No, she wanted to savor the moment. Bram didn't disappoint her. He teased her, licking her, sucking her little clit and tonguing it before he plunged his finger inside her.

She jerked and pressed her hand tighter against her lips. It was a battle, though, because she was panting and needed more air, but moving her hand meant the sounds he was forcing out of her went bouncing around the room.

Bram didn't let up on her, either. Her heart was thumping so hard, she felt like she just might pass out. Not that it mattered. No, she was straining toward him, seeking that last bit of pressure that would push her over the edge into climax.

He made her wait for it, driving a pair of fingers into her with a rhythm that was just shy of being fast enough to make the wave crest. He added a little humming right over her clit that sent her into orbit. She twisted and writhed as pleasure snapped through her like a bullwhip. It was searing and sharp and so intense, she didn't care if she passed out from lack of oxygen.

"Our own place . . . sounds . . . perfect." Bram was smirking.

An arrogant grin curved his lips as he came up and over her.

"Not that I'm altogether upset about our current living arrangements."

She sent her fist into his shoulder, but he was so close, the blow lacked any real force.

"Beast," she muttered, her voice husky with satisfaction.

"Just the way you like me . . ." He growled against her neck.

He really was a beast. At that moment, he was hard, and hovering over her.

"I want to remember you like this . . . wet . . . hot for me . . ."

He pressed her thighs wide, until her knees touched the bed on either side of her. His gaze was on her spread body.

"I want to know you're mine."

Maybe it would have sounded vulgar if the look on his face didn't hit her so hard. He liked what he saw. Wanted to possess her.

*Damn she liked the idea of that . . .*

"Want you to feel what it's like to be mine . . ." he whispered as she stroked his cock.

It was swollen and hard, jutting out from his body. She ached for it, for him and yet, she wouldn't have rushed that moment for anything. It filled her with more confidence than a hundred compliments.

The hunger drawing his features tight was all the assurance she needed to make her believe he wanted more than sex.

No, this was going to be soul deep, just as it always had been.

"Come to me, Bram . . ." Her voice was husky and welcoming. His lips twitched, flashing a smug grin at her before he crawled over her.

"Yes, ma'am . . ."

His breath teased her ear before he angled his face so that he could nip the delicate skin on her neck.

She shuddered.

He was letting her feel him settling on top of her. It was a blunt thing, the way she recognized that she was spreading her thighs wider so that his hips might nestle between them, feeling his hardness as her body accepted him.

She clasped his arms, stroking up and along the corded muscles as his cock slipped between the wet folds of her sex.

"Look at me, Jaelyn . . ."

His tone was full of demand. He threaded his fingers into her hair and clasped it as she forced her eyelids up.

The moment their gazes locked, he pushed into her. She watched his eyes fill with pleasure.

*Raw.*

And that was just the way she wanted him, too.

She lifted her hips to ease his next thrust, noting the wet sound of their flesh meeting.

*Untamed . . .*

She didn't want him tamed.

And the way his features were drawn tight told her he didn't want her civilized, either.

They clashed and collided, and at the same time, moved together in perfect harmony. There was straining and surging and in the end, a hard-won victory that satisfied their cravings at last.

She felt that moment approaching, felt his cock hardening even more. She clasped him to her, squeezing him tightly to her body as she lifted her hips and felt him grinding against her clit. The explosion was mind-shattering. He caught her cry with his hand, clamping it over her lips as he ground his teeth together and she felt him shudder through his release.

A squeal woke Jaelyn at daybreak. She rubbed her eyes and sat up. Several letters were still lying next to her on the bed.

"Vitus!" a woman exclaimed. "I have a list a mile long."

"I've got something really long, too . . ."

Jaelyn opened the door to find Vitus Hale embracing a redheaded woman who was gorgeous. She was squirming against his hold.

"Aw . . . great, you're up," the woman said.

Vitus let out a huff. "She's not the only one up."

"You'll have to excuse my husband," the woman said. "I'm Damascus and we have a hair appointment."

Vitus abandoned his playfulness. "Where?"

"Relax," Damascus said. "My mom brought her own personal hairdresser with her and her escort is going to be there. Bram's daddy said I could invite Jaelyn."

"You heard her." Ginger was coming through the back door of the house, her baby in her arms and Saxon hot on her tail with an identical frown to Vitus's.

The brothers shared a look before they nodded.

Damascus let out a little sound of amused victory before turning and looking at Jaelyn.

"All we need now is the bride."

It was going to be a quiet event, but Jaelyn felt like her heart was going to burst through her chest.

She was preened and the dress pressed. The doors of the church were open wide. A small event meant there was no organ music but Jaelyn decided the sound of the wind was fitting.

Winds of change . . .

"I married Jeanie on a weekday, too." Her grandfather was there, in his Sunday best. He gave her a wink. "I was afraid to close my eyes in case she changed her mind."

"Grandma used to tell me you were lucky she made you marry her."

There was a scuffle and soft sound of conversations as Ginger and Damascus joined an older woman sitting in the pews.

"My eyes must be getting old because I think I've seen that woman before."

"She's Miranda Delacroix," Jaelyn said but had to suck in a deep breath because she was so nervous. "She's running for Congress."

"Well now," Milton muttered as he took her hand and placed it on his arm. "VIPs."

Jaelyn was more conscious of the man waiting for her at the end of the aisle. Bram was looking her way, every inch the man she'd jumped on so recklessly.

Damn right she was going to marry him.

Milton started walking when she did, escorting her through the large double doors that opened into the sanctuary. Their steps were muted by the carpet covering the main aisle but someone was walking in the foyer.

Jaelyn glanced back, hoping LeAnn wasn't making an escape.

There was only a man there. He had a sweatshirt on, crossing the open doorway. She missed a step, making her grandfather look at her. The frantic beating of her heart had her thoughts whirling but something was trying to break through.

A warning . . .

A . . . recognition.

"That's the guy from the hospital parking lot . . ." Jaelyn turned and looked behind her, feeling like she'd turned her back on a lion.

Her voice bounced down the aisle, bringing immediate action. She heard people shifting behind her in the church but the man in front of her turned to look straight at her as he pulled his hand out of his pocket. There was something dark in his hand, about the size of a lemon. He pulled something from it before bringing his hand back and throwing it toward the altar.

"Grenade!" someone yelled behind her.

Her grandfather gave her a surprisingly hard shove that sent her stumbling. She ended up on one knee as an explosion ripped through the church.

A wall of hot air hit her, throwing her backward, and then there was nothing but blackness.

Ricky cussed.

He yanked his gun free and fired off a few rounds as he ducked behind the wall. There were narrow steps leading up to the loft that overlooked the sanctuary. He bounded up them, hitting his knees at the railing.

Perfect.

He could pick them off like rabbits.

Her ears were ringing.

Jaelyn tasted dirt and crushed plaster in her mouth as she opened her eyes. A pile of debris was sitting on her chest, more of it falling like snow throughout the church.

There was an ominous crackling sound as chunks of plaster broke loose and fell down.

"Jaelyn . . . run!"

She heard popping sounds. Not popping . . . gunfire.

Bram was pinned behind the huge altar. Bullets were hitting it, their impact marked by little puffs of plaster.

"Run now!"

She rolled over, feeling like her limbs weren't willing to obey her brain. The shorter length of the fifties-era dress was a lifesaver because she was able to get her feet under her.

She was straining toward the entryway of the church. Digging deep for every last morsel of strength.

"Let go!" Her grandfather was snarling.

Dare Servant didn't pay him any heed. The agent had his hands dug into Milton's clothing at the shoulders and was dragging him back along the wall. Dare looked up at her.

"Get behind cover!"

There was another pop and the whiz of a bullet flying past her. Only this one was going toward whoever had thrown the grenade. Thais was peeking around the doorway, firing toward their unknown assailant to give Jaelyn a chance to escape.

She didn't waste it.

*Why was she the only one without a gun?*


"Hold position, Magnus."

Bram was on his knee, looking down the sights of his gun. Saxon sent him a look. "You'll be cut down before you make it to her."

It was the truth.

One Bram detested.

But he didn't linger on his frustration. Instead, he rolled back, using the shelter of the altar to change clips before judging his avenues of escape. His father was in the doorway of the refectory, blood staining his white hair. He lifted his hand, sending Bram a signal that meant he would cover him.

Bram took off for the side exit of the church. There was a flip of satin as Jaelyn made it into the foyer. He had to fight back the urge to charge out into the open and race around the outside of the church to get to her.

*You can't help anyone if you're dead . . .*

He'd been trained well, taught to ignore emotion, but today, it felt nearly impossible. Saxon made a dash toward Ginger and Damascus who were lying on the floor unconscious from the blast. Vitus tight on his tail. The gunfire increased, giving Bram the chance to slip out of the church.

"This way, ma'am . . ."

Jaelyn was fighting back the terror, trying to keep her wits. The smoke was so thick it stung her eyes, robbing her of her sight, which only further disoriented her.

The man grabbed her by the upper arm, taking control of her in that way Bram and his team members so often did.

"I have to get you to a secure location."

She didn't recognize him but a familiar badge was clipped to his belt.

"Right . . ." She forced the single word past her lips.

The guy was doing most of the work, practically holding her up as she tried not to roll her ankle in her heels.

The gun in his hand chilled her blood.

He was pulling her toward the side of the church, not to the SUVs waiting in the parking lot.

"Where . . . where are you taking me?"

"Move," he ordered her, looking over his shoulder as he pulled her around the corner of the building.

That warning was ringing loud and clear through her brain once more. It conflicted with her logic, which was in favor of leaving the gunfire in the church behind her.

But there was something about the way he kept looking behind him that made her dig her heels in.

"I've never seen you before," she said.

He tightened his grip on her arm, twisting it behind her with a brutality that made her cry out.

"Hold!"

Bram issued the order. She barely recognized his voice. It was hard and unyielding. The man holding her arm twisted around, shoving the muzzle of his gun into the soft flesh beneath her chin.

"One wrong move, Magnus, and she'll be dead before you can get a shot off."

Bram didn't look like he agreed. His grip on his gun was perfect, his head tilted so that he was looking down the barrel.

"Two fingers . . . now . . . or I'll get off a shot before your bullet hit me."

Bram suddenly complied, holding his gun with only two fingers so he couldn't get a shot off. "Tyler Martin."

"Give it up, Martin!" Saxon yelled from the corner of the church.

Tyler's grip tightened. Jaelyn could feel the men of Saxon's team closing in on them.

"Not going to happen, Hale," Tyler declared. "You forget, I trained you."

There was a buzz in the distance. Bram looked toward as Jaelyn recognized the sound.

A helicopter.

"This is how it's going to go, boys," Tyler began. "I'm leaving and she's coming along as insurance."

"There are too many witnesses this time, Martin," Bram warned him.

"None of you will squeal," Martin said as he jerked her closer. "Carl Davis will use an executive order to shut down your precious Shadow Ops teams if you do. I'm taking her as a little insurance that I make it out of here alive and to make sure you give me Sullivan. Keep him quiet or she'll pay the price for it."

The helicopter was swooping in now, kicking up dirt and drowning out any further conversation. It wasn't the threat to her own life that made her get into the aircraft at Tyler's urging.

No, it was the look in Bram's eyes.

He was ready to lunge, the glitter in his eyes telling her he wouldn't hesitate to try and rescue her.

And Tyler just might shoot him before he closed the distance.

It was too horrible for her to accept, so she didn't resist as Tyler shoved her inside the aircraft. It was pulling away from the ground within seconds. She tumbled around inside it, half falling across the long backseat as Tyler turned his attention to shutting the door and reaching for a set of headphones.

She grasped at the seat, pulling herself across it and up so that she could press her face to the glass of the window.

Her reward was sweet. Bram was there, below them, his father fighting to hold him back. The raw strength of the men as they wrestled was impossible to miss, even from her shaky vantage point.

She knew he was furious.

She soaked it up because it helped keep her fear from sweeping in to drown her.

Because there was no doubt in her mind that the man beside her had no reason to keep her alive.

"He can't go far." Bram fought back his rage, reaching down for the composure he'd used in countless missions.

Work the problems . . .

Solve them in order . . .

Claim the victory . . .

Go home alive . . .

His dad was eyeing him as he tugged on his jacket and straightened it.

"If he lands that bird on a military base, he's ours," Bram insisted.

"He'd be a fool to do it," Vitus answered.

The local police were swarming in. Saxon held his badge in hand as he faced them. The tension was high but Bram didn't have time to focus on it.

"Map," he ordered one cop. "I need an area map with fueling stations for helicopters."

"Don't move," one of the cops yelled.

"He took my wife," Bram said with a snarl.

There was a shift and suddenly one of the police officers was striding toward Bram and his team.

"What are you doing, Thornton?"

The officer looked back at his comrades. "I might not have as fancy a badge as these guys but I'll put boot to ass for any man who's trying to protect his family."

Thornton made it to Bram and pulled a map free. "There are only two in range that aren't military."

The map crinkled as it was unfolded. The creases were

marked from heavy use, proving the guy was smart enough to not rely completely on technology.

Dare was splattered with blood.

But the agent was grinning.

So was his suspect.

"Tell me how to track Tyler."

Dare and Sullivan looked up as Bram came up into the loft.

"What's wrong, boy-o?" Ricky grinned showing off the blood in his teeth. "Did he take your girl?"

Bram started forward but Dare stepped into his path. "We need him alive."

Bram only stepped around Dare. "You work for Tyler Martin."

Ricky only snorted and resumed grinning.

"Leave," Dare said to Bram.

Dare cocked his head to one side. Bram turned his head and shot his fellow agent a look.

"I'm not an agent, Dare, so *you* leave."

Ricky's grin melted as he realized exactly what Bram was contemplating.

Bram locked gazes with him. "That's right. I don't have a badge and you've touched my woman . . . twice now . . ."

Dare shook his head. "I can't do it."

"Yes . . . you can," Bram insisted in a low tone. He pointed toward the stairs. "It won't take too long."

He pulled a knife from where it had been strapped to his ankle and tested the edge with his thumb. The look he sent Ricky was enough to make the man shudder.

"Are you still here?" Bram demanded. "Martin has been playing us against our values. I'm done, man, finished toeing a line no one else seems to fucking see. Get out of here. I don't have a badge and maybe I never will but there is one thing I will have . . ." He looked back at Ricky. "And that's the knowledge that Jaelyn didn't die because of my choices."

Dare was frozen for a long moment. "I was never here," he finally declared in a low tone before he turned his back and started toward the stairs.

"Wait . . ." Ricky snarled. "Just . . . you can't fucking leave me with this bastard!"

"What's wrong, Ricky?" Bram asked softly. "Afraid it's come time to pay up?"

Ricky spat on the floor, his body quivering with rage. "Pay up? You fucking prick! What the hell do you know about being tossed under the bus? Tyler left me to rot in a Mexican jail. Hired me to kill your team and then cheerfully left me to die in a hole not fit for a mutt. Why the fuck do you think I'm important enough to him to take your wife?"

Bram stepped closer. "So tell me where he's going . . ." Bram lowered himself onto his haunches and locked gazes with Ricky. "And I'll kill him."

Ricky liked the sound of that. His eyes brightened for a moment before he tightened his expression.

"I could get in touch with him."

Bram flicked his thumb across the edge of the knife again. "I guessed that much."

"But not for nothing," Ricky said. "You're going to . . . unlock me . . ."

Bram shrugged and pushed the knife back into its scabbard. He withdrew a small key and fit it into the handcuffs locked around Ricky's wrists.

"Alright then . . ." Ricky was slightly astounded to be free.

Bram straightened up and sent him a grin. "Looks really bad when a suspect dies in handcuffs. Leaves marks on the wrists that would really be a pain in the ass to explain."

"I'm not going to let you cut me." Ricky snarled as he popped his knuckles. "Try it, glory boy. I'll be happy to give you a taste of what a man like me has to learn to survive."

"Just one question first."

Ricky hesitated.

Bram contemplated him for a moment. "How bad do you want a piece of Tyler Martin?"

Ricky snorted. "I'd suck his cock if it would put me in position to slit his throat."

Bram slowly smiled. "In that case, maybe we should work together."

He wouldn't have any remorse over killing her.

It was a surreal thought, one Jaelyn discovered herself mulling over as she sat across from Tyler Martin.

There was a history between him and Bram. She'd seen it in Bram's eyes.

As well as something that was branded into her memory.

The need to get to her.

So she couldn't die.

*It's not exactly up to you . . .*

Maybe not, but that didn't mean she couldn't do something to even out the odds against her.

*Like what?*

She scoffed at her own lack of confidence. The answer was a simple word: "anything." Anything and everything.

She would not be less than Bram's equal.

Even if it killed her.

He needed Sullivan.

Tyler didn't want to admit it but he hadn't gotten to where he was by ignoring details.

Ricky Sullivan was a very large loose end. One with enough knowledge to sink Carl Davis. It was the social media era, one where a man such as Sullivan might come off as sympathetic.

Martin knew the guy for what he was, a hired dog. Some might call him a prick for labeling Sullivan like that but Tyler found brutal honesty more useful. All the years he'd spent chasing the ideals of honor had left a sour taste in his mouth. One he was enjoying washing out with the help of the expensive whiskey Carl Davis could afford to supply him with.

"Sir, we've got to refuel."

The pilot wasn't asking. Tyler grunted and pushed the button to activate the microphone attached to his headset.

"Someplace quiet. Nonmilitary."

If the pilot had an opinion about the request, he kept it to himself.

"Ten minutes."

The helicopter angled as the pilot changed direction. Below them were the dense forests that had once belonged to native tribes before colonization. There were pockets of civilization but they were still far enough from the coast to make it possible to fall off the radar.

Good, he needed someplace remote.

Someplace where the blood would soak into the ground and the trees would cover the stain.

"We don't have time to pull in resources."

"Agreed," Vitus Hale said. There was an edge that never left a man once he'd been an active SEAL.

Bram liked working with Saxon and Vitus because both of them were razor sharp.

"So we use what we have," Bram stated. "The local police."

"Details," Saxon said, pressing him.

"Unless Tyler is slipping up, he's monitoring the police band. Let's get some chatter going that will make him think Sullivan took a few of us down."

Saxon slowly smiled. "You might be Army but I like you . . . sometimes."

Bram didn't waste time on chitchat. He moved past the area the Shadow Ops team was using to where the police had withdrawn to. Officer Thornton noticed immediately, earning points in Bram's book.

"We need some help."

"If you want the girl back, you'll bring me Sullivan."

Bram didn't have to ask who was calling. Thornton was smirking at him as the airwaves did their work.

"You're a fucking disgrace, Martin." Bram played his part by hissing into the phone.

"Don't be a pussy, Magnus," Tyler retorted. "You tossed in with the Shadow Ops teams knowing we play hard. If you leave your dick out flapping in the breeze by bringing a woman into the mix, don't expect me to kiss your boo-boo."

"I'll be happy to face off with you. I do my fighting man to man."

"So did Saxon and Vitus Hale," Tyler said. "I hope they enjoyed dying for their principles. Personally, I'm planning on enjoying the fruits of my labors for a good long time."

"Not if I take Sullivan here in front of the news camera. In fact Miranda Delacroix is threatening an exclusive; seems she doesn't much care for the fact that you just helped widow her daughter."

"Damascus made her choice," Tyler replied. "If she'd married Carl, she'd have nothing to cry about now."

"Except for having a cold bed. I hear girls aren't his type. In fact, Damascus is pretty emotional right now, and women tend to talk a lot when they're grieving."

"If you want your wife back, you'll get a muzzle on Damascus and Miranda," Tyler warned. "You don't have a badge and your team leader is dead. So let's see what kind of balls you have. Bring me Sullivan and I'll give you your wife. Kagan need never know. One hour. After that, you can join the grieving line of family at the gravesides while you bury your wife."

The line went dead.

Bram looked up and caught the gleam of satisfaction in Saxon's eyes.

Thornton sent them a double-finger salute before Bram moved toward the helicopter where Sullivan was sitting.

Saxon stopped him. "I'm not going to try and talk you out of this."

"Because you know it's not going to do you any good," Bram replied. "And I was there when you were on the run with Ginger."

Saxon muttered a low word of profanity. "We'll be there as soon as we can."

"Not until I have Jaelyn," Bram insisted. "He'll put a slug in her head."

"I know," Saxon agreed. "Kagan is going to give me hell for not calling him, but I don't dare risk Tyler sniffing us out. He'll kill anyone who threatens his plans."

"He's going to have to alter those life plans with Carl Davis," Bram warned ominously. "It's going to be my pleasure to make him see that fact."

Bram refused to allow himself to doubt.

He knew better, knew from experience that focus often meant the difference between life and death. Ricky was pleased with himself, grinning smugly as Bram climbed in beside him and pulled the door shut. He began to power up the bird.

"We have a deal?" Ricky demanded, raising his voice above the sound of the blades as they began to spin.

"I get my wife, you get a shot at Martin."

Bram pulled back on the stick, lifting off the ground.

"And you'll turn your back so I can leave?"

Bram adjusted course before answering. "My first priority is my wife. If you can make use of my distraction, that's up to you."

Ricky snickered. "Bet you didn't tell your buddies that part of the arrangement."

Bram sent him a hard look. "Told you, I'm not an agent yet."

And just might never be. Kagan gave his teams a lot of leash length to play with but there were some things the section leader wouldn't overlook.

Like rogue missions that included high-profile targets, such as the chief of security for the next president.

If that was the price he paid, so be it.

Jaelyn was worth it and more.

He'd bleed out on the ground at Tyler's feet so long as he watched her drawing breath. If Kagan had him prosecuted for murder, he'd take that lump, too. He'd always known the risks. Jaelyn was the innocent one and even if he was going rogue now, he'd always fought for what was right.

He would shelter her.

Even if it meant they would never see each other again.

"Not going to try and make a passionate plea?"

Jaelyn slowly smiled. Tyler Martin had glanced her way a few times but she'd held her silence because she could see he expected something else from her.

"Nope," she muttered. "I'm pretty sure you're beyond hope."

He grunted at her.

"Him on the other hand," she said, looking at the pilot. "He's the kind of person I might make a comment to."

She shrugged and looked away.

"What kind of comment?"

"Why do you care?" she shot back.

Tyler shook his head. "Think you know so much about me?"

"I know you kidnapped me from my own wedding and you're intent on using me to clean up your personal mess." She raked him from head to toe. "You disgust me. I don't see why that pilot can't see you for what you are."

"He knows if he makes a move against me, his entire life will be shattered." Tyler responded in a tone that chilled her blood. "His pension, benefits, everything he's worked for will be overshadowed by disobeying the orders of his commanding officer. Me."

The pilot's face tightened.

"You've got ice where your soul should be," she said.

Tyler snorted at her. Another ripple went down her spine as she realized he liked her description of him.

"You're exactly the sort of romantic Bram Magnus would choose alright," Tyler said as he contemplated her. "All high on glory and service and honor."

"Thank you."

He hadn't meant it as a compliment. Jaelyn smiled at him. Her heart was thumping, fear making it almost impossible to maintain her composure.

Like hell she'd crumble.

Bram wouldn't ever show his fear, so neither would she.

"Helicopter coming in," the pilot said.

Tyler nodded before he pulled his gun from his chest harness.

"Looks like lover boy is coming for you."

"Of course he is," Jaelyn answered. "Bram Magnus doesn't know how to fall short of the mark. Not that I expect you to understand that sort of concept."

Tyler checked his gun and sent her a grin. "I've spent my years living the life Bram has. Let me tell you what I saw. Men like the Hale brothers getting cut down for the men they served." Tyler grabbed her by the arm and pulled her farther onto the surface of the landing pad. "And their widows got their benefits sliced and lived like hamsters while the men who had ordered those honor-serving men into battle bought vacation homes in the tropics where they keep their bikini pets."

He yanked her another couple of steps. "I'm going to have more for the blood I spill."

"You're a sellout."

"Beats being dead like the Hale brothers."

Jaelyn stiffened. Tyler offered her a smug grin. "Sullivan killed them."

"But Sullivan was working for you."

He shrugged as the helicopter came in closer. It was a small, private airfield. There were more rusting airplanes than ones fit to fly. The surface of the landing pad was crisscrossed with cracks that had plants growing up through them.

"And now I'm going to kill him," Tyler informed her without a shred of remorse. He tightened his grip on her arm, pulling her into tight contact with his body as he used her as a shield and shoved the barrel of his gun beneath her chin.

"One wrong move, and you die, too."

Bram was flying the helicopter. It gave her a moment of relief from the fear that was trying to cripple her. She watched the way he angled the aircraft and brought it down with what looked like a delicate touch.

Damn, he was everything she'd ever dreamed of.

*Soak it up . . .*

She listened to her inner voice because it beat dwelling on the feeling of Tyler against her.

The guy made her flesh crawl.

The helicopter rotor slowed down. Bram left the cockpit before it finished, completely at ease with the machine. He moved around and opened the passenger side door.

A moment later he was hauling a handcuffed man away from the helicopter.

But Bram was taking Sullivan toward the only building on the site. He'd landed the helicopter between where Tyler was holding her and the building.

Brilliant.

She let out a soft sound of mirth as Bram disappeared inside the building, denying Tyler complete compliance.

"Shut up." Tyler growled.

"Guess you're not going to be able to just shoot Sullivan from behind me," she said in spite of his warning. "You might just have to face Bram, man to man."

"You know, there are things worse than dying." Tyler's tone had crossed into the creepy zone. "I know places where I could sell a woman like you. While you still have your looks, you'd be in a brothel. But after starvation takes its toll, you'll end up behind a wall, your legs in stirrups as man after man uses you for release. Drug bosses like to make sure their underlings have a glory hole to make them feel appreciated."

"Bram is going to kill you."

She'd never been so sure of anything in her life. Never craved bloodletting as much as she did at that moment. It was strange the way she mentally crossed the line and there wasn't a shred of remorse in her for the way she felt.

Bram emerged from the building, bracing his feet apart and holding position as he looked toward Tyler.

"Bring me Sullivan!" Tyler yelled.

"Come and get him," Bram responded.

Tyler pulled the gun out from beneath her chin and leveled it at her temple.

Bram pulled his own gun and aimed it at Tyler.

"You're fucked," she said to Tyler. "He's not stupid enough to bring Sullivan into the open for you to just kill."

"You might be right," Tyler remarked. "I'm going to have to change my tactics."

The gun went off. She smelled the powder as a searing pain went through her leg. She crumpled, hitting her face on the ground because her hands were still handcuffed behind her.

"Bring me Sullivan!" Tyler bellowed.

She'd never felt pain like this before.

This was a whole new level of agony. The bullet had passed through her calf like a red hot iron. The scent of fresh blood filled her senses as she watched the way the blood flowed across her skin.

And something snapped inside her.

All of a sudden, the pain didn't bother her. No, she had strength surging through her making her feel like she could fly if needed. Tyler was bringing the gun up again, taking aim at her arm.

Jaelyn lunged herself at him, a cry of rage coming from her that made her feel even better. She collided with him as his gun went off again. This time the bullet burned a path across her shoulder but she had the satisfaction of feeling Tyler recoil from her attack.

She rolled right over her shoulder and came up onto her feet. Bram was running toward her and it seemed the most natural thing to spring toward him. Time was moving slower for some odd reason, allowing her to notice every step. In fact, she was aware of the way her foot pushed off the ground, when her heel lifted and then the sensation of using the front of her foot to push herself forward.

Bram was lifting his gun and she dove into another roll out of instinct. She heard a bullet fly past her as she came up again and closed the distance more.

So close.

He was so near . . .

Jaelyn strained toward Bram, reaching him the only thought in her mind. The sun was blocked out as the shadow of the building covered her. Bram caught her shoulder and pushed her behind him. She landed against the side of the building, lifting her head in time to see Bram knocking the gun from Tyler's hand.

It went sailing through the air, landing with a clatter.

Tyler recoiled, but Bram followed him. Flesh hit flesh, the two men doing their best to kill each other.

"Get back, Jaelyn!" Bram snarled.

Tyler was charging at Bram, trying to move him aside and get closer to her.

Her feet slipped as she tried to move farther along the side of the building. Tyler was coming for her, and she felt the dread knotting in her belly as the scent of her own blood drove home how easy it would be for him to kill Bram.

So she fought.

Fought to move faster . . .

Fought to gain more distance . . .

An inch might make all the difference.

There was a pop and a shower of glass. It fell from the upper floor of the building as someone jumped through the shattered window.

"You wanted to see me, Martin?"

Ricky Sullivan landed on his feet just behind Tyler.

"I want to see you, too."

Jaelyn was jerked around as Bram retreated. Ricky shoved a knife into Tyler Martin's back. He grunted as Tyler made a wounded sound. Bram was torn but he came toward her, lifting her up and off her feet and onto his shoulder so he could get her away from Tyler and Ricky.

She lifted her head, watching the battle with morbid fascination.

Ricky drove his knife into him over and over like a boxer pummeling a pinned opponent. Tyler was convulsing, turning and trying to pull another gun from where it was shoved into his waistband.

Bram let her down at last, turning to watch the two men trying to kill each other.

Not trying.

No.

They were succeeding.

Blood was staining Martin's shirt, coating the knife still clutched so tightly in Ricky's hand. Ricky grinned, showing off blood in his teeth. He staggered back as Tyler's knees gave out, his eyes gleaming with satisfaction as he watched Tyler convulse.

"No one . . . fucks over a Sullivan."

Ricky's eyes shone with satisfaction a moment before there was a second helicopter coming toward them.

And a third.

"Here comes the cavalry, baby." Bram said.

And then she was being crushed against him.

The scent of his skin replacing the smell of fresh blood.

He was the cure for the insanity around her.

"Let me look at you . . ." Bram was lifting her off her feet and lowering her to the ground as he started to access her wounds.

There was a ripping sound as he tore a length off her skirt and used it to stop the bleeding.

The two helicopters touched down, men jumping from them before the rotors stopped turning. They had their guns drawn as Bram looked up.

"Clear!" he bellowed over the sound of the aircraft. "Medic!"

"I'm fine," she said.

He locked gazes with her. For a moment, he was still

hiding behind his stone expression, but his lips twitched. "Not too bad, Jaelyn. Who taught you to roll?"

"My grandfather," she replied as Saxon Hale came close enough for her to recognize him. She gasped. "You're alive."

Saxon pulled his shades off as Vitus knelt behind her and unlocked the cuffs still binding her wrists.

"Can't believe everything you hear," Saxon replied with a smirk. "It was your hubby's idea, though."

She suddenly narrowed her eyes. "Except, you're not my husband."

"Not yet," Bram agreed. He scooped her up and started to carry her toward the helicopter. "Seems Tyler has managed one last interruption in our lives."

She looked past him to where Saxon and Vitus were looking at Tyler Martin's body.

"His last one," she said.

Bram placed a kiss against her temple. "That's for sure."

He reached behind her to pull the straps of the chest harness over her shoulders. There was a click as he secured the buckle. He cupped the side of her face.

"I have to stay here, baby, and you need a hospital."

She reached out and caught his chest harness. Big fat tears were suddenly welling up in her eyes. "What's wrong?"

"Your grandfather will meet you."

He wasn't going to tell her.

"I'm only going to marry a partner, Bram Magnus, so you'd better start singing. What's wrong?"

Dare Servant was sitting beside the pilot and she heard him snicker.

But her attention was all on Bram.

He grunted and looked away before returning his gaze

to hers. "I disobeyed chain of command to come after you and I don't regret it. I love you, Jaelyn. Nothing was going to stand between me and getting to you, but I need to face the consequences of my actions. Saxon's commanding officer will be here shortly. I plan to face him."

Of course he did.

At his core he was solid, with the sort of integrity she'd witnessed in her grandfather and had been holding out for until she met him. She reached out and grabbed his body armor, pulling him toward her so she could kiss him. Bram didn't need any further encouragement. He kissed her back with all of the hunger and need she felt herself.

"I love you, too," she whispered as he pulled away.

He shut the sliding door and stepped away from the aircraft but there was a grin on his face, one she liked a whole hell of a lot.

The sound of the rotor starting up filled her ears. Bram backed up, the wind whipping at his pants. The pilot lifted off a few moments later, giving her nothing to do but watch as Bram was left behind.

He was in his element.

And she was so scared he would be kicked out of it over her.

Saxon was on his phone. He finished and looked toward Bram.

"Kagan is on his way."

Bram didn't show any response. His teammates knew him too well, though. Or perhaps it was more precise to say, they knew they'd have done the same. It was the reason they were teammates, their values ran soul deep.

"You did what you had to," Vitus remarked. "I'd have done the same."

"She's safe," Bram remarked. "And Tyler isn't going to be hunting any of us again. Did you get Sullivan?"

"Your dad shackled him," Saxon said. "Word is, he's pissed."

"Ricky knows where your command center is. We couldn't let him go. His loyalties go to the highest bidder," Bram said. "I'm taking the responsibility for this."

Saxon wasn't comfortable with Bram's statement. But Bram sent him a stern look. "It was my wife this time."

"Tyler took a shot at both of our wives, too," Vitus said, joining the conversation.

"So tell my dad to give Ricky a shot of whiskey."

Saxon snorted. "I wager the good colonel already deduced that."

Bram nodded. He looked back at Tyler's body.

He wouldn't regret any of it.

Because the fact was, he'd do it again and more if that's what it took to safeguard Jaelyn.

It would be better if Kagan understood that now.

It might cost him a future with the Shadow Ops but he'd shoulder that load. A badge with Kagan was all he'd worked toward getting for a long time. Now, it seemed there was more to life than the team.

Jaelyn . . .

Yeah, she was a whole hell of a lot more.

Enough to fill a lifetime.

Kagan was looking at Tyler Martin's body. But Bram's arrival caught the section leader's attention.

"Guess it looks sort of strange to see me so fascinated." Kagan spoke before he rose to his full height.

Bram shared a look with him, one that only a few men truly understood. "Mr. Sondors said there were times when a good man has to go to war," Bram said. He looked back at Tyler's open eyes. "He took out your men for his own gain. Can't really blame you for enjoying the fact that he's dead. Fact is, I'm going to sleep better knowing it myself."

The scene was blocked off from sight now. Huge cargo nets had been suspended above the body and walls were erected to keep the curious television news helicopters from seeing what had happened. It would have been cleaned away if Kagan hadn't wanted to see it himself.

"He betrayed every ideal I expect my men to shed blood for," Kagan explained in a deep tone as he came closer. He stopped and dug something out of the breast pocket of his suit jacket. "If you accept this, know that I want you to feel the burden of that morality."

Kagan held a badge out. Bram clenched his hands into fists.

"I disobeyed chain of command."

Kagan's lips twitched. "You dealt with the situation as it was presented to you. Tyler had his fingers in too many pies. I agree with you on the information blackout." He held up a finger. "Just don't make a habit of it."

"I've got a wife now."

"So does Hale." Kagan pushed the badge into Bram's chest. "And as you've illustrated, Dare and Thais don't want to play house just yet, so you get to help bring that command center up. Once it is, I'm going to need men like you who can smell an evidence trail when everyone else dismisses the situation as insignificant. There is a place for you on this team, Magnus, take the badge. You've earned it."

Satisfaction was filling him. Bram took the badge as

Kagan shifted back, revealing the rest of the team. They grinned at him and came forward to shake his hand.

"Welcome to the team," Kagan said.

Bram stopped him from leaving. "Tyler said Carl Davis was going to sign an executive order disbanding the Shadow Ops teams."

Kagan pursed his lips together and rocked back on his heels, slowly thinking over what Bram had said.

"I've heard him say the same." Kagan looked at his men for a long moment. "I'll look into it."

He nodded before disappearing. The cleanup teams were just waiting for Kagan to go. They started forward as the section leader ducked into a truck with tinted windows and started the engine.

"Carl is leading in the polls," Vitus said. "We'd better have a bugout plan in place in case he puts a hit out on all of us."

Bram felt the weight of reality on his shoulders. Taking chances with his own life was one thing, but now he had Jaelyn.

He secured the badge to his belt.

They were a team and there was safety in numbers.

Carl had better learn to leave well enough alone.


Kagan made sure Carl Davis could see him.

Another fundraiser, this one with a fancy meal that cost five thousand dollars a plate.

Carl was performing well. Shaking hands, looking as though he was listening intently as his supporters explained what they thought was important.

Hell, maybe the guy was sincere. Kagan didn't know. Some men were so focused on their goal, so convinced of their own ability to do good, that they justified the means of getting into position.

Carl might be one of those.

Perhaps Tyler Martin had just been jaded.

Not that Kagan failed to see Tyler's point. It was hard not to drool a little. Men like Tyler and himself were face-to-face with the wealth and privilege that many would never taste. Including himself. It was the sort of knowledge that would rot a man's soul if he didn't check himself.

"Kagan," Carl said as he flashed his practiced smile. "It's a real privilege to see you tonight."

The press was on them but with a wave of Carl's hand, they were pushed back.

Kagan fell into step beside Carl, crossing out of the ballroom where the event was being held and down the hall to where Carl had private rooms.

The door shut with a firm sound. Carl didn't look at him but his lips took on a pinched appearance as he went to the bar and poured himself a whiskey. He tossed it down before refilling the glass and turning to face Kagan.

"Is he dead?"

Kagan nodded.

The ice clinked inside the glass in Carl's hand. "I gather you're enjoying telling me."

Kagan shook his head. "Tyler said you were going to shut down the Shadow Ops teams."

Carl's pallor lost its grayness. Confidence returned to his eyes as he raised his glass. "There isn't much you could do to stop me."

Kagan slowly grinned. The glass went smashing onto the floor as Carl went ash gray again.

"Now . . . we can discuss this." Carl struggled to find the tone he used so often with the public.

Kagan moved toward him. His steps didn't make a sound and Carl was leaning back against the bar by the time Kagan stopped.

"I'm not going to kill you, Carl."

There was an audible sound from the presidential hopeful.

"See," Kagan continued, "that's the difference between men like Tyler Martin and myself . . . and the Hale brothers. It's the substance you really should cultivate in your team." Kagan reached out and ran the tip of his finger down Carl's lapel.

"Honor."

The word was a whisper but it penetrated soul deep because of the look in Kagan's eyes when he spoke it.

More than a word, it was an ideal, a way of life.

"I can't kill you," Kagan explained, "because that would make me no better than Tyler Martin." He let it sink in for a moment. "And I believe that no matter how unfair life can be, there is still a good helping of karma out there."

Kagan retraced his path to the door. He stopped with his hand on the knob. "Something to think about, on your road to the White House. Men like me and those on my teams are the ones you really want watching your back. We never sell out. You'll sleep better with us as your friends than knowing we're looking for the man who didn't see any value in our dedication."


"Home sweet home . . ."

Bram drove her to a slightly different location a week later.

"Home sweet . . . mobile unit . . . ," Jaelyn remarked.

A new mobile housing unit had arrived. This one was covered by a cargo net as well but set a good two hundred feet away from Saxon Hale's home.

"Do you mind?" Bram asked. "That it's not a house?"

Jaelyn sent him a wicked look. "We're beyond the boulder fence. Sure you want to encourage me to misbehave?"

Bram sent her a grin. "Yes, ma'am."

She winked at him. "Guess it's a good thing you married me."

"I'm grateful the reverend agreed," Bram said. "We nearly destroyed his church."

Her grandfather was pulling her door open, a smile on his lips. LeAnn was watching from nearby.

"Well, it looked like repairs were well underway." Jaelyn tried not to wince as she put her weight on her leg. Whatever strange surge of adrenaline had given her the strength to ignore pain while fighting with Tyler Martin was long gone now.

"Shadow Ops teams know how to erase the marks they make."

Bram scooped her off her feet and carried her to the steps of their new home. But he didn't go inside. He sat her down and sent her a wink.

"Milton," Bram began. "Now that you've taken off your wedding ring, I think it's time you gave Jaelyn and me a little space."

Jaelyn narrowed her eyes while the growing crowd accumulating around them made her bite her lip.

Bram was up to something.

There was the sound of a car coming around the house. As it came into sight, her grandfather let out a whoop.

Vitus Hale drove the honeybee right up to Milton. The dust settled, showing off the fully restored paint and body of the VW van.

"You'll be needing this to do that getting-on-with-life part," Bram said.

"Sweet God . . ." Milton was circling the van, reaching out to touch the shiny chrome work and the new tires.

Bram reached out and pulled the side door open. Every inch was restored. "We made a few upgrades, but she's ready to roll."

Her grandfather was beside himself. He climbed up inside the honeybee to tinker with the seats that folded down into the bed.

"I might have already stocked it with coffee," Bram told her as he joined her on the steps.

"You're perfect, Bram Magnus," she said.

Absolutely perfect!

There were places time forgot.

Kagan slipped into a tunnel left from the Prohibition era. It was lined with crumbling concrete that was moldy. The thing was, the dark splats of growth were actually sort of worthy of respect for being tenacious enough to grow so far belowground.

He walked through the maze by memory, emerging in the basement of a building that hadn't been in use in two decades. Here there was the buzz of old florescent lights. Some of them flickered and there were more than a few burned out.

He moved along toward a door that was chained shut. He fit a key into the lock and turned it, swinging the huge metal door open. Behind it was a shelter, built to withstand a nuclear blast. The walls were three feet thick, the air circulation system the only sound.

"Is it visitation day?" Ricky Sullivan had been lying on a sofa.

The shelter was like a small apartment with living room, kitchen, and bedroom.

"Come to check on your pet?"

Kagan sat a backpack down on the floor. It was heavy with provisions.

"It's better than a Mexican jail."

Ricky sent him a snarl.

"Or a grave."

"I'm not so sure about that," Ricky grumbled.

Kagan retraced his steps toward the door. "Maybe you could ask Tyler Martin his opinion."

Ricky was watching him, judging the distance between the door and Kagan.

Kagan shook his head. "Told you before, Sullivan. There's a timer on the entrance to this floor. If I don't cross back out within a few minutes, this building will be leveled by a blast from the C-4 buried beneath that sofa."

"Might be worth it," Ricky said as he plucked the backpack off the floor.

Kagan only sent him an unsympathetic look.

"I know you're just keeping me alive in case you need me to rat on Carl Davis. Don't be too sure I will!"

Kagan secured the lock without a shred of remorse. He moved back toward the control panel and typed in his code. Even the knowledge that Sullivan would starve to death if something happened to him didn't keep him from rethinking his plans.

Carl Davis needed to be kept at bay.

And Sullivan was a hit man at best. He was lucky to still be drawing breath.

Ricky dropped the backpack and left it lying on the floor for the next hour.

He'd be fucked if he was going to be grateful for scraps.

But even he got tired of his own company. He went over to the bag out of boredom. Carrying it to the tiny kitchen where he opened it and pulled out his food for the next . . . well, he didn't know exactly how long. Kagan never came on the same day.

It forced Ricky to eat only what he had to, in case he had to stretch his resources.

He fucking hated the way it excited him to see what was inside the bag. Kagan always packed it full. There was food, a bunch of it dehydrated rations from military stock. He tossed the little foil packets onto the counter, digging for the heavier items.

Tooth powder.

The little tin looked like it was as old as Kagan.

Razors.

A roll of toilet paper.

In the bottom was a plastic case with several movies on DVDs inside it. The apartment was cut off from the rest of the world. He read through the titles, sickened by how much he anticipated having some fresh entertainment.

He finished and looked at the backpack. His mind buzzed with ideas of how to take it apart and begin making a net. He'd be able to trap Kagan in it on one of his visits.

But he knew the rules.

There was a security box in the wall. He had to put the

backpack and his dirty clothing into it or Kagan would cut off his supply of water.

He wasn't ready to die yet.

No, where there was life, there was hope.

And he really hoped he got the chance to kill Carl Davis.

"Liberation papers have arrived." Dare Servant was grinning as he walked toward Thais. "We're shipping out."

He was as giddy as a child making ready to dive into his pile of birthday presents.

"Sure you're not going to miss this place?"

Her implication wasn't lost on her fellow agent. In the distance, LeAnn was busy sorting through boxes of supplies for her glass-making shop. She had rock music blaring as she worked her head with the beat. More than one of the men working on the site were having trouble keeping their attention off her bouncing derriere.

"Told you, Thais, it's not my cup of tea . . . settling down." Dare turned his back on LeAnn. "Why all the concern over my attachments to case subjects? Are you longing for the married life?"

Thais sent him a warning look. "I've had my fill of that."

Dare lifted a dark eyebrow. "Really? Who's the idiot who let you go?"

"I chewed through my chain," she said venomously. "Didn't you just say you could do without it?"

The amount of emotion was more telling than what she said because Thais never let her feelings show.

He admitted to being curious but the promise of a new case also brought with it more time with Thais Sinclair. Women tended to talk when they felt comfortable.

Thais wouldn't be any different.

Or maybe she would prove him wrong. Truth was, he forgot from time to time that she was a woman.

His job was holding the line between the innocent and villians. Thais was competent and an asset to the team. Those were the qualities he kept foremost in his mind about her.

Dare liked the word "villain," too. The men he went head to head against were evil. Plain and simple. They weren't just criminals.

*Villains . . .*

And he was going back out because three good men were digging in now, their days as street agents over. He glanced over at Saxon and Bram. They were deep in discussion, intent on the project of creating a command center out of the silo. Dare didn't dispute the need for it, either.

Only that his contributions weren't needed.

No, he had more villains to catch.

And he couldn't wait to begin.

Yeah, it might get him killed.

But that was just half the fun.


She really shouldn't take the opportunity to poke him.

Miranda Delacroix had spent over twenty-five years playing it safe, keeping her chin down and her expression free of her true feelings.

Tonight, looking at Carl Davis, she found her resolve being tested.

He'd ordered her baby to be abducted.

That was the real problem with keeping her distance from the man. Carl had touched her daughter, Damascus, and a mother's instinct to protect was just too strong.

Carl didn't miss the attention she was giving him,

either. All around them the fundraiser was proceeding smoothly. Waiting staff delivered beverages while the band played flawlessly and Carl . . . well, he was shaking hands, laughing at jokes, all the while calculating the amount each guest was going to contribute to his campaign.

"I appreciate your support, Madam Delacroix."

Miranda offered a practiced smile that faded the moment she realized Carl had made sure to come over to her when they were mostly shielded from the rest of the guests.

"Wouldn't miss it," she replied before dropping her voice. "The chance to see you without Tyler Martin was worth the expense."

Carl flinched. But he recovered quickly. "Yes, I am sure you're relieved to know about his departure from my service."

Miranda didn't rise to the bait. She'd shot her late husband and no one was ever going to find out. A mother did what she had to do.

She sent Carl a hard glare before departing. Life was too short to waste her time and Carl Davis was definitely that.

"Yes, sir?"

Carl considered the man who'd answered his summons. There was an empty whiskey glass on his desk as he swept the man from head to toe.

The man stood still, which helped Carl cultivate confidence in his decision to ask the guy into his private office.

Tyler was gone. But Carl still needed a man at his side who wouldn't cringe over getting his hands dirty.

"I'm looking to fill a position."

The man slowly grinned. The expression sent just enough of a chill down Carl's back to make him return it.

"I need Miranda Delacroix off the radar."

The man's expression tightened. Carl watched as he thought about the assignment.

"Let me check some resources."

That wasn't what Carl wanted to hear and the guy read the disappointment clearly.

"I don't make promises I can't keep. You ask for something, I'm going to make sure I can deliver. That's where Tyler slipped up. He took assignments before checking the situation out. Sometimes, the risk outweighs the gain."

Carl leaned back in his chair, thinking the matter through. "Right." The springs on the chair groaned as he stood and offered his hand on the deal. "I think you just might be who I'm looking for, Geyer."

Eric Geyer shook his hand before turning and leaving.

"You'll need this," Carl wrote something down before offering the slip of paper to his new head of security. "All the funds you might need."

Geyer nodded and slipped it into his pocket. There was a soft click as the door closed behind him. Carl grabbed the glass and walked over to where a cabinet held his private stock of whiskey. The ice clinked against the crystal before the scent of the liquor teased his nose while he poured it.

Tyler had just been a guard dog.

A good one but replaceable in the end. A master had to know where the people around him ranked.

It was a lesson Miranda Delacroix needed.

He was going to enjoy schooling her.

* * *

"You've got to let him go."

Jaelyn huffed at her new husband. "He's almost eighty."

Bram shrugged. "According to the doctor, he's in great health." He came forward and dropped his arms around her from behind as she watched her grandfather drive the honeybee down the road toward the open highway.

"I wouldn't have restored that thing if the doctor had said there was an issue with him driving it. The honeybee is a camper van, Jaelyn, and I swear he looks ten years younger behind the wheel. Don't worry, I put a tracking beacon in it."

"I know," she mumbled. "You check your details."

He kissed her head. "I do. So don't think I overlooked making sure you have something to do while Milton is beach bumming."

Bram turned her loose and pointed across the space between the house and the construction site.

"LeAnn claims you two used to enjoy blowing glass together." He leaned over and kissed her again, this time on the lips.

LeAnn was waving at her from where their ovens were set up. There was a red glow coming from around the edges of the closed door on the crucible where the clear glass was held.

"We've got connections with art galleries or at least people who do." He dropped another kiss on her head. "Go make something to sell. We need some income to build a real house."

She slowly grinned. "In that case . . . stop distracting me, I've got work to do."

"I love you, too."

Jaelyn ended up turning around and watching her husband leave.

He melted her heart every time he said that, leaving her just a little pile of mush as he walked away.

But he'd be back.

She slowly smiled, feeling the tingle of anticipation. It would grow throughout the day, blooming when the sun started to set and she knew he was coming back to her.

Would it ever get old?

If she was lucky, no.

And honestly, she was the luckiest damn person on the face of the planet. Because she was in love with a man who loved her back.

It just didn't get any better than that.

Read on for an excerpt from Dawn Ryder's
next Unbroken Heroes series

# Close to the Edge

Coming soon from St. Martin's Paperbacks

*You're playing with fire . . . .*

His words and very, very true.

The problem was, fire was fascinating. Oh so tantalizing. Just like Dare Servant. Was it his real name? She found herself pondering that question as he pulled up to the Cliffside restaurant and the valet opened her door.

It would be nice to think she knew something about him.

*Dangerous too.*

Yeah, well, bench warmers never were the life of the party.

Paul and Sam moved ahead to talk to the host.

"What are you doing?" she asked.

"You wanted to see if you had my attention."

He'd eased close, playing his part perfectly. It was a tad disappointing because there was part of her that didn't want him to be fake. He noticed too, looked like he read her thoughts right off her face.

Maybe he did, it wasn't like she had a whole lot of experience in playing cloak and dagger games.

He did though.

Dare recovered in a flash, gently settling his hand on the small of her back as he guided her towards the table.

Her heart rate tripled.

She likely should have been offended over how easily he touched her. There was just one tiny problem with that.

She liked it.

Sure, there were a few, unflattering things that might be said about her in response but she'd always been a realist. One plus one equaled two and she found the guy hot. Overbearing men had never struck her that way before but Dare, well, her hormones were having a field day at her expense.

He even smelled good.

She caught the hint of his scent as he settled down next to her. Sam was already signaling the waiter.

"We need wine." Sam declared in a jovial tone. "Really good wine."

And she needed a prayer, because divine intervention was really the only thing she might count on to shield her from Dare's affect.

But the wine was a pretty good alternative.

It left her more relaxed as the evening progressed. Sure she was more susceptible to his charm but there was a point in every great adventure where you just grabbed hold and hung on while you enjoyed the ride.

By the time they made it home, she was sure restlessness wouldn't be a problem tonight. Sam and Paul hightailed it to their car with very poorly disguised intent to leave her alone with Dare. The smile her friends face sent her behind Dare's back was more than suggestive, it was almost a shove towards him.

Under different circumstances, embracing her impulses might have been an option.

But hard reality cut through the wine, leaving her facing a man who had spent the evening with her with the sole intention of intimidating her and undermining her sense of security.

*That sucked.*

She really didn't like to think about him like that. Jenna turned and unlocked her door. She left it open behind her as she went into her living room.

"Not finished pressing me beneath your thumb special agent?" she asked when he followed her inside. "I rather hoped you were. It's disappointing but you have my attention. So say what you think you need to."

Jenna tossed her purse down and faced him squarely. She wasn't sure if it was her wording or the sound of her voice that gave him pause. Something did though. He'd closed the door and turned to face her, his expression warning her he was making ready to try and squish her.

It wasn't that she doubted he could, the night spent in his custody had proved it to her. He froze though, fixing her with his dark stare as he contemplated her with eyes she had no doubt saw a whole lot more than most men did.

The guy was just off the scale in every department.

"Disappointing?" he asked. "Why does my behavior matter to you?"

He sounded sincere, and she shrugged, uncertain as how to proceed.

A conversation.

A sincere conversation, now that was something she hadn't seen coming. She didn't have a plan for dealing with this part of his personality but she realized she felt privileged to glimpse it.

"Call me old fashioned but I still actually believe men who earn badges want to be good guys."

He liked what she said. There was a flash of approval in his eyes that he covered pretty quick.

"Well, do whatever floats your boat, just don't . . ." she ended up biting her lip as she contemplated whether or not to finish her thought. She lost the battle though because no matter how exposing it might be for her, part of her really wanted him to hear what she had to say.

"That was for all intents and purposes my family you just inserted yourself into, don't be a dick." She said and looked him straight in the eye as she spoke. She didn't think she'd meant something so much in her life.

Or wanted someone to not disappoint her so much.

He didn't brush her words off either. For a moment, she watched him absorb them, like her opinion actually mattered. "I don't work with the run of the mill bad guys Jenna. Being a dick, keeps me alive. It also helps me hold a line that ensures you get to have the life you do."

A strange little shiver went across her skin, like she was getting a rare glimpse at his personal nature.

"There's a difference and you know it." She opened her hands up wide. "Right here, it's just you and me. Fine, you came over here to make a point, one you feel justified in making for my own good. I get it. I'm never going to know just what motivates you and I'm better off understanding that ignorance is bliss."

His lips twitched, curving up into a grin. It warmed her insides and that was a fact.

She savored it. Letting it burn away the tension that had kept her in its grasp most of the evening. Of course that just left her prey to the flood of hormones she'd been attempting to ignore. She indulged in a long look at him, knowing it was going to be her last.

Like everything else, he noticed.

She watched the way his keen stare picked up the fact that she was looking at him, his eyes narrowing as his complexion darkened. A twist of sensation went through her insides and she realized it was anticipation.

Of what?

Hell if she knew, but she was breathless.

That word had never really held any true meaning to her before. Now? Dare Servant somehow managed to embody it.

*Tall, dark, dangerous . . .*

Everything a girl dreamed about in those hours after midnight and before dawn when reality arrived to make her realize the sensible guy sleeping next to her was the best choice. Like he'd said, he didn't work with the run of the mill bad guys and work followed everyone home from time to time.

"Ignorance is bliss darling . . ."

He moved toward her, freezing the breath in her chest.

"I don't suffer ignorance very well though . . . always have needed to try things myself . . . ..like you . . . .I want to know what you taste like Jenna Henson . . . ."

He caught her nape, with a grip that was soft enough to spare her pain but strong enough to remind her he could hold her.

He was going to kiss her.

She recognized that fact a moment before he angled his head and pressed his mouth to hers. There was a hint of wine on his lips as he pressed his against hers, insisting on more than just a compression. He took her mouth, and she opened hers out of sheer need to taste more of him.

*Insanity . . .*

Another word she was learning the true meaning of with the help of Dare Servant.

Reality melted away as she reached for him, pushing her fingers into his hair as she kissed him back. She needed more of his taste, more of his scent, more of his skin. It was a frantic urge, beating at her from some place deep inside her that she'd never really realized yearned for freedom.

But he pulled back. Muttering a soft word of profanity beneath his breath.

"You're right . . ." his voice was a mere rasp. "I shouldn't be a dick but I'm not sorry I kissed you."

He was gone a moment later, leaving her alone as he covered the distance to his car with strides that showed her how powerful he was. He didn't do anything like the men she'd known in her life. Nope. Nothing. There was a rawness about him which captivated her. An ease with the darkness which was hypnotic.

Jenna watched him go. Her entire body was tingling long after he'd cleared out of her driveway.

*There's your lesson girl . . . .*

A man like Dare Servant wasn't going to stick around.

*Yeah? Well in that case, she was glad she'd kissed him back.*